ZARA DUSK

A Court of Fur and Fangs

This is for the powerful women who still need a little wolf in their lives.

Contents

Leif

Shifting into my wolf form was a sweet relief.

My stress melted away. The pressures and responsibilities of being thrust into the role of alpha shed from me as my fur grew and my muscles lengthened and thickened.

As soon as I emerged from the moonway, brushing through the thick dark foliage in the forest, I stripped and shifted, leaving a puddle of clothing on the leaf litter. My muscles coiled then released, my paws on the mulchy undergrowth like thunder in the silent woods. Every stride pounded away my anger and fear, muting it. At least for now.

The Lakehouse was a distant speck on the far side of the lake. Often I swam across, but today I needed to run. The path through the forest was not discernible to the fae eye, but as a wolf, the trail was clear, a track of familiar scents I knew like the back of my paw. I'd trodden it a thousand times.

When I emerged from the forest, the Lakehouse looked somber and still, as black and dead as my heart. If there was one thing I'd learned these past few months, it was that danger lurked everywhere. Even here at the Lakehouse, the sanctuary for me and my four best friends, the other heirs to the thrones in the Realm of Verda...Even here, I couldn't relax.

I climbed the stairs to the Lakehouse deck, shifting into fae form. It used to be fun, and I'd set myself challenges. Could I transform while running? Could I shift while swimming? While climbing stairs?

Like everything else, I now knew how stupid and childish that was. The ability to change forms wasn't a game but a war skill, every bit as important as my claws and fangs and as valuable as my know-how with the sword.

I stood momentarily on the deck, staring across the black lake. Its surface was perfectly still, like a glass mirror reflecting back the stars. The trees lining the shore reached for the sky, their piney scent mingling with damp earth and moss. In that moment, it seemed like I could dive in and swim down, down, plunging the depths, and never reaching the bottom.

The house behind me was just as dark, the floor-to-ceiling glass windows reflecting that same sliver of moon in their black surface.

In fae form, my responsibilities dragged on me, and the pit of heat in my belly started to flame. I was naked, of course. Nudity didn't bother me—I used to love seeing the look of shock on my friends' faces. Even my best buddies, the other heirs to the thrones of Verda, always reacted strongly. A smirk, a laugh, a scowl. I did anything to steal their attention.

It felt like years ago when my biggest concern was whether I could convince one of the heirs to sleep with me and what food I could scrounge from Dion.

But in the weeks since Mom died, my whole world had changed. I'd grown up a whole lot. I realized now those were childish games, the efforts of a damn court jester.

Today, turning up naked wasn't a ploy for attention or sex but because I didn't care. I didn't give a fuck.

Sliding open the glass door, I stepped inside the main room

and instantly froze. Somebody was there. My ears pricked up, and my hackles rose, my wolf instincts suddenly on high alert.

Sometimes Shadow Walkers lurked in the gloom, so I'd learned to be afraid of the dark.

I summoned a globe of light, casting a weak warm glow about the room, looking for the source of my tension.

It was just Gabrelle. She lay on her glass chaise longue, looking beautiful and elegant even in sleep. Her soft pink hair cascaded around her brown shoulders, and her soft, plump lips were slightly ajar as though inviting a kiss. She wore a cream négligée that pulled awkwardly across her belly and slipped sideways, revealing a flash of light brown breast, with a soft blue blanket covering her legs. A hint of passionfruit wafted around her.

Gabrelle was the heir of House Allura, the house of beauty. If she was a goddess, she'd be Aphrodite. As the heir of the house of sensuality, I'd spent my whole life trying to get in Gabrelle's pants.

Dion had invented some no-sex pact, claiming that we heirs shouldn't screw each other because that might complicate life when our time came to jointly rule.

But he was a freaking idiot who didn't even know that Gabrelle and Ronan used to fuck like rabbits whenever they got drunk.

My footsteps echoed through the silent Lakehouse as I approached Gabrelle. The weight of my newfound responsibilities bore down on me, intensifying my simmering anger. I paused, my eyes locked on Gabrelle's peaceful form on the chaise longue. The soft glow of the moon highlighted the vulnerability woven on her face.

My heart clenched, torn between the desire to protect her

and the bitterness that threatened to consume me. Slowly, I reached out and brushed a lock of pink hair behind her perfect pointed ear.

Gabrelle stirred, her eyes fluttering open, her soft pink eyes blinking up at me. Confusion clouded her gaze for a moment, but her lack of composure only lasted a moment before she snapped herself together. It was impressive, really, her ability to maintain her façade of perfection, even while the world around her crumbled.

She patted down the soft blue blanket that covered her legs. "You're here."

The well of angry heat in my belly throbbed, and I barked a reply. "How observant." The anger in my tone was unmistakable. Even when I tried to sound calm, my inner, unquenchable rage shone through every word.

The air between us crackled with unspoken words and the weight of our shared past. "So bitter," she finally said.

"You don't understand, Gabrelle," I whispered. "The danger we face, the Shadow Walkers...It's unlike anything we've encountered before."

Gabrelle sat up, her expression a mixture of concern and defiance. "Leif, we're not strangers to danger. We've faced challenges together, and we can face this too. But you have to let us in, let us help you carry this burden."

My fists clenched at my sides, my inner wolf wrestling with my desire to protect and the bitter knowledge of my failures. I took a step back, my voice raw. "You can't help."

Gabrelle looked at me in silence. Our history filled the space between us, but all those moments of laughter couldn't fill up the gnawing emptiness in my heart.

She changed tactics and rose to her feet in a smooth, elegant motion. Her cream négligée hugged her curves like milk, and she plastered a deliberately sinful smile on her plum lips. "I was just dreaming about you, Leif."

My eyes narrowed. She looked hot as fuck, a walking embodiment of a bunch of dreams I'd had over the years. "You were?" I couldn't detect any arousal mixed into her usual passionfruit scent, but perhaps it was coming.

She lifted a shoulder. "Shall we call a halt to the pact, just for this evening? I'm in the mood for a little fun." She smiled seductively. "It might lessen your load."

She glanced down at my naked dick, which immediately hardened. I'd spent my life trying to bed this Gaia-be-damned female, and now that I'd finally come to my senses and realized there was more to life than screwing around, she finally offered herself up.

A deep growl rumbled from my throat, and I stepped closer, towering over her. "Be careful what you wish for, Gabrelle," I warned.

She took it as a game. I could tell she was just trying to stir me back to my old self, her playmate who used to joke and laugh about sex all the time, but she was dealing with something dangerous.

I wasn't the fae I used to be.

She wriggled slightly, her brown skin wafting sensuality. Just being this close to her made me hard.

But she was dealing with a beast now, not a faeling.

In an instant, I was by her side. I flipped her around and pressed her back against me, poking my cock into her silk negligee, hard. Her ass was soft and giving and felt fantastic against my aching dick. I fisted her luscious pink hair in one hand and transformed one single forefinger into a sharp claw,

5

which I held at her throat. "Are you sure, princess? My sexual appetites have gotten a lot darker recently."

The little cub deep inside me whimpered silently at this interaction. My inner pup wanted to play with Gabrelle, maybe rub up against her and have her stroke my fur or tease me about chasing balls. She would swat me on the nose and call me a bad dog, and I'd whine to apologize.

But that inner pup was gone. I had to be an alpha now.

So I would take her if she let me. But it would be punishing and brutal, not playful.

Her body was pressed against mine, soft and supple, molding against my hardness perfectly. Her breathing came faster, but it wasn't desire. Her anger met mine, and she elbowed me in the belly with all the force of a trained warrior. "Fuck off, wolf boy."

She danced out of my reach, and I laughed. I didn't recognize the fae I was becoming. Didn't recognize the cold, hard bark of laughter, but I knew this was me now. That the scales had fallen from my eyes, that I now saw the world as it was.

Mom had protected me from so much. I'd laughed about the Shadow Walkers, avoided any responsibility, and hadn't lifted a finger to help her deal with them. Then she was slaughtered by them on a trip out East. And where was I at the time? Drinking with my friends, of course, like a fucking child.

Well, I'd grown up a lot these past few weeks. I might not yet sit upon the Verdan throne, but I was already the alpha of my pack. The only fae standing between my wolves and the Shadow Walkers was me. Responsibility weighed heavily on my shoulders, dragging me down, and turning me from a playful cub into a strict alpha. I might not like it, but it was who I had to be.

Perhaps Gabrelle noticed my inner turmoil. Her dusty pink eyes softened, and she flicked a lock of dusty pink hair over her shoulder. "You don't have to do this, Leif. Don't have to become this...this...whatever you're becoming. You aren't alone. Ronan, D, Neela, we're all on your side. I know you were thrust into a role you don't want, Alpha of your pack, and you—"

Her pity fueled my rage. "You don't have a clue, beauty queen. You'll be there to hold my hand during a foot race or a magical trial, but this isn't the classroom anymore. I'm facing a full-scale threat from beings we know nothing about who are targeting shifters. Targeting my pack. I am responsible for every single wolf in the realm. So don't tell me you understand or that you will help, because you can't do either."

Her mouth hung open, and regret tried to pierce my anger but failed.

I turned and left. No idea why I even came here. Some lingering part of me thought to seek refuge at the Lakehouse, where I'd spent so many happy hours hanging out with my friends, but there was nothing for me there. Just memories and the past.

I extinguished my light as I stepped outside and slammed the glass door behind me, leaving Gabrelle alone in the dark.

Alara

Pa looked sicker every day.

His hair, which used to be the same shade of flaming orange as mine, was fading into bone white, and his nut-brown skin looked sallow. He sat by the fire, soaking up its warmth with the blanket over his knee, and when he called my name, I willed up a smile.

I turned from the sink where I was rinsing out a glass. "Yes, Pa?"

"The faelings are playing games down on the beach today, Al. You should join them."

"I'm not a child, Pa. I'm twenty-three."

He patted down his blanket. "Even more reason to join in, Alara. You need all the skills and practice you can get before you ascend."

"No." I shook my head. "There's too much to do here. This den won't clean itself, you know."

I strove for a jovial tone to jolly him off course, but he was determined. "This den is spotless, and you know it. Even if I was wading up to my knees in trash, I'd still say it was more important for you to wrestle and tussle with your peers. How else will you ever figure out where you fit into the pack?"

I busied my hands with the tea towel while thinking of an

original response. We'd had this conversation so many times in so many different forms over the years that it tasted stale. "I don't need to fit in with the pack. I can go my own way."

Pa bristled, and a shadow of his old self shone through. "You are a shifter. Pack is everything. Hierarchy is everything. You know that, so stop playing the fool."

His words stung. My lack of participation in the pack's fun and games marked me as an outcast, and I had to put up with jibes and barbs from my peers. The last thing I wanted was to endure them at home as well.

I slammed the glass on the kitchen counter. I took some deep breaths to pull myself together. Smoke from the fire mingled with the roasting beef, making the den smell delicious. Our den was small but cozy, a one-room cottage with aged wood. "What about Valann Croft? She doesn't fit in with the pack, and you have plenty of respect for her."

Pa tilted his head like he was trying really hard to understand me. His wispy white hair floated in the heat from the fire. "Valann Croft is as crazy as a box of kittens. You don't want to turn out like her, do you?"

I pictured the old shifter in her filthy den, babbling nonsense to anybody who would listen.

No, I definitely didn't want to turn out like her. But nor did I want to chase a ball and wrestle other Unascended wolves so we could sort out some bullshit hierarchy.

Pa's voice was softer but more dangerous. "Your mother would have wanted you to go."

I bit back a sigh. He was playing the dead-mom card, and it was a trump. She died when I was five years old, and I barely remembered her, but I still felt duty-bound to honor her wishes.

It was just Pa and me now; he was all I had in the world. I loved him fiercely, and I'd run out of excuses.

But I wouldn't go graciously. In frustration, I flung the tea towel to the floor. "Fine. I'll head down to the beach," I declared before storming out of our den, slamming the door behind me, and stepping onto the small porch.

The little cottage den that Pa and I shared was right on a windy clifftop overlooking the magnificent Omber Strait. I closed my eyes for a few seconds and relished the cool air on my face. A stiff wind brought a strong salty taste and blew my orange hair across my face.

Stepping off the porch, I followed the winding track along the clifftop and headed toward town. Self-loathing gnawed at me, amplifying the biting wind that whipped against my face. I was such a bitch. My dad was dying, visibly weakening every single day, and I was having a little temper tantrum about playing with my friends. Like all sick wolves, he needed physical affection, and I was storming away. Usually, I found the constant rumble of waves crashing against the shore calming, but today it fueled my self-loathing.

Shoving my hands in my pockets and putting down my head against the wind, I swore to do better. Be a better daughter. Who cared if I had to spend the afternoon baring my fangs and jostling others to the ground?

At least I wouldn't have to put up with this shit once I'd ascended. The first Ascension rite after a shifter turned twenty-five, they had to confront Gaia, the Earth Goddess. If she deemed them worthy, they ascended into the full potential of their magical power, becoming stronger.

If Gaia deemed them unworthy, they died. Risking our lives was the price we fae had to pay for our power.

Thankfully, most shifters passed their Ascension rite, so I wasn't too worried. But perhaps I would be when my twenty-fifth birthday crept closer.

It wasn't just wolves who ascended. Other fae faced the Ascension rite, too, the non-shifters. Or so I'd heard. I'd only met a few non-shifters in my life, so everything I knew about them was hearsay. And I knew even less about the humans who lived on the other side of the barrier across the Requin Sea; all I knew was that their hair was dull and the color didn't match their eyes, which must look super weird, and that they had round ears and no magic.

The wind tried to rip off my heavy blue wool coat, so I tugged it tighter around me. This was perfect weather for tucking up with a good book or trying to decipher an Eldralith scroll. I could settle down in front of the fire and unravel the clues of the ancient language, passing on any interesting findings to Pa while he read his own book.

But I told Pa I'd go to the beach, so the beach it was. I could read later—after I'd given Pa a good long cuddle and apologized for my outburst.

As I neared the beach, the cacophony of yelps and howls of victory reached my ears, a sure sign that the lively games were already in full swing. Then my peers' scents mingled with the salty air, all blended together in a smell soup.

Then I saw them, down on the beach below me. They were playing some kind of chasing game that involved snatching a parcel from each others' razor-sharp claws and sprinting in circles.

And I got to join in. Yippee.

My control over my wolf form was dismal. Worse than most other Unascended shifters. After my Ascension, I'd have complete control and be able to shift at will, but until then, I had to make do with a crazy inner beast who only emerged when I was in danger. I felt like a thirteen-year-old male with an overactive dick, except my shame manifested as a mid-sized orange-furred wolf instead of an unwelcome erection. Even harder to ignore.

I was so focused on the game on the beach below me that I almost jumped out of my skin when a stick cracked behind me. My hackles rose, and I whirled around to find myself face-to-face with a muscular black shifter in wolf form. He stood on the narrow path behind me with his ears forward, his fangs bared in a vicious smile. Ruben Rootswold, the Unascended shifter with irritatingly good control over his wolf and a bone-deep hatred for me. Shit.

He shifted into fae form, no doubt so he could torment me verbally before he got physical. His nose had a hook big enough to catch a shark, so I called him fishy back when we were cubs. I didn't know he'd grow into a burly beta with a strong vengeance streak and a good memory.

His black hair was long and lank with sweat, and he smelled like he'd just lost a wrestling contest with a pig. "Where's your book today, word girl?"

I cocked out a hip. "Word-girl? Seriously? That's the best you can do?"

A warning rumbled from the back of his throat. "Don't talk back to me, bitch, or you'll get what's coming."

I smirked. "Bitch? Come on, you can do better than that. At least word-girl was original."

He was bigger than me, stronger than me, faster than me, and a shitload meaner than me. So why the hell was I goading him? Because I was a mouthy bitch with a self-control problem.

And every sign of his growing anger, that stupid animalistic growl, those hunching shoulders, and his reddening face, just make me want to hurt him more.

I smiled calmly. "And let me see, what else did you say? Oh yes, I'll get what's coming. Well, that seems fairly self-evident, but good on you for figuring it out."

Ruben growled. "Bitch," he repeated, and I couldn't help laughing.

"Shouldn't you be off seducing somebody's mate?" I asked. Last month, Ruben tried to sleep with Krista, and her mate had gone absolutely wild and almost killed him. Jealousy was rare among wolves, mostly we were happy to screw anybody, and nobody minded. But newly mated shifters were the exception, and everyone knew to steer clear of them for at least a few months. Except for Fishy, apparently.

He'd been the town's laughingstock ever since his stupid error, and he clearly didn't like being reminded of it. He snarled and lunged at me. His control over his wolf wasn't refined enough that he could shift mid-leap, so the spikes that dug into my throat were fae fingernails, not wolf claws. Thank Gaia for that; otherwise, this could end very differently.

"You fucking outsider," he warned, calling me the worst name he could think of. Most wolves despised the idea of being different, of not wanting to join in. But it wasn't an insult to me. If his fingers weren't closing around my throat and making it hard to breathe, I might have laughed. Heat rushed to my face as I struggled to suck in oxygen.

Ruben squeezed his eyes shut, his face etched with visible strain as he attempted to shift forms. Being Unascended, the transformation wasn't yet second nature for him. It gave me a moment to escape, and I squirmed out of his clutches and backed away, gulping down air and wondering what on earth to do next.

He was faster, stronger, and meaner. But also dumber. I folded my arms across my chest, going for a confident air I didn't feel. "Did you hear about the new arrivals from Verda City?"

Pa had been around a long time, formed a lot of connections, and had a lot of friends in the pack. The older ones visited with him every day, bringing him all the latest gossip, so I latched onto a piece of news and tried to sell it as interesting.

Ruben had shifted by now, a hulking black wolf with fur just as lanky as the hair on his head. He didn't pounce but cocked his head, listening. At least in wolf form, he couldn't talk, so that was a positive.

"Apparently, they're emissaries from the alpha of alphas." Our village, Sylverclyff, was run by Alpha Blackwood, but every pack in the realm answered to House Caro, and the alpha from the capital was the alpha of alphas.

The whiff of power and hierarchy got Ruben salivating. He probably had a raging hard-on underneath that lank black fur.

I pretended to think hard while seagulls crooned and cartwheeled in the sky. "I wonder why the city shifters are here. I heard they're going to pick his next betas."

That last part was a lie, but it had the desired effect. Ruben puffed out his chest and tried to rub his two brain cells together to deduce what that might mean for him. He might be chosen as a beta for the alpha from Verda City.

His attention veered from me, and he looked off toward the village as though he could see through the thick scrubby bush. A seagull squawked loudly. Then he bounded away, weaving through the stunted trees.

I couldn't help it. I called after him, "Good boy, fishy."

My adrenaline subsided as I picked my way down through the rocks to the beach to join the games, but they were already over. A steady stream of shifters flowed toward the village square, their colorful heads bobbing and chatting excitedly. Two powder-blue braids atop a snow-white body drew my attention, and I slotted in beside my friend, Selene.

"What's happening? What happened to chase-the-leader? Or were you playing snatch-the-ball today?"

She gave me a half-hearted scowl. Selene loved beach games as much as the next wolf, but at least she respected my aversion to them. "The visitors from Verda City want everyone to gather in the town."

"So?"

Two gulls screeched overhead. "So, we're gathering." She sounded exasperated.

I looked around at the excited chattering of the other fae heading our way. "All this fuss for a couple of visitors from the big smoke?"

"It's not just that." My friend's voice was terse, her words sharp. Selene could be relied on to be ultra-relaxed, so her tension was unnerving.

"What do you mean?" I whispered.

"They're taking volunteers." She made air quotes around the last word, then she bent down to brush sand off her legs.

I brushed some sand off her back, then slapped the gritty grains off my hands. "Volunteers for what?"

She glanced at me, her powder-blue eyes tight and tense. "They're conscripting shifters for the alpha of alpha's army."

I tripped over a log half-buried in the cool sand and hopped a couple of paces, clutching my big toe. "Conscripting? Like, taking fae against their will?"

She nodded.

"What the fuck?" I shouted, making no effort to mask my words, even though we were in the thick scrubby trees and just around the bend from the village. If these superior assholes from the capital city tried to come in here and take our shifters, they would damn well hear my thoughts on the matter.

Selene grabbed my hand. Like all wolves, I calmed down at physical touch, so I rubbed my bare arm against hers, soaking it up. But my serenity fled when she dug her fingernails into my palm. "Shut up. You don't want to draw their attention," she hissed.

True enough. I absolutely did not want to be forced to join the alpha's army. I got that his mom had just died, and he probably wanted to make a mark and build the strongest shifter army in history, or some shit like that, but I would not be part of it.

I was the closest thing to a pacifist you could get and still be born to fangs and fur. "Do you know who they're choosing?"

Selene's powder-blue eyes locked onto me. "Every family must send an Ascended wolf. Every family."

My feet crunched over the leaves fallen on the sandy ground, and I breathed in the salt spray, blended with the smells of the other villagers I knew so well.

Every family had to send an Ascended wolf. For most fae, that wouldn't be a problem. Most families had ten or twenty members, and at least one of them was a meathead enough to want to go to war. Ruben and his brothers would probably fight for the privilege.

But not me. It was just me and Pa, and I wasn't Ascended.

We stepped into the bright sunshine, and the sand underfoot

was replaced by gravel. Sweat trickled on my brow.

Selene squeezed my hand. "I'm sure they'll excuse your dad, hon." She knew me well enough to understand exactly where my thoughts had gone.

I snorted. "Right, because Verda City wolves are so famous for being relaxed."

City shifters had a terrible reputation for mixing their hedonism with strict punishment for anyone who strayed from the pack's plan. Leif Caro hadn't been Alpha of Alphas for long, but word had already reached us that he was the biggest prick of the bunch.

I'd never been so reluctant to enter my own village, but as I approached, even the gulls stopped screeching. A sense of dread settled in my limbs, and I had to force myself to keep moving.

I would never let them take Pa. He wouldn't survive twenty-four hours away from home. He didn't even go to the village for the annual Ascension party anymore. If they needed a wolf from my family, they would have to take me.

I might not actually be Ascended, but I was fucking good at lying.

Alara

Underneath the scorching sun, five unfamiliar shifters stood in a loose circle before the small, ramshackle building that housed Kenny's bar. The air was thick with the lingering sour smell of stale beer, as usual, and the gravel road sparkled in the intense sunlight like a carpet of silver coins. On either side of the road were small shops and cozy dens. This open space in the center of the village was the closest thing we had to a town square, where fae usually gathered and lurked when there was gossip to share.

So why did I feel like a lamb being herded for slaughter? Instead of excitement, I couldn't shake off the nagging feeling of impending doom.

The five shifters watched us file in and fill the square, leaving plenty of space around the strangers.

City wolves. They had the loose limbs and steel spines of shifters, but their faces were stony and solemn. Most of my fellow villagers instinctively averted their gazes, displaying submission to the newcomers. Unlike them, I locked eyes with each shifter, studying their every move. The one who seemed to hold authority was a formidable female, her broad shoulders and pale blue skin contrasting with vibrant violet hair and eyes. The other four glanced up at her at intervals, following her lead. Once we all assembled in the square, she nodded, and the tension in my nerves spiraled tighter.

A younger fae, a male with dark brown skin and curly flaxen hair, stepped forward, managing to look down on all of us at once. He produced a scroll and began reading, explaining exactly what Selene already told me. Every family in Sylverclyff must commit one Ascended wolf to the alpha of alphas.

His final two words sent a shiver through me. "No exceptions."

Selene's reassuring grip on my arm provided a comforting anchor amidst the turmoil. Wolves were touchy-feely creatures, even outsiders like me, and physical affection was worth a thousand supportive words. But her words mattered too. "We'll tell them you're part of my family," she whispered. "Nobody will call us out on it because everybody loves your Pa."

Everybody loved Pa, true enough. His beloved status within the community offered a potential loophole. While they might not lie for me, they would do it for him. Lie to the city wolves. Let them believe I was part of Selene's family. The realization ignited a flicker of warmth within me as I gained a newfound appreciation for the strength of our pack.

My thoughts were interrupted as the flaxen-haired male resumed reading from his scroll. "Artemis."

Shit. That scroll contained a list of the families in Sylverclyff. I clung onto Selene's wrist like a lifeline, hoping her ruse would work.

The Artemis twins stepped forward when their family name was called. Twins were so rare among fae that these guys were practically famous throughout the realm, and their mere existence was one of our village's proudest achievements.

However, their mother pushed them back and stepped forward, calling loudly, "Get back in line, you two. You're not a day over twenty, and you're not going anywhere." She held her head high. "I am."

The flaxen-haired city shifter continued down the list, naming every family in Sylverclyff. When he called, "Everly," I took a deep breath and stepped forward, my heart stuttering. My name was on the list. There was no escaping.

A low murmur rippled through my brethren. Pity rolled off them in waves, mingling with the sour beer from Kenny's bar and the underlying scent of their fear. They knew my situation. They knew I wasn't Ascended and that sending my father would be tantamount to sending him to his death.

The list-obsessed city shifter barked the same question he'd asked everyone. "Are you Ascended?"

I glanced around, catching the shifting weight of my fellow villagers, the slight scuffle of boots on gravel, and the distant croon of seagulls.

I threw back my shoulders, mustering courage. "Yes."

I waited for the fae to nod me toward the group of conscripts like he did after every other name, but he seemed to be extending the silence, toying with me.

Could he hear the blood pounding through my veins? Could he sense the tension in the square? Could he read the knowledge in every villager's mind that I was lying?

I exchanged a glance with Fishy. Ruben Rootswold. He'd obviously figured out the city fae weren't here to select betas and that I had lied to him. He held my gaze and smiled slowly, a dirty smile that showed he intended to rat me out. To tell the city shifters I was lying.

My heart pounded as Ruben raised his head and cleared his

throat. "She's not—"

His father elbowed him sharply in the ribs, shutting him up. I'd never liked that family, but suddenly I loved his dad.

The flaxen-haired guard looked between Ruben and me, then stared me down, assessing me. "What is your Ascended power?"

"Lupus," I said quickly, knowing that was the correct answer. Every wolf ascended into Lupus; otherwise, they were kicked out of the pack.

"Do you have a secondary power?"

Fuck. I should have thought this through. I didn't know they'd ask what my secondary magic was, but of course, they would need that information to use us properly.

I looked around desperately, and my eyes landed on Selene's. "War," I blurted out, naming the power that my best friend wielded.

The city fae narrowed his eyes at me. "You're not very strong, are you?"

Fae hated conversing with War wielders because the gaze of War was unsettling. The strongest wielders could make you feel like your life was in danger just by looking at you. Clearly, I didn't impress this male much.

From the corner of my eye, I noticed Selene staring at him intently, so hopefully, he'd feel some measure of discomfort under her gaze that he would attribute to me.

Finally, he nodded me toward the other conscripts.

I tried not to breathe as I crunched across the gravel toward the chosen group. My blood pounded in my ears, and I concentrated on staying upright while the city wolf read out name after name, and fae stepped forward with varying degrees of reluctance or excitement.

I'd saved Pa, but I hadn't thought it through. What was I supposed to do now? I wasn't Ascended, I had no special magic and could barely control my wolf; all I had was a weak ability to decipher languages and a sassy mouth. How the fuck was that going to help me in Verda City?

The selection process was over, and the flaxen-haired fae barked out one final command. "War wielders, follow me. The rest of you, go with Commander Peterson."

Oh, good. The War wielders were being separated from the pack. Of course, they were—this was an army. Fucking brilliant.

At least Selene was in my group. She squeezed my hand briefly and gave me a tight smile as we fell into step behind the flaxen-haired fae.

Our little group of War wielders.

There were only three of us, plus the flaxen-haired city wolf who introduced himself as Onyx.

"Are we supposed to just call you Onyx?" Selene asked.

He gave her a flat look. "Well, that is my name."

"It's kind of a stupid name, that's all, hon," Selene muttered.

Of the two of us, I was usually the one who ran my mouth off, but I was so busy not looking at the guard so he wouldn't notice my missing War that I couldn't engage. Fear of discovery made me keep my head down and my mouth zipped.

"The alpha doesn't tolerate backchat," Onyx snarled. "So you'd better cut your attitude, or he'll cut out your tongue."

That was almost enough to make me join in the conversation. I was a member of the most hierarchical group of creatures in the known universe, but I hated authority. That was a problem. That had always been a problem for me. And if I had to spend any time with this authoritarian alpha asshole, it would be the biggest problem. I kept my eyes on the sand and my mouth sewn, but who knew how long I could keep it up.

The other member of our elite crew of War wielders was Johnson Jacobs, a middle-aged male with a couple of hundred years behind his belt and a resting smile face, which set him apart from most wolves around here.

Selene and I called him Weiner behind his back, of course. I mean, Johnson, come on, right?

"Keep it civil, Selene," Weiner warned.

Selene may not have much respect for this Onyx dude, but she did for Weiner, so she held her tongue.

Onyx glared at me, and I felt a needle pushing into my wrist. I couldn't help glancing down, expecting to see a thin metal rod protruding from my skin and blood trickling out, but of course, it was just an illusion. Onyx must be powerful in War to manifest such an intense physical sensation. "You have half an hour to gather your belongings and say your farewells." He released me from his gaze, and the needle at my wrist disappeared. "Don't be late," he barked.

Selene gave me a quick smile and then jogged in the direction of her home. Weiner raised his eyebrows at me but kept my secret before stripping naked and shifting, then bounding inland toward his family's den.

I jogged back toward the scrubby coastal forest, heading vaguely northerly, but I wasn't going home.

I couldn't tell Pa what I'd done. He would never let me go. He would climb to his spindly frail legs and offer himself up as a conscript before allowing me to put myself in danger. But he wouldn't make it a thousand steps before he keeled over in the sand, and I couldn't live the rest of my life knowing I could have gone instead.

So I had to keep away from my den, keep away from Pa.

But it killed me not to say goodbye. I spent a half-hour in the forest, shaking, having the conversation in my head where I gave Pa a massive hug, he squeezed me tight and told me he was proud of me, then kissed me goodbye.

As farewells went, an imaginary one was pretty shit, but it would have to do.

A glinting light caught my eye, and I saw a tiny bird in the trees, encrusted with jewels and reflecting sunlight into a rainbow of colors. A jewelwing. Most fae thought they were extinct, and I'd read about them in some old texts and always hoped to see one. Maybe this was Gaia's way of bidding me farewell. It looked at glittering among the dull green leaves of the shrubby trees, and it seemed to look right back.

"Goodbye, jewelwing," I said, feeling calmer and more sure that I was doing the right thing, making the right choice.

I ran back to the village square, my feet crunching over the gravel, signaling my approach. Most dens had an ocean of gravel around them as a courtesy to warn inhabitants of approaching fae, and we applied the same principles to the common spaces of Sylverclyff.

Consequently, every shifter in the square looked up at my approach, and I nodded a confident farewell to some of them while I trotted toward my elite squad of Warriors.

Onyx seemed to see right through me. "Where are your personal belongings?"

I shrugged, trying to look calm. "I like to travel light."

Onyx looked me up and down. "Just as well because we're running."

He meant we were running as wolves. Shifted. Which was

as easy as breathing for Ascended wolves, and like pulling lightning from a stone for me.

"In wolf form?" I asked, playing dumb and playing for time. Selene glared at me, looking all kinds of feral. I knew she was trying to support me, that she was freaking out for me, but she just looked terrifying.

"Obviously," Onyx barked. "Strip."

Alara

I'd never been in a moonway, but obviously, I knew about them. They were the fastest way to travel through the six fae realms, Verda, Fen, Caprice, Ourea, Brume, and the Unseelie Realm of Dust. Moonways were magical shortcuts across the land and could theoretically be built to connect any two places in Arathay, from the far North of Fen to the deepest South of Dust, or from our little coast in Verda to the Ourean mountains in the West.

But our tiny village of Sylverclyff on the eastern coast of Verda was a two-hour run from the nearest moonway. Which was why I'd never been in one. Because a two-hour run in wolf form was a five-hour walk in fae form. And I couldn't shift.

Which was a real fucking problem because I'd just told this Onyx guy that I was Ascended, so my wolf should be under my perfect control.

But it wasn't. My wolf was a rebellious teenager.

Onyx shifted into a sleek black wolf, far leaner and more attractive than Ruben's oily one, then he snatched up his bundle of clothes in his big jaws and pounded away toward the West without a backward glance.

Weiner wasted no time in stripping down and adding his clothes to his bag of belongings, shifting into his gray wolf, grabbing up the bag in his jaws, and running after Onyx.

"I guess we're getting naked," I sighed. Most shifters were super comfortable with nudity, but I'd always been odd, and another one of my peculiarities was my reluctance to flaunt my naked body in front of the whole town.

Still, if I shifted without stripping, my clothes would tear and I'd have nothing to put on at the other end.

That was if I could shift at all.

Selene stripped naked and looked at me, her snow-white skin glowing under the sun and her powder-blue braids caressing her full curves. "Are you sure you want to go through with this, hon? You won't be able to hide being Unascended for long, and when the alpha of alphas finds out...."

I kicked off my shoes. "Trust me, the last thing I want to do is go play soldiers in the city. And I know I can't get away with it forever. But I have to follow Onyx, or they'll send back guards and take Pa. I have to go with him." I unbuttoned my tight jeans and shimmied out of them, letting them drop to the gravel. "Besides, I'll steer clear of Alpha Caro. I'll do my best to blend in and stay out of the way. You know me, I'm an expert at not joining in."

Selene was completely naked, and the high sun cast strong shadows across her snowy skin. The triangle of blue hair at the apex of her thighs was a shade darker than the hair on her head, and I glanced away. "Okay. Just keep your head down."

I yanked off my white singlet top fast, and Selene stared at me for a moment, waiting for me to take off my underwear.

"Hurry up, hon," she said with a grin. "Your squeamishness will have to wait. I don't want to lose Onyx. He'll probably accuse us of going AWOL."

I tore off my panties, whipped off my bra, and then bundled

it all together. Standing naked in front of the whole village was a nightmare but not exactly life-threatening.

"Come on, wolf," I muttered to myself. I closed my eyes and thought wolfish thoughts, like how good fish smelled and how lovely and bouncy balls were, but it was no good. I clenched my fists and imagined fur sprouting from my skin, but when I peeked open one eye, my usual nut-brown skin was as hairless as ever.

"Shit," I muttered.

Selene looked at me with a feral expression in her powder-blue eyes. "If you don't shift, we will both fucking die," she hissed. My friend shifted expertly into a sleek white wolf with a hint of pale blue at the tips of her fur. I would have called her beautiful if she didn't shove her sharp jaws in my face and snarl ferociously. Her breath was hot, and for one single moment, I thought she was going to bite me.

The adrenaline was enough to shock my wolf into appearing, and the transformation came over my body in one jolting movement. Suddenly, I was no longer myself but a wild wolf with dark red fur and a carefree heart.

I howled in success, and Selene lowered her head for an instant, then bounded away after Onyx and Wiener. I snatched up my pile of clothing, smelling my own panties quite strongly now I was a wolf, then I broke into a sprint after Selene, chasing her blue-white fur as she raced uphill through the scrubby bushland.

My legs coiled and sprang, and I raced joyfully, feeling the freedom and rush of being a dominant predator, powering my way over the earth. I would never get sick of this, and after I turned twenty-five, I might become one of those weirdos who lived full-time in wolf form.

Fatigue set in after about an hour, but Selene and I had caught up with Onyx and Weiner by then, and all of us settled into a loping gait, not as frenzied or fast as at first. We were passing through lands I'd never visited, greener and more lush than the coastal village I called home. A copse of golden trees glinted under the warm sun, and I detected the scents of creatures living there that I'd never smelled before.

How many wonders were waiting for me beyond the confines of my tiny town? Perhaps this conscription was a blessing. This could be a fun adventure if I could steer clear of the alpha and keep my head down.

Onyx stopped by a purple flowering shrub that glinted metallically. He shifted into fae form and looked at us, his middling dick bouncing against his balls. "This is the entrance to the moonway."

Weiner nodded sharply, and I knew Selene had been here before, so I hid my confusion at seeing nothing resembling a magical pathway to the city.

"You may shift and dress."

Thank fuck for that. I did not want to turn up Verda City naked. Luckily, shifting to fae form was easy, even for me, because it was my natural state. I stayed half a step behind Selene and changed as fast as possible, buttoning my tight jeans like lightning and pulling on my white singlet top inside out.

"Follow me." Onyx stepped forward and appeared to blur. This must be the moonway.

Weiner followed immediately, and Selene looked at me, winking. "Inside out," she said with a nod toward my top, then she stepped onto the invisible path.

I placed my foot exactly where Selene had, and then I was

in. The others were ahead of me, and I jogged to catch up with Selene, marveling at how every step of mine took me yards through the field. The orange grass beside me blurred as I walked, and I couldn't help the little giggle that bubbled out of me.

Selene grinned. "Pretty cool, huh?"

"Super cool."

After half an hour, the fields around us disappeared, and blurred buildings took their place. The moonway spilled us out onto a broad paved area with a copse of trees behind us and a magnificent black marble building before us.

The majestic black marble building towered, its intricate carvings and porticos standing out against the bright sky. It was breathtaking. Even the granite slabs beneath my feet were polished to perfection.

"This is Alpha's den," Onyx said.

I couldn't hold in my gasp. It was so enormous, so stupidly spectacular, so wonderful. I could fit my entire hut in the front room of that place and still have enough space to hold a dance party.

"Impressive," Weiner said.

I couldn't agree more. I wanted to get on my knees and bow down to that building, but then I remembered it was home to an asshole who was recruiting us without our consent, and I wiped the grin off my face.

Two dozen fae stood outside the building, looking as lost as I felt. From the prickles and physical sensations all over my body, I could tell they wielded War. An army gathered from throughout the realm to serve as Alpha Caro's personal guard. Against their will.

Asshole.

Another Caro pack member started barking commands, making us recruits all line up in a row. It wasn't until I heard the words, "Alpha will be here soon," that I realized just how much shit I was in.

My entire survival plan was to avoid the prince and keep my head low, and apparently, he would be here within the hour. Shit buckets.

We didn't even have to wait an hour. Three minutes later, Prince Caro, Alpha of Alphas and heir to the Verdan throne, strode out of his den. He was tall and broad, with creamy skin. He wore a suit of midnight armor, a black leather jacket, and pants that swallowed every particle of light. His face was strong and handsome, but his gaze held more than just beauty—it hinted at danger and mystery.

His silver hair cascaded down his back like a river of light. Even from the far end of the line, I could see his cruel eyes flashing silver with anger. Like a god carved from glinting steel, he exuded power and control. But despite his size, every step he took looked graceful and precise.

At the sight of him, his betas cowered, shrinking ever so slightly into themselves and lowering their heads.

They knew this male. They knew exactly how angry and cruel he was, and they were clearly scared. So he was clearly charming.

With so many Wars present, I didn't worry too much about the effect my gaze would have on the king—or rather, wouldn't have. Somebody would be looking at him at all times, so he must be swimming in creepy sensations.

So I looked at him openly as he came down the line, inspecting us. As he got close, I saw the brutal cut of his jaw, his lips pressed in displeasure. When he got to Selene, he paused, drinking her in from head to toe. My friend was gorgeous, sculpted and lean, with large boobs and long, long legs that drew a lot of attention. Her snowy skin played off her powder-blue hair and eyes.

That was exactly the look the prince was giving her. Lascivious. Sexual.

He didn't even address her but jerked a finger her way and spoke to a beta. "This one."

I had a vision of him taking her against her will, her squirming and writhing, and him not caring if he hurt her.

I stepped forward, yelling. "No! You can't have her. She won't go anywhere with you."

The alpha of alphas turned his focus to me, and a bolt of pure pleasure shot through me. He was the highest member of House Caro, the house of sensuality, and I knew that being near him would be... pleasurable...but I hadn't known it would be like being drenched in a lust potion.

His silver eyes flashed. "You dare to speak to your alpha this way?"

He stepped closer, and the wet heat in my pussy dripped. "You're not my alpha. Alpha Blackwood is back home in Sylverclyff."

Way to keep my head down. Not only had I drawn the prince's attention, but I'd followed it up with an insult. Clever.

His face drained of blood. "I am the alpha of all Verda. Your Blackwood crawls on her belly before me, and you should do likewise."

"I've never been very good at crawling."

You will learn how to crawl, even if I have to shove you to your knees to teach you."

The heat in my pussy grew at that image, but I knew it was

just the effect of his House's power. I refused to be cowed by him. The more powerful the bully, the more I rallied against him, and the alpha of alphas was the most powerful bully of all.

I opened my mouth to reply, but the prince jabbed his finger at me, clocking me painfully in the chest. "This one, too," he barked over his shoulder. "I need to teach her some manners."

Alara

Of the dozens of War wielders presented to the alpha, he selected three for further investigation. Or interrogation. Or, in my case, to teach me some manners.

Me, Selene, and a slim male with bronzed skin and lean muscles who shook his head frantically when I asked his name.

Prince Leif Caro, Alpha of Alphas, heir to the throne of Verda, led the three of us inside and then spun around. Without a word, he pointed at me and beckoned me to follow him, leaving Selene and the terrified male behind.

"Good luck, hon," Selene mouthed.

The alpha led me along a corridor that began as a grand, tapestry-lined hallway, but as we followed its twists and turns, it became more like a tunnel carved through the rock.

We reached a flight of stone stairs that spiraled down into darkness, and at their base, he paused and let me pass. He smelled of spice and leather. Just being this close to the Head of House Caro, the master of sensuality, was enough to make my panties soak through.

I paused on the threshold to the room, my mouth parted. Even from here, I could see the walls were stacked stone, smoothed and carved, comforting in their heaviness. Wolves liked to surround themselves in sturdy rock, and this would be an excellent place to relax if it wasn't for the leather restraints, whips, and paddles hanging off pegs on the walls. And the ceiling mirror suspended over the padded table in the room's center.

The alpha shoved me in the small of the back. His touch was hard and brief, but it sang through me. I stumbled a few paces into the room and realized only three walls were made of gray stone. The fourth was a floor-to-ceiling mirror.

"Um..." I was overcome with eloquence while I stared around, taking it in. Several suspended globes of contained Lightning, presumably sourced from the Realm of Caprice, lit the space and cast shadows of the curving arches that spread from floor to ceiling.

This was a sex dungeon. Sex. Dungeon. The pulsing between my legs was real, but it didn't mean I would spread them for a male I'd just met.

I found my tongue. "What am I doing here?" I wrapped my arms across my body protectively, but they just swiped my nipples and made me more aware of my excited state. Over the earthy scent of leather from the room's equipment, I could make out the alpha's musky arousal. Annoyingly, that made me more excited but also more irritated.

"I'm not going to have sex with you," I blurted out. "I don't care who you are or why I've been recruited, you can't force me to do anything."

The alpha ignored me, removed his black leather jacket, and then tugged off his silver shirt, pulling it over his head. For one glorious moment, his face was covered, and I could stare at his bare chest, at his small pink nipples and the way his muscles bunched and rolled with every movement, rippling beneath his smooth skin. Sculpted muscles and a highly fuckable body.

When he flung his shirt at the wall, letting it drop into a puddle on the floor, I looked away. He had the body of a God, but I wouldn't give him the pleasure of noticing how much I liked it. But his broad chest and the muscular curve of his shoulder were seared on my memory, and I was aware of every particle of air between us.

Slowly, so slowly, he circled the room, wearing just his black leather pants, inspecting the implements hanging from the walls. Was he choosing one to use on me? Was there anything I could do about it if he decided to fuck me? And did I even want to stop him?

My body was definitely on board with whatever weird sex dungeon we were in, it was soaking and hot, and I could barely keep my panting in check. The alpha's sexual magic was intense, and my emotions were already in turmoil after the day I'd had. Maybe a good fuck was exactly what I needed. And the longer he took inspecting his weapons, the longer I could watch the lean muscles of his back flex and release.

He picked up a tool with a long handle and a broad padded circle on one end. He whacked it firmly against his thigh, testing it out. The slap of the paddle meeting his leather pants made me jump, but he didn't turn to see my reaction.

"Strip," he barked, not even bothering to make eye contact. "Then lie on the table, face up. I want you watching yourself in the ceiling mirror as I teach you how to behave."

The word "strip" had my traitorous pussy hot and wet, but I had no intention of doing anything this obnoxious male said. Not if I had a choice.

"No."

He rounded on me. In the flickering Lightning, shadows danced on his pale face. He kept his intense silver gaze on mine and slowly stalked closer.

I was already regretting my hasty decision. Maybe a quick fuck with the super alpha wouldn't be so bad. He closed the space between us with deliberate slowness, playing out his authority, and my skin got hot and tight.

"Get on the fucking table, pup."

The murderous glint in his eyes and his cruel tone hardened my spine, and I managed to fold my arms across my chest, enjoying the pressure of my forearms against my nipples. "Are you in the habit of taking females without their consent?"

He growled. "I always have consent."

"Not this time."

I must have been the only shifter in Arathay who was brave enough to deny the alpha of alphas, the heir to the throne, the prince of sensuality. I breathed deeply, expanding my chest, letting my nipples rub against my arms to relieve some of the ache.

Correction. I was the only shifter stupid enough to deny him. Deny myself.

In a smooth action, he picked me up and tossed me over his shoulder so my hair dangled down his back and my ass was in the air. His skin was warm, and his spicy musk was even more potent up close. His hard muscles bunched, and I placed a hand on his butt to keep myself from sliding off sideways since he wasn't holding my legs in place, just letting them flounder against his chest.

An unsophisticated shriek flew from my mouth before I could stop it, then he crossed the room in a few short strides. His shoulder pressed against my pelvis, and the heat in his skin inflamed my own.

Was he really going to take me against my will? I would

fucking kill him if he did. Seriously. I would nurse my fury and revenge for years, if necessary, until I got the chance to carve out his heart and slice off his cock.

The plans were forming so nicely in my head that I was almost disappointed when he deposited me on a red velvet lounge in the corner.

Another unsophisticated shriek, a couple of ungainly kicks in the air, and I managed to right myself.

The alpha looked like an avenging God. Like the Father of Death himself, Mortia, had just discovered his favorite Unseelie had been kidnapped. Like an asshole who would whip me with one of those handy leather straps if I left my seat.

I stayed in my seat.

The prince turned his back on me, and his hands bunched and released, fisting nothing, but the veins in his forearms showed how fucking pissed he was. I tucked my knees up against my chest and rested my back against the cool stone wall, keeping a wary eye on the alpha as he inspected the sex weapons, simmering in barely controlled rage.

How would this play out? Would we stay here until I gave in and consented to sex? If so, we'd be a long, long time. Maybe we'd both die of thirst.

He pulled a tennis ball out of somewhere and stared at it for a moment like he was about to throw it. It was so out of place, that ordinary-looking toy among all these sexual ones. He inspected the ball and tensed the muscles in his forearm, but instead of throwing the ball, he crushed it into dust inside his fist.

I jumped when the door swung open. A wolf entered, slinking in like a sleek predator. She was dark-skinned and beautiful, her eyes and hair glowing like molten gold. Her lips were full and inviting, and she moved with a seductive grace as she stepped closer to the prince.

He greeted her with a long lick up her neck, and her musk instantly filled the room, mixing with his and mine. She ran her fingers through his silver hair and murmured something in his ear that made him smile.

Heat bloomed in my chest that had nothing to do with lust or arousal. It was closer to jealousy, but wolves never got jealous, so it couldn't be that. The two of them were oblivious to me, locked in conversation and touching each other in a suddenly intimate way.

She ran her hands over his sculpted chest, around his sides, and down his back. His eyes closed in pleasure, and he groaned softly as she moved her hands lower.

My stomach twisted as I watched them together, feeling like an intruder into something that should have been private. I shifted uncomfortably on the lounge, wishing I was anywhere else but there.

But at the same time, my skin reacted as if I were the one being caressed, a trail of fire across my nerves.

I couldn't drag my eyes away from the scene. The female's hands paused at the waistband of his black leather pants, and she looked up into his face expectantly. He nodded ever so slightly.

She kneeled on the cold hard ground, her face level with his waist, and she carefully unzipped his fly. His cock sprang free, and a strong pulse thrummed through my body at the sight of it, and when the female leaned in close and licked him from balls to tip, I shivered.

She worked him delicately before taking his cock in her mouth with a passionate intensity that left me breathless.

His body tensed as if her movements made him crazy, and he closed his eyes in pleasure.

He caressed her head, and she pleasured him, his hand fisted in her golden hair. Then, without warning, he snapped her head away from his cock, leaving her panting and wanting more.

His cock was erect, enormous, standing out of the zipped-open pants and glistening with the she-wolf's saliva. She was still on her knees, panting, dripping with desire, her head pulled back at an angle by his firm grip on her golden hair.

I was panting just as much.

My body was alive with heat, burning in a way I had never experienced before. The sight of them together stirred something deep and primal in me, something that wanted to be released and explored.

Leif gestured for the she-wolf to stand, then he took a leather restraint from the wall and commanded her to strip. She obeyed without question, slipping off her clothes with an enviable grace that made my mouth water.

She stood against the wall naked and exposed, her body a feast. Her curves were perfect, lush breasts topped by pert nipples begging for attention. My gaze lingered on the patch of golden curls between her dark thighs; it was so inviting and yet forbidden.

The alpha stepped beside her and bound both of her wrists in the leather restraint, then he moved his hands around her waist as if measuring her for something. He smiled down at her possessively while he attached the bond to the stone wall above her head, forcing her breasts out and forward. He then bent and forced her legs apart roughly, and she glanced down at his head between her thighs with clear longing, but he didn't linger. He secured each of her ankles to the leather buckles on the wall, then stepped away.

The she-wolf looked so vulnerable standing there with her arms bound above her head, her legs apart, her back flush against the cold stone wall, exposed and aroused. I couldn't take my eyes away from her; watching them together had twisted something inside me that I didn't know existed. Nudged my inner wolf.

My heart pounded as the silver prince moved closer to the naked female, his hard cock still on show, his pants loose about his hips.

He flicked the shifter's nipple, and she cried out, shuddering. My body was alive with heat. Leif leaned in and took the wolf's injured nipple gently in his mouth, and my own breast ached with need at the sight.

I reached a hand under my top, up along my smooth, warm skin, and around the swell of my breast. I clasped it hard, trying to ease the aching need. My fingers tingled with unspent energy as I caught my nipple between them. My own moan was inaudible against the groans of the trussed-up female.

The intensity in the room was palpable; it seemed like everything else had faded away while the alpha and his victim were lost in their private world together.

They didn't seem aware of my presence at all. She stood with her back arched, trying to get her restrained body closer to his, her full breasts reaching for him while her wrists and ankles were bound to the wall. His expression was cold and calculating as if he were conducting a punishment, but his cock was hard, and the muscles of his back were coiled and firm.

The prince pulled a black leather whip from the wall and flicked it against the female's other nipple. She moaned, and his cock jumped, and my pussy throbbed.

My mouth watered, and I ached to taste the salt glistening on his skin. Every inch of his body rippled with hard muscle and strength.

The alpha's focus was so intensely on his beta as he contin-ued to strike her with his whip and then appease her with his tongue, that I felt invisible enough to unbutton my own jeans and slide a hand down to my wet, wet pussy.

I closed my eyes, letting myself get lost in the intensity of the moment, picturing the prince's hands on me instead of her. I imagined his tongue licking and exploring my body, his fingers delving deep inside me. With each stroke of his whip, I felt a wave of heat radiating through my core that caused me to throb even harder.

I shifted my hips, rubbing my clit as I imagined what it would feel like to be in the female shifter's place; to feel that whip on my nipples and his tongue atoning for its sins.

But I couldn't stop now; too much energy coursed through me, and with the alpha's relentless assault on his captive's body, I was lost in pleasure. His touch was rough but full of passion, igniting something inside me that demanded release.

I had never felt so alive or so desperate for release. The air around us was electrified, as though the Lightning had escaped from the globes, and all I wanted was for it all to be directed at me.

Leif

Raven was bound to the wall by her wrists and ankles. She was naked and sexy, and I was hot enough to burst and spray her with cum.

But I wanted to draw this out some more first. My dick was hard and coated in Raven's saliva with some pre-cum thrown in for fun. I used to be all about jokes and laughter, now hardcore sex was the only fun I got.

So I had to make it last.

I traced the fringed tip of my whip down Raven's body, following the curve of her waist and hip. When I reached her golden triangle, I flicked it inward and caught a few golden hairs with an expert snap of my wrist.

She cried out in pain, and my cock got even harder.

I used the whip to guide her hips into a thrusting motion. Her hips moved back and forth, gently fucking the air, and I had a delightful time making her do it.

I started at her right foot and moved the whip up her leg, twisting her foot and ankle into a sexy position. I moved on to her left foot and did the same thing so her legs were spread wide enough to see her clit. It was enlarged, and her pussy lips were too.

"Please, fuck me."

I looked at her wide golden eyes, staring at me with desperate desire. "Please, Leif."

I smirked and moved the whip up her body. She was held tight to the wall, so there was no place for her to escape. Her knees were bent, and her pussy was on display.

Raven was a good fuck-buddy, always enthusiastic and bouncing with anticipation.

Not like the fucking country bumpkin who refused to be dominated by me. Who called me out in front of my pack and looked me in the damn eyes with impunity.

Well, she'd find herself punished. Anger swept through me that the bumpkin had even refused to have sex with me. Her alpha. Her fucking prince.

I'd intended to punish her with a whip, but I wasn't a fucking rapist, so I was venting my anger on Raven instead. The country bumpkin's punishment was to watch and not be touched. I could smell her arousal from here, even stronger and headier than Raven's. That country bitch was as turned on as I was, and I hoped she'd never orgasm again so she could stay in that tortured state forever.

In the meantime, I'd put on a good show.

I leaned in and flicked Raven's nipple with the whip, much harder than before. She was still sensitive, and she shuddered. A thin trail of blood oozed out from the wound and ran down her breast.

I licked the blood off the whip. "You taste good, Raven." My pleasures were getting darker every day. Was this what my father was like?

"Thank you, Alpha."

"Do you want to come for me?"

"Yes, Leif."

Stepping back, I took a few practice swings with the whip. Raven was my puppet, and I could do whatever I wanted to her, which made me feel powerful. I swung the whip at her pussy.

The leather caught her right on her clit, and she screamed out.

I hit her again, right on the same spot. She was enjoying it, so I didn't need to rein myself it. We were both consenting, Ascended fae.

"You want to come, don't you?" I asked.

"Yes, Alpha."

"Then ask me."

I increased the power of my whip a few notches and struck her lightly on the stomach, making the muscles contract.

I used to like the sound of my pack's moans, their groans, their sensual whimpers. Now, I only wanted to hear them scream.

"Let me come, Alpha. Please," she said, shivering, crying out in pleasure and pain.

But I couldn't finish yet. My observer's punishment wasn't complete. The country bumpkin from the coast who dared to defy me then refused to fuck me. Her punishment might never be finished.

I leaned in and grabbed Raven's ass cheek, squeezing it hard enough to leave a mark.

"Pain is pleasure, isn't it?" I asked, leaning in to whisper into her ear.

"Yes."

"So, who do you belong to?" I asked.

"You, Alpha."

"Who owns your pussy?"

She hesitated.

I squeezed her ass cheek even harder.

"You, Alpha."

"Who owns your nipples?"

"You, Alpha."

I smiled. "Who owns your ass?"

"You, Alpha."

"Who owns your throat? Your belly? Your thighs?"

"You, Alpha. All of it is yours."

I was so hard I could feel pre-cum leaking out.

But my attention wasn't focused on the naked female before me, tied up, writhing in pleasure, leaking blood. It was on the damn coastal wolf seated behind me on the red velvet lounge.

She wielded War. And I didn't feel a lick of discomfort, so she wasn't watching me. Which pissed me off even more. I could smell her arousal, but she wasn't watching.

Well, I'd damn well get her attention.

Stalking closer to Raven, I threw aside the whip and ran my fingers over her smooth, hot skin. She felt good. I plunged a finger inside her pussy, and she moaned in ecstasy, rocking her hips forward to take more of me.

"Naughty little wolf," I teased, pulling out my fingers and licking them slowly. "But tasty little wolf."

I slowly traced my fingers around her breasts and up her arms, then released her wrists from their leather restraint, keeping her ankles locked.

I stepped behind her so my butt was flush with the cold rock wall, and I pushed her forward into downward dog. Her ankles were still bound to the wall, so she couldn't go far, but her ass tilted tantalizingly up, begging me to take her.

Lining up my cock with her dripping wet pussy, I plunged into her at the same moment I snapped my gaze to the country bumpkin on the lounge.

She was watching. Not only watching, but she also had one hand deep inside her own pussy and the other clutching her breast under her white singlet top, writhing like she was in heat.

She faltered when she saw me look at her as though she hadn't expected me to be able to see her. Did she think she was fucking invisible? Her musky arousal was so intense I could practically taste her, and the look of desire on her face made me harder than ever.

I thrust into Raven but kept my gaze locked on the bumpkin. Her lips parted in a hungry O, and her hand moved faster between her legs as I picked up my pace and speared my beta, her tight wetness was exactly what my dick needed.

I didn't give the country bumpkin a chance to look away. I grabbed Raven's hips and pounded into her. I didn't give a fuck how good her pussy felt, my focus wasn't on her.

I was angry, my cock hard and ready to come, and I wanted to punish the country bumpkin for daring to defy me. I wanted to show her she couldn't say no to me. I wanted to remind her that I was her alpha. Her prince.

I fucked Raven hard, slamming my cock in and out of her tight, slim body so hard my flesh smacked against her. I could hear her muffled gasps for breath, solely for my benefit.

The bumpkin kept her eyes locked on mine, her expression needy where mine must have been angry. She was enjoying my show. I used to love when my pack fucked in public, showed off, and made a spectacle of themselves. Now, I only wanted them to watch me.

And I only wanted to watch her.

When the country bumpkin threw back her head and cried

out, her orange hair splaying against the dark stone wall behind her, I exploded inside my beta, hard and fast, slapping her ass as I watched the bumpkin fall apart.

She collapsed against the red lounge, breathing hard, sweat glistening on her skin, the sound of her panting making me wish I had my face buried between her legs.

But only for a moment. She righted herself quickly and did up the buttons on her jeans, wiped her hand on the sofa like a fucking animal, and resumed looking at me with disdain.

This was supposed to be her punishment, and somehow she'd ended up with a reward, and I was the one gagging for more.

I strode to the blood-red door at the end of the dungeon.

"Where are you going?" Raven asked from her bondage, her voice strangled. "You can't leave me like this."

I clicked the lock on the door. "Watch me."

Perhaps I was talking to Raven. Perhaps I meant the country bumpkin with the disrespect for authority. Disrespect for me. Either way, I was leaving.

Leif

The following day, I bounded into the Lakehouse in wolf form, with my worries sluicing from my silver fur like the lake's water. Gabrelle stood on the deck, clad in her fighting leathers, firing arrows across the lake.

I loped right up to her and nudged her groin with my muzzle, taking a whiff of her familiar, comforting scent. She smelled like home.

She tutted and swatted my head aside sharply. "Bad dog."

A grin lit me up on the inside, and for a moment, it felt like old times when I annoyed the fuck out of my friends, and they tolerated it. Good times.

I shifted into fae form with the ghost of a grin still on my face. "Standard wolf greeting, babe. You know that."

Gabrelle cocked out a hip. "Not a wolf, dog boy. You know that." She said it with a slight smile.

She was fucking sexy, just curves upon curves, and my dick twitched as I took in her pose. Dark leathers that hugged her and a fierce warrior's stare that softened as we bantered. "You could get some wolf in you," I teased.

She leaned against the balcony railing, and the early morning sun trickled down her body. "Maybe I should."

That comment snapped me out of my nostalgia. This wasn't

old times when we were all heirs with open futures, our responsibilities firmly in our parents' laps, leaving us to mess around and screw up and flirt and banter.

We could no longer spend our days chatting and laughing, hanging out, drinking, discussing our sexual conquests, vying for position.

The heirs had a no-screwing pact. I could fuck anybody in Arathay except Gabrelle, Dion, Ronan, or Neela. But the only one of us who ignored that rule was me. I was the sole asshole who constantly tried to bed them all; I was the joker. Their role was to turn me down.

So why was Gabrelle offering herself to me? Because she pitied me. She fucking pitied me, Alpha of all Verdan Alphas, Head of House Caro, heir to the throne, a fucking prince.

How dare she pity me?

My good mood soured. Every ounce of relief disappeared as my responsibilities came crashing onto my shoulders. I refused to be pitied by anyone.

I had to recover my pride and claw back an ounce of my dignity.

"Sorry, babe, I'm not interested." I turned my back on Gabrelle, but not before I saw the flicker of offense cross her features.

She was an ice queen, a master of containing her emotions, so I took it as a win that I could draw some sensation from her.

It was early, but Dion was here too, cooking up a storm in the kitchen, which was part of the grand open-plan room with the floor-to-ceiling glass overlooking the balcony and lake. His hair was pale yellow and curled in around his ears like shaved butter.

Dion had ascended a few years ago, and, to nobody's surprise, he chose to become a Magirus. The best chefs in Arathay. He imbued magical intent into his cooking, so he could make peanut butter toast taste like a mountain in winter if he wanted to. Like all Magirus's, his hair and eyes changed color to reflect what he'd most recently eaten, so I figured he'd swallowed a gob of margarine for breakfast.

My mood lifted at seeing him. My pals always had that effect on me, but it never lasted. "Please tell me you're cooking for me, bro."

He grinned. "Scrambled eggs, baby." He slid a plate of steaming goodness across the kitchen counter, and I took a greedy bite.

"Tastes like a celebration." I turned the creamy mixture over in my mouth, letting it roll over my tongue, trying to figure out exactly what I was tasting.

Dion nodded, his pale yellow eyes lit with excitement. "Yep. Which celebration?"

I took another bite. "I'm getting elements of excited faelings, with a note of waterslides." I swallowed. "It's the Summer Song!"

Dion leaned his elbows on the kitchen counter, wafting his eggy smell toward me. The scent of a Magirus changed whenever they ate too. "I was going for that first time we ever attended the Summer Song together when we were nine. Do you remember? You licked one of the door dudes, and he wouldn't sell us a ticket, so we had to sneak over the fence to get in." He started laughing at the memory, but I didn't join in.

I pushed the plate away, the crockery singing across the wooden table. My friends meant well, trying to jolly me along and cheer me up, but it just reminded me how carefree they were...and how full of cares I was.

Gabrelle came in from outside, bringing a gust of wind as she slid the glass doors open. Dion shoved a plate of eggs across the kitchen counter, which she delicately picked up and then carried to the dining table. "Let's eat like civilized fae, shall we?"

I shrugged and scooped a huge spoonful of eggs into my gob, but the ice queen just glowered at me until I picked up my plate and joined her at the table.

Dion slid in beside Gabrelle, looking at her in anticipation as she tried the meal he'd prepared. "Well, how is it?" he asked.

"It's fine."

"Fine? What does it taste like?"

"Eggs."

Dion heaved a sigh. "Behind the eggs. What does it conjure up in your mind?" He looked at me. "Help me out here, buddy."

A small part of me wanted to join in the banter, to make fun of Dion or to niggle Gabrelle until she admitted it tasted like the Summer Song. That tiny cub inside me who still wanted to wrestle with my buddies and sniff their crotches while they were distracted. But that little part had shrunk so small, wasting away under the mantle of responsibility, that I just scowled. "It's the Summer Song."

Dion pouted that I'd given the game away. "Spoilsport."

Gabrelle was clearly in a mood, too, because she just said, "I'm only getting eggs." Or maybe she was being her usual ice-bitch self.

Dion slid his arm around Gabrelle's shoulders, and she rubbed her face into his chest like a cat. Damned if I could work out what she was trying to communicate with that gesture.

"You're losing your touch, D," she said.

He pinched her arm. "I'm getting better at cooking every day."

She raised a shoulder, making the gesture look elegant. "I tasted the celebration, but I thought it was the Wild Hunt of Fen." She shot me a wicked glance, dripping with seduction.

My dick jumped. Fen hosted one of Arathay's biggest events, a raucous fairground of decadence and debauchery, where fae could dress in whatever and fuck whoever they wanted for a few days straight. It was held in the Realm of Fen, which bordered Verda to the North. Fen was the truth-telling realm, and anybody within its borders could not speak a lie. Most fae from there were uptight bastards, but man, they could really let loose. I'd only attended the Wild Hunt once, about five years ago, and my dick was so sore afterward that I hadn't been able to piss for two days.

"I might go to the Wild Hunt this year," Gabrelle mused. "Anything to get away from Mother for a while."

Shit. A tiny stab of jealousy skewered me. It wasn't jealousy of Gabrelle. I didn't even want her anymore. It wasn't even jealousy of her still having a mother, although if I thought about Mom's loss for too long, heat pricked my eyes, exposing weakness—which is why I avoided thinking of her.

No, it was jealousy of my friend's freedom.

The Wild Hunt of Fen was a decadent event, and as Alpha of Alphas, Head of House Caro, heir to the throne, and Prince of Verda, I couldn't just piss off to a fuckfest.

I had to stay and look after my pack. Figure out how to keep them in line. Strategize against the Shadow Walkers.

Dion spread his arms along the back of the neighboring dining chairs. "Sounds fun, count me in. You should come along, Leif."

This had the scent of an orchestrated tactic, like they'd planned this whole conversation in advance. Why were my friends constantly trying to undermine my responsibilities? Didn't they know it was already hard enough to bear them and that being invited to fuckfests only made it harder?

"No," I growled, sounding meaner than I'd intended. The wooden chair felt hard beneath my butt, and I wriggled in place.

The front door swung open, and two voices drifted down the hallway, the deep rumble of Ronan Mentium and the lighter bubbling tone of Neela Flora, heirs to the Mentium and Floran thrones.

Ronan appeared first, his black hair slightly disheveled and his coal-black eyes sparkling with joy. "No what?" he asked, joining in the tail end of our conversation. He brought a strawberry scent to the room.

"We were just discussing the Wild Hunt of Fen," Gabrelle explained silkily, sitting gracefully with her long legs crossed and her hands folded in her lap.

Neela crossed and tousled my hair in greeting, and I leaned into it. She was vanilla and musk, a scent I had grown to love over the past year. "The Wild Hunt of what-now?" Neela asked. She was the heir to House Flora and the younger sister of the heir we'd grown up with. She had been squirreled away in the mortal realm for her own safety, for protection against Gaia's curse, and had reappeared after her brother, Sebarah, died. It was fair to say we didn't exactly welcome her with open arms when she first came to Verda, but she'd proven her worth, and now we accepted her as one of our own.

Ronan more than accepted her. He lived with her, screwed

her, and adored her. He'd been prepared to sacrifice his life for her, but in the end, he had only sacrificed his fortune and was now penniless. But Neela acted as his sugar mommy, and he didn't seem to mind a bit.

Being a recent arrival to the realm—and only just realizing she was fae—there was a lot Neela didn't know about. Including the Wild Hunt. Dion and Ronan explained it to her, and Gabrelle summarized it briefly as "A debaucherous event where the uptight fae of Fen get to screw away their stress."

The innocent cub inside me panted with excitement, wanting to go camp out in Green Valley so I wouldn't miss the start of the Wild Hunt.

It was harder to keep that inner cub under control while I was near Ronan. He was the heir to Mentium, the house of mood, and since hooking up with Neela, he was always happy. It was infectious. Literally. Like a disease. So with him bubbling with joy beside me and the heir to the house of beauty planning a trip to a fuckfest, it was hard to keep myself aloof.

I ran a finger along the smooth wooden table, trying to ground myself.

"That's decided, then. We're all going to Green Valley next year," Ronan declared.

Neela got some cutlery from the kitchen and, while she was there, grabbed a spare tennis ball from a drawer. "Catch," she yelled and tossed the ball to me.

Out of instinct, I caught the ball. It was firm and slightly spongy, and I squeezed it. On instinct, I tossed it in a well-practiced move, skimming the ceiling, and caught it while Ronan and Neela pulled up chairs and dived into their own plates of scrambled eggs.

All four sets of eyes landed on me, waiting for me to agree to join next year's Wild Hunt. They had definitely pre-planned this.

"What is this?" I growled, catching the tennis ball and squeezing it hard. "A fucking intervention? I'm not going to some faeling's party while the world is burning. I have a pack to look after. Every pack in Verda, actually, and we're being hunted by Shadow Walkers. It's not that hard to understand, and I don't know why you keep trying to derail me. It's hard enough as it is." I slammed the tennis ball into the dining table hard enough that the ball split in two.

Silence followed my outburst, and I hoped they felt guilty. Gabrelle leaned forward and placed an ice-cold hand over mine. "We know you have a lot going on. But we're worried about you."

"You should have worried about Mom. I'm not the one who got killed by a Walker. Now there's only three rulers left, so if you don't worry about them, you'll be facing up to the same shitstorm as me soon."

Verda was ruled jointly by five monarchs, one king or queen from each of the Royal Houses. My four buddies and I would slot into those roles when the majority of our parents died.

Two of the five were already dead. Neela's mom from Flora, and my mom from Caro. One more death, and all five of us useless heirs would be propelled onto the thrones. We no longer had the luxury to act like faelings.

Neela leaned forward, her sky-blue hair matching her sky-blue eyes. "We know. We're sorry about your mom. Ronan and I spend hours every week in the Library of Whispers looking for answers, hoping to find something that will defeat the Shadow Walkers."

"We've scoured the damn place," Ronan agreed. "I've never

read so many books. Especially ones that bite."

"And bodyguards are watching over Ronan's dad, Gabrelle's mom, and D's dad," Neela continued. "But you need to let loose sometimes. You can't keep all that anger inside."

I scraped out my chair and stood, looming over them all, my mind suddenly turned to that irritating country bumpkin whose name, I discovered, was Alara. A truckload of my anger was directed her way, and I had no intention of keeping it inside.

"Don't worry about that. My anger seeps out of every pore of my body."

"Just go easy on them," Ronan said as I turned to leave.

"What?" I said, dangerously quiet.

"Go easy on your pack. They mean well."

"Oh, good. That'll keep the Shadow Walkers at bay. My pack means well. They shouldn't be punished if they screw up or break the hierarchy or let a shitload of Walkers through our defenses. As long as they mean well."

I stalked away and slammed the glass door behind me so hard it shattered. The moss and the earthy tones of the forest assaulted my nose, calling to me. I shifted into wolf form without undressing, so shreds of material scattered across the deck as I leaped over the balcony and into the cold, dark water.

Leif

I returned to Mom's den—no, *my* den—and headed straight to my room. I had the largest bedroom, with a bed big enough to fit twenty, though these days, I rarely used it for anything except sleeping. I kept my sex drive in the playroom.

The only other shifters on the same level were the Wars in my personal guard. I looked in on the bedroom they shared, with an oversized mattress in each of the four corners plus plenty of thick rugs on the floor in case of an emergency fuck. Big windows overlooked the lawn out the back, letting bright streams of sunshine into the black-and-cream marbled room.

It was empty. Apart from one lone wolf sitting on a red velvet pouf staring out the window.

"What a surprise," I growled. "The country bumpkin doesn't have any friends."

She called over her shoulder without doing me the courtesy of meeting my eye. "What a surprise, Alpha doesn't have any manners."

My hands curled into fists, drawing blood from my palms. "You will respect me, bumpkin, or I'll hog-tie you in my dungeon and leave you for days."

She turned and slowly got to her feet, making her submission seem like a power play. "My name is Alara, Leif."

"Call me Alpha," I barked.

Her gaze was unwavering, and her posture remained confident. "I'll call you by your name or not at all."

I took a step forward, towering over her small frame. "You forget your place, pup. I am the alpha here, and you will do as I say."

Alara stood up, her own hands balling into fists. "I know my place, and it's not to be your punching bag."

I sneered at her. "You are nothing without me. I keep you safe, I provide for you."

She stepped closer, not backing down. "I can handle myself. And I don't need your protection or your provisions."

I grabbed her by the collar, pulling her face close to mine. "You think you can stand up to me? You think you're strong enough?"

Her eyes bored into mine. "I know I am."

I pushed her away, and she stumbled a few steps, tripping over the leather seat and tumbling onto her ass on the cold marble floor.

Alara scrambled to her feet, her eyes still fixated on mine. I could see the anger and defiance in her gaze, but I refused to back down. I was the alpha, the one in charge. No one, especially not some young War wielder, would challenge me and get away with it. I'd learned the hard way the importance of keeping a hierarchy in place, and I'd paid for the lesson in death. My wolves, my Mom.

"You're nothing but a pup. Do you think you can take on the alpha? You have a lot to learn," I spat at her.

Alara's lips twisted into a smirk. "Maybe I do, but at least I'm not a coward hiding behind my anger and fear."

My blood boiled at her words. Who did she think she was? I

had the power here, not her. I took a step closer to her, looming over her petite frame.

"You know nothing about me," I growled at her.

"Then show me," she challenged.

Without thinking, I grabbed her by the waist, pulling her close. Our bodies were pressed together, and heat emanated from her skin. I leaned in, my lips dangerously close to hers. My anger snapped into desire at one whiff of her citrus scent.

"Is this what you want?" I whispered, my voice heavy with longing. I was practically begging for consent to kiss her, and I hated her power over me.

Alara's breath hitched, and she met my gaze with a fiery intensity. "I don't want anything from you."

I ignored her words and pressed my lips to hers, kissing her with a ferocity that surprised me. I hadn't planned to kiss her until she said I could. But she responded eagerly, her hands winding around my neck. I gripped her hips, pulling her closer.

For a moment, all the anger and fear that had been consuming me dissipated, replaced by an intense desire that left me dizzy with need. But as the kiss deepened, a nagging voice in the back of my mind reminded me of who I was and what I stood for. I pulled away from Alara abruptly, my chest heaving with exertion.

Alara looked up at me, her eyes filled with desire and confusion. "What was that?"

I didn't have an answer for her. All I knew was that I was the alpha, and I couldn't let my guard down like that again. I had an entire pack of wolves to protect, and I wouldn't do it by losing my mind. "Get out," I growled at her.

"Like hell," she said, scowling up at me, her flaming orange hair lit by the sun streaming through the window. "This is my room. You get out."

Anger swept over me, uncontrollable and ferocious, mixing with the lust in my blood. I snatched her up, sat on the leather chair, and lay her across my knee.

"Call me Alpha," I growled.

Her musky scent deepened, mixing with her natural citrus notes, making her arousal crystal clear. "Fuck off," she spat.

I slapped her hard, watching with satisfaction as her ass jiggled under the force of my hand.

The little cub inside me, the sweet faeling who made friends with everybody and always cracked a joke, whimpered under my treatment of her. He wanted me to lick her wounds, ask if she was okay, and maybe convince her to have sweet sex.

But I couldn't be that cub anymore. I was an alpha now. I had to be strong and couldn't tolerate a lack of respect. That was the very thing that let the Walkers through to my den and killed one in every four of my pack's shifters. Lack of structure and obedience was the reason my Mom died on a visit out East. I couldn't tolerate it,

Even so, I would have stopped if I hadn't smelled Alara's heady arousal. But as I brought my hand down to her tight ass, her musk strengthened, and she panted, though she tried to cover it by wriggling free.

I yanked down her pants, tearing the thick denim, revealing her pale brown ass. I slapped her again, harder this time, watching as her pink flesh turned red. "Your body betrays you, pup. You can't deny how much you want this."

I hit her again, my hand landing on her left cheek this time. "Tell me you want this."

Her body tensed up, and she gritted her teeth. "I don't," she said through clenched teeth.

I slapped the other cheek, leaving a matching pair of hand prints. "Then stop moving."

She kept squirming. "But you're hurting me."

"It hurts good, bumpkin."

Her arousal was the strongest I'd ever scented, and when she peeked up at me, I noticed her eyes were glassy with lust. She was as turned on as I was.

"If you'd consented yesterday, we would have agreed on a safe word," I said. "But you gave up that opportunity. Now, the only way this ends is when I say so."

She flailed on my lap, trying to escape, and her wriggling arm brushed against my hard cock. I groaned, struggling to maintain control. But I had to prove I was the master and she was the slave, not vice versa.

I kept one arm firmly across her back, pushing her down, while I caressed her ass cheeks with the other. Round, firm, luscious, and marked with my hand.

"I will mark you every fucking day, pup," I growled, loving the sight of my handprint on her flesh, wanting to make it permanent. Wanting my sign on her body forever, hating that I wanted it so badly.

"I hate you," she panted.

I cupped her ass with my hand, squeezing gently. "But you want me," I said, moving my hand between her legs and pushing forward, stroking her pussy.

This was the worst kind of torture, her wet heat mere inches from my cock, and I wanted to thrust deep into her, to feel her muscles tighten around me. I wanted to plunge my cock into her until she cried out my name, until she begged for mercy, until she forgot to hate me.

I pulled my fingers from her wet, wet pussy, and she moaned.

I slapped her again and again until she was gasping for breath and writhing on my lap. Then I lifted her up, pressing her against me, pulling her back against my chest, her ass wedged against my cock. Her tight jeans constrained her legs, and she had no leverage to move, so she was trapped.

"I am in control of your body," I growled in her ear.

"Fuck you," she snarled back.

I slapped her thigh lightly, then held her tight against me, my cock throbbing against her ass and back.

"There are several ways we can do this, pup," I said, my voice low and husky with desire. "I can tease you until you can't take it anymore, until you beg me to let you come."

I ground my hips against her ass, and she let out a long, low moan.

"Or I can fuck you right now," I said, imagining slamming into her tight pussy, marking her with my cock.

She ground out her words breathily and slowly, as though she didn't want to say them at all. "I. Do. Not. Consent."

In an instant, I shoved her away, suddenly wanting nothing to do with her. How dare she refuse me? How dare she deny me? I was the head of the house of sensuality, her alpha, and she didn't fucking consent?

She rolled across the ground, showing flashes of her red ass and her ripe pussy, her torn jeans. She scrambled to the closest mattress and pulled the blankets over herself while I did everything I could to ignore her.

Ignore her scent, ignore her heat, ignore her disrespect.

I looked out the window at the lawn, taking in the scene she'd been watching when I arrived. The young betas were playing ball in the garden, racing across the grass to retrieve it, jockeying for position in the pack's hierarchy.

"You should be out there," I said. I sucked down the jealousy of my betas and tried to silence the inner cub who wanted nothing more than to join his pack outside and race after a ball.

"I'm not much of a joiner," Alara said.

"I noticed."

"I didn't think you noticed anything except your fawning betas and fuck toys."

I laughed in her face, feeling cruel but not stopping myself. "You're a naive little girl, Alara. You have no idea what it takes to be an alpha."

She hugged the blanket closer to her body. "Maybe not. But I do know what it takes to be a leader. And it's not about being the strongest or the meanest. It's about having faith in your pack, trusting them, and delegating. Respect is a two-way street, you know."

I sprang across the room and landed on the mattress beside her, making a big dent. I let my saliva fleck over her as I snarled. "Don't lecture me about respect, bumpkin. You're the most disrespectful wolf I ever saw."

She glared at me. "Two-way street," she repeated.

Under the weight of her stare, I noticed the lack of discomfort. She was a War wielder, so she should cause me some irritation, even if she was weak.

"Do you really wield War?" I asked, and she blanched. "If you've been lying, you will learn what real punishment is. And consent has nothing to do with it."

I left her then, quivering under her blankets like a mouse, and stalked to my own chambers next door to take my straining cock into my own hands.

Alara

It was official. Leif—whom I refused to call by his damn title—was a bastard. Asshole. Dickwipe. He was so caught up in my so-called disrespect that he completely failed to see the ocean of disrespect he made his pack swim in.

But that didn't make me any smarter than him. I spent the afternoon in bed, trying to read a book about ciphers I'd found in the den's library, but mostly cursing myself for drawing so much damn attention. After he'd slapped me silly and made me horny enough to fuck a true dog, he questioned whether I really wielded War. Man, I was an idiot. I should have kept my head low and my mouth shut as I had planned. Now I was in serious danger of being discovered as the liar I was.

From now on, I would keep quiet about all the hundreds of ways Leif Caro was an arrogant prick and keep myself out of his focus. I might even join in with some stupid games to fit in with the pack.

The afternoon wore into evening, and I welcomed the rest of the Wars to the bedroom. At least I wouldn't be alone if Leif came past again. Selene came in, laughing with the bronzed male who'd been chosen by the alpha on day one for further interrogation—or, as it turned out, dungeon sex, although he and Selene had avoided that fate. I'd since learned the not-always terrified male's name was Kellan, and in the two days we'd been in Verda City, he seemed nice enough.

Selene tossed me a bread roll and a chicken leg. "You missed dinner again, hon. You know, you'll have to face the whole pack one day. Sooner rather than later." She flicked a long powder-blue braid over her snow-white shoulder.

I nodded. "Yes. Starting tomorrow, I'll be a good little cub." She raised her eyebrows, radiating skepticism. "Truly," I promised. "I will."

Dinner was good, but I was ready when the time came to sleep. It had been a big few days, and fatigue wormed into my brain. But drifting off wasn't easy.

Sleeping in a room full of hormone-fueled wolf shifters was like trying to nap on a galloping horse while all the nearby stallions and mares were trying to have sex with you. It only worked if you ignored the constant jostling, the array of giant dicks, and all that hair.

I wasn't a virgin, obviously. I slayed my virginity years ago, but that didn't mean I wanted sex twenty-four seven. Although, since arriving here, I'd thought about it a lot more than usual. Probably because that asshole alpha kept showing me his cock.

I found a nook on the massive mattress right next to the wall, and Selene was happy to act as a barrier between me and the rest of the pack. "Gives me first pick," she said with a wink.

This was my second night in the room, so I knew what to expect. Screwing and moaning for a few hours before everybody fell into a coma, then a bit more playing around at dawn.

I missed my den. Missed my single bed, my own blankets, missed the hell out of my dad. For a fae who didn't like joining in, being forced to live alongside a bunch of strangers wasn't my idea of fun.

I woke early to shower and dress before the adjoining bathroom became a flesh zoo, then I made my way downstairs in search of breakfast.

The opulence of this den would never get tiring. Marble walls and floors that alternated between stone, mosaic, and wood paneling. Each room was different from the last and furnished grandly, from ornate fireplaces to elegant chandeliers. Somehow the heavy rock made it feel cozy despite its massive size.

The kitchen was equally impressive. The counters were a light granite that contrasted perfectly with the dark wood cabinets above, while copper fixtures hung from the ceiling and illuminated every corner of the room. In one corner sat an enormous bank of stoves with dozens of burners, while a pair of huge refrigerators stood against another wall, and an open door revealed part of the pantry with shelves stocked with enough food to feed an army. Wolves were good eaters.

When I entered, a shifter with chartreuse eyes and a narrow chin looked up. "I'm sorry, but the kitchen isn't open yet."

My belly growled loudly. Good timing.

The cook looked down at my gut, then answered as if it had spoken to him. "You're supposed to wait until breakfast time. Alpha's orders."

Fantastic. Prince Asshole was taking his despotic rule of the pack to a new extreme. I'd be lucky to get a cup of water.

"Is it okay if I take a seat? I'll just wait for the other Wars to come downstairs."

"Oh, you have War?"

"Yep." I glanced away quickly, remembering too late that if I

67

looked directly at anyone, they'd expect to feel uncomfortable.

"In that case, help yourself." He pulled a basket of fresh eggs from under the counter. "The alpha said you needed protein for your testing. Eat up."

"He asked you to do this?" I asked, peering into the basket. I expected the eggs to be raw, but they were all cooked.

"Not just for you. For all the War wielders, so you have energy for the test."

"The test?"

He tilted his head, and a lock of chartreuse hair fell across his eye. "Apparently, Alpha wants to test your strength."

"Oh, fuck."

I thought I saw a glimmer of understanding in the young chef's eyes, then he turned away. Maybe he knew what it was like to be conscripted. Maybe he was an exile like me. Maybe he was just nosy.

"Thanks for the food," I told him, grabbing a large egg and wandering through to the adjacent dining cave, where the marble walls were veined with orange. I sat down to eat my egg and waited for the full menu to open.

I didn't feel bad about lying to the cook about being Ascended or wielding War. I was here against my will, conscripted into the alpha's army for no good reason, torn from my family, and forced to lie to protect my dad.

I didn't owe these assholes anything. So I would keep lying through my teeth for as long as it kept Pa safe.

Wolves trickled into the kitchen, and Selene walked through to the dining cave with a massive smile on her dial and plonked herself onto the chair opposite mine. "I'm starving. Sex really takes it out of you, doesn't it?" Her powder-blue eyes had a satisfied glow.

"I wouldn't know."

"Goody two-shoes," she teased.

"Slut," I replied with a grin.

She nodded a tiny bow. "Thank you." She looked around. "Where's your food?"

"Oh, when I came in, it wasn't ready, so..."

She grabbed my hand. "Well, it's ready now, let's go get some."

We lined up at the buffet and took brimming plates back to our table. The food was amazing, beef and rowenut souffle and an exquisite breakfast meringue that was more delicious than any healthy food had the right to be.

"Fuck Gaia, this is tasty," Selene said through a mouthful of plumple tart.

"They sure know how to cook," I agreed.

Kellan, who had taken the seat to my left and was happily listening in, snorted a laugh. "Alpha has a Magirus on staff, you country bumpkins." His bronze eyes glimmered in amusement.

Oh, that made a lot of sense. And it definitely made me look like an idiot. Also, it explained why Prince Alphahole kept calling me "bumpkin" in such a rude tone of voice.

I shrugged. "Better than being a city dick, I suppose."

Selene laughed, and Kellan smiled. He could have taken offense, but he chose to find the humor in my comment. I was starting to like this guy. He reminded me of a wooden doll, with his hair, eyes, and skin all the color of bronze, but his personality was way better.

After my plate was clean, I lowered my voice. "Apparently, we're being tested for our War strength today."

Selene's jaw dropped. "Oh, shit." She immediately snaked

out an arm and lay a comforting hand over mine, and I soaked up what comfort I could. "Are you okay, hon?"

Kellan was still right next to me, and the dozens of wolves in the dining cave would hear even if I whispered. We couldn't speak freely about how bad that was for me, how it would end with me being discovered and punished. Maybe Pa too. All we could do was look at each other, me with fear and Selene with pity and horror.

"Bring it on, I say," Kellan said, flexing his bicep. That started a round of muscle tensing and general showing off, which Selene nor I joined.

As the shifters around us finished their meals, the simmering anxiety in my gut grew into boiling fear. How would I prove my War ability? I knew Selene would do everything she could to help, I just hoped that would be enough.

I dreaded to think how Leif would react to discovering I'd lied about wielding War. Lied about being Ascended. My legs were shaky as I rose to follow the rest of the new recruits outside, ready to face my trials.

The air outside was heavy with humidity and the sweet musk of the nearby woods. Everything felt alive and electric, buzzing with birdlife. I surveyed the scene, wondering if I should make a run for it. The forest was lush and thick, but I couldn't even shift into my wolf form without being in mortal peril, so I wouldn't get more than twenty feet before I was pummeled to the ground by an angry pursuer. Then Alpha would really have a reason to suspect me.

Leif stood before us, a tall figure swathed in silver leathers and a high silver cowl. He didn't need to speak for us to feel his presence and power. He paced around us, assessing our strength and beauty as if we were nothing more than wild animals up for sale at a market. I wished he would move fast so I wouldn't have to feel those cold silver eyes on me.

Finally, he stopped before me, his face an unreadable mask. "You claim you can wield War?" he asked, his voice low but loud enough to be heard by everyone.

I nodded slowly, my throat tight with fear. He held my gaze for what felt like an eternity before finally giving a single curt nod and continuing around the circle of Wars assembled in front of him.

He didn't single anybody else out.

"Today," he began, "you will be tested for your War strength. You will each be taken away one by one for testing."

He glanced around the circle of wolves expectantly. No one moved or spoke. This was a disaster. If we were tested individually, Selene couldn't help me in any way. Sweat formed on my brow, and I tried to keep my breathing calm and not draw attention to myself.

Finally, he pointed his silver-tipped staff at me. "You first."

Anxiety coursed through my veins as he gestured for me to follow him. He suspected me. He must. Otherwise, why did he suddenly decide to test us all? And why choose me first?

He passed an object to his black-skinned, black-haired black-dressed beta, and I squinted to make out what it was, but I failed.

I trailed my alpha into the forest beyond the grassy lawn and down a dark winding path where sunlight didn't penetrate. The trees were bone white, and when we reached a small, damp clearing, it smelled of decay.

Leif nodded toward an altar in the center of the glade. It was dark red, dripping with blood-colored wax. Leif nodded toward it. "This is your first test. We will move on to larger prey until we find your maximum strength."

My stomach dropped. A small white rabbit was tied to the blood-red altar, its nose twitching pathetically. I felt sick. I was supposed to slaughter some poor animal as an offering to Gaia.

Leif's silver eyes gleamed like beacons of death and destruction in the dappled sunlight. Like he wanted me to fail and was just waiting to see it play out.

I had no problem killing the creature. I'd hunted plenty of animals in my time. Like most shifters, I enjoyed the kill. But a War wielder should be able to do it by just slicing a finger through the air.

"I can't do it if you're watching me," I said, playing for time, swallowing the lump in my throat.

The prince stared at me, reeking of distrust. "I don't think you can do it at all."

The rabbit twitched its nose, and my heart stuttered. "Just leave the glade, and I'll get it done."

"I'm not going anywhere, bumpkin."

I bristled. "Stop calling me that."

"Or what?"

"Or I'll call you a city dick, city dick." My mouth was running off, just making things worse for me when I needed some way to escape this situation. But I had nowhere to hide, and my gut was filled with bile.

Leif got up in my face, towering over me, his chest level with my eyes. When would I learn to control my damn tongue?

"Stop trying to distract me and get on with your test. Either separate that rabbit's head from its body or admit you can't."

I ran through the options in my head, trying to think through the cotton wool in my head. Plan A, stand there like an idiot, waving my finger through the air and hoping to manifest some War through sheer force of will. Or Plan B, confess to lying to the alpha of alphas. Shit. Neither option sounded great, but at least Plan B had me in control and not waving my hand around like an idiot.

Throwing as much sass into it as I could, I thrust out a hip and placed my hand on it. My heart was rattling at a million miles an hour, but I tried to sound casual, tried to hide my pounding fear. "The thing is, I haven't actually ascended yet, so—"

The alpha roared so loudly that the trees shook, and a dark purple leaf fluttered past his rage-filled face. "You haven't ascended?"

"Let me explain. I—"

"I'll never let you do anything again, bitch." He lowered his face to mine, his silver eyes glowing with hatred, his chiseled jaw working with fury. Something softer glinted behind his rage, perhaps something closer to disappointment and regret, but his facade of fury covered it. "I will lock you in my cells, and the only thing you will ever do again is breathe, eat, and shit, and only when I tell you to. Nobody defies me and lies to me and gets away with it. Especially not a nobody bottom-feeding wolf pup from nowhere."

He clicked his fingers, and a beta emerged from the forest's darkness. Dread filled me. What would happen to me? Was he about to order my death?

Leif stared at me, his eyes narrowed slits of silver in the dark clearing. "Take her away," he said without dropping my gaze. "Lock her in the smallest, dampest cell and give her nothing to eat or drink until I say so."

This alpha might be an asshole, but he had his pack's respect.

My pack back home in Sylverclyff never showed me an ounce of the deference or dignity that every single wolf showed Leif. This was no exception. The beta leaped to obey the prince, grabbing me roughly and forcing me to walk ahead of him along the forest path.

It could have been worse. He could have struck me down right there for lying to him. But he was only taking me away to a cell. To lock me away without giving me a chance to say goodbye to Selene.

Adrenaline simmered in my veins, boiling away my fear and leaving only anger.

Leif might be respected, but he was still a city dick.

Alara

The beta led me back to the den and into a side passage so we didn't pass by the other War wielders. Selene wouldn't know where I'd disappeared to, but at least I wasn't marching past them all with my dignity in tatters.

The lickspittle shoved me down narrow stone stairs to a proper underground jail with cells carved out of the cold, damp stone.

He unlocked the tiniest cell and pushed me inside, then clicked the lock shut and left me in the dark.

The cell was a tight space in the stone, barely wide enough to let me stretch out and stand simultaneously. The walls were chipped and covered in old splotches of who knows what. Blood, probably. Or semen. The iron bars that made up the door were rusted but still strong enough to hold me in.

It didn't take long to figure out I was alone down there. The other cells were empty. There was no talking of prisoners or shuffling, no clanging doors or footsteps, just the dull echoing of silence and my own shallow breaths. Thank Gaia for the Lightning globe glowing from the corner. Without it, I'd spend all my time and energy trying to produce light, a spell I was particularly terrible at.

I sat on the cold stone floor, my back against the wall, and hugged my knees close to my chest. A wave of exhaustion washed over me, and my head felt heavy as I closed my eyes.

Doubts crept into my mind, whispering that maybe I wasn't cut out for this struggle against the hierarchy and that I was destined to fail. Who was I to fight the alpha of alphas? The weight of uncertainty settled heavily on my chest, and I battled to silence the nagging voice that threatened to shatter my confidence.

Minutes passed, then hours. An entire night, probably. Maybe two. My only marker of time was my stomach, which growled painfully, and my throat, which was scratchy and dry. My mind began to wander, and I found myself thinking of Selene. Was she safe? Had she managed to pass the War trial?

I tried to focus on my breathing, to keep my mind off the thirst that threatened to overwhelm me. But the silence was deafening, and the darkness was suffocating. I couldn't shake off the feeling of being trapped and at the mercy of the alpha and his wolves.

There was no telling what the alpha had planned for me. Would he keep me here until I died of starvation and dehydration? Or would he come down here and torture me for his own amusement?

The silence and darkness were suffocating. I hugged my knees closer, feeling the cold seep into my skin. Every creak and distant echo made my heart race, while the dampness of the cell penetrated my bones, mirroring the fear that threatened to consume me. I fought to keep my composure but couldn't stop my hands from trembling.

Then, suddenly, I heard a noise. Did I imagine it? Footsteps echoed off the stone walls. The heavy thud of boots got closer until they stopped in front of my cell.

Two guards—a burly male dressed in sleek black leather and a petite female wearing nothing but an exquisite red corset and thigh-high stockings.

The female smiled. "Follow us."

We moved through winding stone hallways lined with flickering Lightning globes, making our way deeper into the depths of the den. The air was scented with smoke and sweat and arousal. I followed closely behind the guards as they opened door after door until we reached a rubber-lined cubicle.

The female guard knelt before me as though she were bowing at my feet, her hands clasped behind her back and her eyes cast demurely to the ground. "The alpha requests that you shower."

She and the male guard retreated, closing the cubicle door behind them, which I now realized was a shower. I stripped off and turned on the faucets, then drank greedily, filling my mouth with the delicious pure water.

When I'd had my fill, I turned up the heat and stepped under the flow, relishing the feeling of being surrounded by water. Scented oils and creams were available, so I washed my hair and scrubbed my body. It was bliss.

A fluffy white towel hung on a hook, so I dried myself and looked around for my clothes. They were missing. The female guard opened the door, so I wrapped the towel around my body.

"Towel, please," she said, holding out a hand.

I didn't exactly have the power here, so I reluctantly passed it to her, feeling vulnerable and extremely naked. Even her thigh-high stockings were preferable to being nude.

"Follow me."

She paraded me down the hallways, completely naked. I

threw back my shoulders and tried to walk proudly, but I was aware of my nudity, and the cold air brushed my nipples into peaks.

We emerged in the lush sex dungeon I'd been to earlier, where Leif had fucked his beta while I'd touched myself in the corner. Same curving arches of stone, cold gray walls with hanging leather restraints, whips, and paddles. And that wall of windows that I knew contained the observation chamber, whatever that was.

Something was different this time. The padded table in the room's center, beneath the large mirrored ceiling, was dressed in a tablecloth and laid with a feast. My mouth watered.

Leif stood beside the table, looking poised and composed, not as fiercely angry as when I last saw him. He wore casual light-gray sweatpants that sat low around his hips, highlighting the silver in his hair and eyes. That was all he wore, so his glorious bare chest was on full display. He looked me up and down slowly, taking in every inch of my nudity. It took every ounce of my concentration not to throw my arms across my chest to cover myself, but I refused to appear weak.

Finally, he gestured toward the table. "Help yourself, Alara."

I might be a proud bitch, but I was also starving, so I pounced on the table and ate my fill. The alpha watched me the whole time, his silver eyes never leaving me. The longer I stood there eating, the heavier his gaze became. When my appetite was sated, I ate slowly, trying to delay whatever he had planned next. Finally, I had to stop.

When I looked up at him, he spoke. "Now, Alara," he said, his voice low and commanding. "It's time for our session." He moved closer, and my body tensed as his gaze roved over me. "You will submit to me completely," he said, silver eyes glinting with anticipation.

"I..." I didn't have a choice. Or maybe I did. But the pulse of desire coming from the Head of House Caro was hard to resist...and I was done with resisting.

He stepped forward and placed a hand on my shoulder, the warmth of it radiating through me. Then he motioned for me to turn around so that my back was facing him. As I did, he grabbed a length of rope from another corner and bound my hands tightly together behind my back. It felt sublime to relinquish control, just for a few moments. Just this once. To let somebody else take charge. I'd spent so long looking after Pa, so long worrying about my place in the pack, and, more recently, how to avoid raising Leif's suspicion. But now, all I had to do was follow his instructions.

He pulled me over to the padded table in the center of the room, which he cleared with a long swipe so food and plates clattered onto the ground.

He guided me onto the table, turning me onto my stomach with my hands still bound behind my back. His fingers trailed down the curves of my body, igniting a fire within me that spread throughout every inch of flesh. Then he took some nylon straps from a drawer beneath the table and used them to tie my ankles securely to opposite sides of the bed, ensuring they were tight enough that there was no movement. My legs were splayed wide, my ankles firmly attached to the table, and my hands restrained behind my back.

I was naked. He was bare-chested but fully clothed where it counted—down south. I had never felt so vulnerable. And yet I felt the heat of my desire for him burning deep inside me. All of my anger had melted into goo, and I was liquid beneath his touch. His hands felt solid and warm against my body. He pressed his fingers into my flesh, and I exhaled a quiet moan. I hated him, but Gaia-be-damned, I also wanted him.

"You're a wicked pup, Alara," he said, his voice deep and commanding. He massaged my ass, running his hands over their curves, pressing his thumbs into my flesh. He bent down and kissed between my shoulders, then began to suckle on my flesh, lightly at first, then harder.

"You're going to learn to be obedient," he said, pulling his face back to leave a trail of kisses down my spine. He sucked on my flesh so hard I moaned again. His hand slid down my waist, over the curve of my ass. He slapped me hard. I gasped as a sharp pain followed the hot sting of his hand. He slapped me again and again, quick and fast, making me moan.

I never imagined being so aroused by pain, but I was. The knowledge that he controlled me and the surety that he would never go too far. Somehow I knew that, and it kept me warm.

I tried to shift, but my movements were restricted. He was forcing me to stay in this spread-eagle position, and I couldn't move.

My pussy was dripping. I could feel the juices trickling down my thighs. Alpha moved closer and climbed onto the table behind me. He straddled me, still fully dressed. His muscular thighs pressed against the insides of my own, the fabric of his sweat pants rough against my skin, and the weight of him pushing me down.

I moaned as he scooped his fingers into my pussy and spread my juices, getting me ready. My clit throbbed, and my body quivered with unbearable anticipation. I whimpered, and he lifted his fingers to his lips, sucking the wetness from them.

Then he pinched my clit, and I cried out.

"Are you going to be a good little shifter from now on?" he

growled.

"Yes."

"Yes, what?"

"Yes, Leif." I couldn't help the little moment of disobedience. I knew he wanted me to call him Alpha, but my tongue had a mind of its own.

He shifted his weight, moving down my body, crawling backward and planting kisses down my spine, over my bound hands. He sucked on one of my fingers, hard, then disappeared, not touching me at all. My wet finger was cold in the air, and I tried to look around to see him, but he growled, so I stopped moving.

I gasped as his tongue, warm and wet, lapped at my pussy out of nowhere, teasing the sensitive flesh.

Then he bit me on the inner thigh, hard enough to draw blood.

"Fuck," I yelled out.

"That's for your disrespect."

He ran a tongue over the wound, licking up the blood, then traced higher, suckling on my pussy. He spoke into it, and his words went through me like deep vibrations. "Will you be a good girl?"

"Yes," I breathed.

He withdrew his mouth and got off the table, leaving me alone and desperate for more. "Yes, what?" he asked dangerously.

This lack of affection, this withdrawal of his touch, was a far worse punishment than his biting. "Yes, Alpha," I moaned. It was all I could do to stop myself from begging.

I felt his hands at my back, and he unfastened my wrists, then he lifted my arms up and bound them to the top of the table. He loosened the bindings at my ankles and pulled me along the table so my chin was level with the edge, and I could see down to the cold stone floor. My hands were bound near my shoulders, and my ankles still fastened. I was a starfish, naked and panting.

Every sense of vulnerability had vanished; now, I was ablaze with desire.

Leif moved around the table, and I heard him removing his pants. The sound of them hitting the floor, and his musky arousal, ignited my lust even more.

He moved and stood before me.

My eyes moved from his feet up to take in every inch of his body. He was naked and glorious; his muscles, sleek and toned, bunched as he stepped in closer. His cock was long, hard, and ready for me.

He stepped closer, his cock right at the level of my face. I wanted it. In my pussy, on my body, all over my skin, in my mouth.

"Do you want it?"

"Yes, Alpha. Now."

I hated asking nicely. It was too close to begging, and I fucking hated it. And this made me hate the prince more, but right now, I needed his cock more than I hated him.

He put the head of his cock in my mouth, pausing for a moment to let me lick. It was hard, but the skin was soft. He pushed it further down my throat, thrusting toward me, and I had no control over the tempo or the motion. But for once, I didn't need control.

I moaned around him, pleasure radiating through me. He moved slowly at first, then increased his pace as he thrust deeper into my mouth.

My tongue flicked across the underside of his shaft as I sucked him in and out of my mouth. His taste was intoxicating, salty but sweet, with a hint of musk that left me salivating for more.

My pussy throbbed, and I was leaving a damn puddle on the table. My breasts rubbed against the padded table, getting what relief they could from their aching.

His thrusts were slow and deliberate, pushing me further into submission, and I couldn't bring myself to care.

I just wanted him to keep going.

He continued to thrust into my throat until I felt him swell even more inside me, then suddenly, he erupted with a deep guttural moan that reverberated through the room. I lapped up every drop until he softened in release and finally pulled away.

He left me bound on the table, literally gagged and gagging for it.

"No orgasm for you, little bumpkin," he said cruelly, wiping his cock on my shoulder. "You'll have to submit much better than that if you want release."

Then he pulled on his gray sweatpants and left me lying naked on the table. Just fucking walked out of the room, leaving me bound and unable to take care of myself. Asshole.

Leif

Patrolling the perimeter of my pack's lands helped to calm me because at least I was doing something to protect against the threat of Shadow Walkers. At least my feet were moving.

My top beta, Jet, trotted by my side. He was tall and lean with onyx skin and, when he shifted, jet-black fur. With black hair and eyes, he blended into the shadows.

Having him with me kept the worst of my thoughts at bay. Stopped me from picturing how I'd just left Alara bound on the padded table earlier in the day, although I'd sent somebody to untie her. I supposed she was sleeping by now, still in her cramped little cell. The thought made my skin crawl, so I shook it away and focused on the forest.

Jet and I moved in sync, with our senses attuned to the slightest rustle of leaves or snap of a twig. The night was still, except for the occasional owl hooting. We were on high alert because anything could lurk in the darkness.

Jet's deep voice broke the silence. "Leif, you've been getting more and more irritable lately. Is everything okay?"

It was true, but I didn't want to discuss it. I just grunted in reply.

"Leif, I know you're worried about the Shadow Walkers, but you have to trust in the pack. We have the strongest warriors and the most advanced security systems. We can handle anything that comes our way."

"Security systems don't do shit against Walkers. Or have you already forgotten how they walked right into the den, my den, and slaughtered one in four of my shifters? One-quarter of our pack dead in one night." Anger simmered through my voice as I remembered that awful night last year, and I clenched my fists.

We kept within the shadows of the trees, dodging the moonlight. The crunch of leaves under our boots was the only sound that disturbed the calm of the night. I shoved my curled hands into my pockets.

"I haven't forgotten," Jet said. He clocked my mood and kept his voice low. Then, as if the night's music had called him, Jet began to sing. His deep baritone filled the air around us, its melodic tones lilting through each branch and leaf.

It was a call of joy and sorrow—a reminder that beauty still existed in this shithouse world. My fists unclenched in my pockets as the song rolled through me.

A light glinted in a treetop, turning the moon's silvery light into a rainbow of colors as it reflected off the bejeweled wings of a tiny bird. I stopped and held out a hand to Jet, who paused beside me and stopped singing, peering in the same direction. It was a jewelwing, a tiny bird that was encrusted with rubies and pearls.

After a few moments, it flew away, and I released a breath. "That was pretty cool," I said. "I've never seen one of those before."

"One of what? What did you see?"

I rounded on him. "You didn't see it? The jewelwing! It was right there in that tree, then it flew away. Come on, it was as bright as a torch, you must have seen it."

Jet shrugged. "Nope. I thought they were extinct."

The tiny bird must have been attracted by Jet's song, and when he resumed singing, my heart was light.

As we rounded the bend in our patrol, a lone wolf howled in the distance. My heart jumped into my throat. Jet's song stopped, and he was immediately alert. We exchanged a look, then we were running, shifting as we sprinted, tearing our clothes to shreds, darting between trees, our muscles bunching and releasing.

A second howl joined the first, then a third. Calls of desperation, not joy. My hackles were raised, and my silver fur was erect as I streamed out ahead of Jet, racing to get home to protect the pack.

Thoughts of the Shadow Walkers chased me through the trees, but somehow my mind turned to Alara. The insubordinate bottom-dwelling shifter who had tested my patience one too many times. The one who always asked questions and didn't follow orders, who taunted me and challenged me every chance she got.

A strange pang of worry stirred in my chest—why was I thinking about her when the whole pack was in danger? I shook my head. Hopefully, the Shadow Walkers would tear Alara apart, coat her in their darkness and feast on her soul.

Fuck, my mind was going dark. Who was I turning into? I'd never known my dad, but he had the reputation of being a sick fuck, and maybe it was my destiny to become just like him. Perhaps he was only like that because he needed brutal strength to keep the pack safe.

The howls grew louder, making me run faster, fueled by fear and determination.

Finally, I reached the edge of the woods and saw our den. It looked quiet, bathed in a protective light, completely normal. Relief rolled over me.

But as we padded closer, a chill ran through my veins. Something felt off. It was too quiet; not even a whisper of wind stirred, or the rustle of leaves broke the stillness. Just a group of fae standing on the lawn like statues.

There, on the ground. Taal lay still, coated in blood. Her wiry strength was gone, and her nut-brown skin bleached in the moonlight. Dead. She was one of the betas I used to share a bedroom with when I was just another beta, just the alpha's son. When I was carefree, an expert at avoiding work.

I knew Taal inside and out. Literally. I'd fucked her many times and appreciated her tight brown ass and her small pert boobs. The cub inside me howled in grief and fell to the grass in a puddle of tears, and I couldn't help stepping forward and nuzzling her still-warm body, letting out a slight whine.

But I was Alpha now, and I had to act the part.

I shifted into fae form, the moonlight turning my naked body silver. "Who was on lookout duty?" I growled.

A dozen pack members stood around Taal's blood-soaked body, and every one of them curled in on themselves instead of stepping forward.

"Who takes responsibility for this?" I boomed. I'd spent a lifetime avoiding my obligations, and my mom had paid the ultimate price—her life. I wouldn't tolerate the same mistake in others.

"Who should have been watching the grounds?" I demanded. "Who the fuck is responsible for Taal's death? Step forward now, or you will be ostracized from the pack. Permanently."

One of the newly-Ascended wolves, Petra, stepped forward

with her head bowed in submission. "I—I was on watch, Alpha."

My breaths came fast and deep. "So, why weren't you watching?"

She risked a glance at another shifter, Lucas, but didn't dare to answer my question.

Rage built inside me. "Were you rutting Lucas instead of keeping my den safe?"

She nodded, a tiny gesture that would be easy to miss. Still, she didn't speak, didn't offer an apology, and didn't grovel at my feet like she should have.

I felt the power of my wolf-self rising in my chest, and I threw back my head and unleashed a roar that shook the trees around us. I was furious at Petra. No one could have predicted the Shadow Walkers would attack, but still—she had failed in her duty, and there were consequences.

"You are ostracized from this pack," I growled.

I turned my back on her, and every pack member did likewise, a wall of indifference.

She was dead to us. I felt her fear, sharp as a blade, as she backed away from me in horror. A shifter without a pack was nothing, and she howled and sobbed, begging for mercy.

But I had to teach her a lesson. Teach everyone a lesson.

A strange tapping sound grabbed my attention. The dead body on the ground was twitching. Taal. Her body was reanimating, her dead eyes rolling back in her head until they were completely white. She rose to her feet and began to stagger toward us. She hissed and let out a long, menacing growl before launching at me with her claws extended.

My pack reacted instantly, transforming into their beast forms and roaring with anger. Jet tossed me a sword that gleamed silver in the moonlight. I plunged it into Taal's heart, wincing at the sickening feeling of parting flesh and the sloshing of her blood.

Withdrawing the sword, I swiftly severed Taal's head from her body. She toppled to the grass, lifeless.

"Salt her and burn her," I barked at Lucas. "And don't fuck it up."

Petra was still wailing at being excluded from the pack, but every single wolf ignored her, as was the custom. It was a harsh punishment, but no worse than she deserved. I'd told her I would ostracize her if she didn't step forward, but I never said I wouldn't if she did.

"I want double patrols around the den all night," I barked at Jet, who could be trusted to make it happen. He was a competent second, an excellent beta.

I raised my voice, making sure everyone could hear. "The next shifter who fucks up won't just be chucked out of the pack. I'll shred their heart with my claws."

Alara

The bastard screwed me and then had me taken back to the tiny cell. Fucked me, then fucked me. I wasn't even clean anymore after the shower because food from the table was smeared down my front, and my pussy and thighs were dripping.

The cell shrank before my eyes, suffocating me with its oppressive walls and thick, dank air. A chill raced down my spine as I surveyed the four enclosing walls, the solitary window perched high above, and the door guarded by rusted steel bars—a constant reminder that my fate remained at Leif's whims.

Just thinking his name filled me with rage. How dare he use me like this? I was nothing more than a toy to him. His games were designed to make me suffer, and that's precisely what they did.

I felt violated, like he'd used me without my consent and without my pleasure. It was always about punishing me, never about pleasing me or giving me what I wanted. In the dungeon, it was all about how much pain he could inflict upon me—mentally and physically—while still keeping himself entertained.

And worst of all, he didn't even let me orgasm. He got off on watching my suffering but wouldn't give anything back in return—not even a chance to enjoy some of the pleasure I was enduring for his amusement. But instead, I just lay there in a state of perpetual arousal until Leif finished with me and sent me back to this wretched place.

He didn't care about my needs and desires; he just wanted to control another human being and use that power for his own gain. The more I thought about him, the more I hated him—though my stupid pussy got hotter and wetter.

It was all his fault that I was here. If not for him and his power-hungry ambition, I wouldn't be stuck in a rat-infested cell in Verda City, separated from my family, away from my sick father who needed my care. He conscripted me into his egotistical personal bodyguard, and I felt nothing but bitterness toward him.

My life in Sylverclyff wasn't perfect, but it was peaceful, and I lived it on my own terms. Now I was stuck here dealing with the consequences of the mighty prince's greed and pride. Each torment felt calculated to push me closer to the precipice of my sanity.

But no matter how hard he tried to break me, deep down inside I knew that one day I would escape this place—and when that time came around, I would make Leif pay.

Thoughts of Selene kept me going, even as the night got colder and darker. How was she doing? She was a competent War, and I was sure she had passed Leif's War trial. Hopefully, she was living a good life upstairs in the beta dormitory and not worrying too much about me.

Selene was always brave and strong, capable of enduring anything life threw her way. I'd seen her at her weakest moments, and still she managed to find something inside her to carry on—a strength that inspired me. She would be fine.

She had to be.

Selene had always had the pack's respect. She was a joiner, she had fast reflexes, and she liked chasing balls. Not me. I preferred reading books and deciphering ancient scrolls, not acting like a damn animal. The only balls I chased were attached to attractive males.

This prison cell was shitty times a million, but it gave me an odd appreciation of my life in Sylverclyff—at least I'd had the freedom to live as I chose. I'd been an outsider in my own way, but at least my confinement didn't involve rusty iron bars and slimy stone.

My thoughts inevitably circled back to Leif and his asshole games—and the uncertainty that loomed ahead. What might he do next? Would he move me from this cell? Would he let me go? Or would he keep me here forever, doomed to suffer his sickening desires?

A faint rattling sound shook me from my thoughts. It came from outside my cell. I opened my eyes and looked around, but I couldn't see anything in the darkness. Then I heard it again—and this time, there was something else: a glint of bright silver in the shadows.

I bum-shuffled across the cell to look closer. Somebody had slid an old-fashioned iron key along the stone floor outside my cell. It was just out of reach, but if I lay down and smooshed my face against the bars while stretching out an arm, I could grab it. I slid to my belly and snatched the key from the floor without thinking twice.

The moment the cold metal touched my skin, a spark of hope ignited in my heart. My mind raced with possibilities, my heart thudding. Freedom. Taking a deep breath, I turned the key in the lock. It clicked open, and the heavy cell door swung open.

I looked around to see who had delivered the key, but nobody was there. My mysterious do-gooder wanted to stay anonymous, which made me slightly anxious. Was this a trick of Leif's, trying to find some new excuse to punish me?

It didn't matter; I had to try.

I stepped out of the cell and headed down the underground corridors, taking care to be as quiet as possible. Every step was a leap of faith, and I knew that one wrong move would cost me dearly. I made my way up the winding stone stairs to the first floor and headed to the side door that led outside—the one Leif had sneaked me in through when I failed his War trial.

With one hand on the door, I paused. There was one fae I needed to know was okay. Selene. For all I knew, she'd pissed off Alpha and was rotting away in some other dungeon or being raped and beaten. I couldn't leave her. Not until I knew for sure she was all right.

Even if it meant risking Leif's wrath, there was no way I would abandon her.

"Damn idiot," I muttered, then turned on my heel and sneaked through the corridors to the main staircase.

Steeling myself with determination, I climbed slowly. It took every ounce of courage and willpower I possessed not to sprint up those steps—not only because noise needed to be kept at a minimum but also because each step brought me one step closer to Selene.

As soon as I set foot inside my old bedroom, the beta dorm where I hoped Selene still slept, I felt a presence in the air that made my hairs stand on end. A power took hold of me, freezing me in place. I tried to take another step into the dormitory, but my soles were frozen to the plush rug.

Pulse thudding, I tried to figure out what was happening. I

must have set off the defensive spells that protected the betas. The magical wards were designed to detect the presence of any creature who wasn't a member of the pack.

Which apparently included me.

The ward was powerful and overwhelming, like it had been waiting for me for years—as if it knew my every thought and intention. The air around me was alive with pulsing energy, and my strength drained from my limbs. I couldn't take another step.

A high-pitched screech suddenly pierced the air, and I couldn't move my hands to cover my ears. The sound was disorienting, making it difficult to think.

I was stuck in place. Couldn't move, couldn't think.

Black spots appeared before my eyes, and I scanned the room quickly, looking for Selene. She turned at the piercing siren, her powder-blue hair messy around her face, and her jaw dropped.

"Alara? Are you okay, hon?"

I must have looked like crap, so I tried to reassure her. "Yearimfiiine."

She looked healthy and well, so that was something. "I'll call for help," she said, then started moving.

"No, Imheretoresssccue..."

As I began to lose consciousness, something deep within me stirred—my inner wolf responding to the call of this magical force. With every breath, my animal instincts came more alive. Finally, all reason faded away, and only instinct remained.

Then, out of the corner of my eye, I spotted a massive figure in the doorway. Leif. He did not look happy. He looked like a damn hunter, and no prizes for guessing who his prey was.

With a slight growl, he stepped forward and confronted me.

"What do you think you're doing? You have no right to be here." His voice was low and menacing, trying to intimidate me into submission.

But this time, my inner wolf was prepared to fight back. With a wave of his hand, the magical ward dissolved, and my strength returned. As soon as my eyes met his, a surge of courage ran through me, and I embraced the wildness inside me.

I bared my teeth and snarled at him fiercely, ready to defend myself against attack. My wolf instincts were taking over, and I knew there was no turning back now—if I wanted freedom, I would have to fight for it with every breath.

My wolf took over, and the shift came easily. I lunged at him, my fangs bared and my claws outstretched. I would teach him I was a force to be reckoned with. But Leif had the advantage of strength and size, combined with a skill honed from many years of experience in battle—something I had never faced.

He batted me away with one arm. "You can't beat me, pup," he snarled, dripping with condescension.

He shifted into wolf form, too, his fur glinting in the moonlight like liquid silver. I lunged again, and he swatted me aside with a single paw, and I flew across the room and landed splayed over the cold marble floor. Should've aimed for the rug.

Leif's steel eyes were fierce and unyielding, daring me to challenge him again. I knew I could never beat him in this form—it would take more than physical strength now.

But I refused to give up. As long as I still had breath, I would continue fighting for freedom until the very last moment of my life.

The floor was cold, even through my fur. The sleep-rumpled

betas stood around watching, not daring to intervene. Selene had her hand over her mouth, her powder-blue eyes wide, but some of the others were grinning at the show.

The alpha prowled closer like he was stalking prey and then pounced, his heavy body landing over mine, pinning my fur to the floor with his sharp claws. He growled, exposing sharp white fangs, which he clamped around my neck.

He bit hard, pressing against my windpipe until I struggled to breathe. Then harder, his fangs piercing my skin, so blood matted my fur.

Was he going to kill me? I couldn't just lie there and take it.

Thinking fast, I shifted into fae form, so I was smaller and had more space to move. I slid my throat out of his jaw and started wiggling away, scrambling to get out from under him, but he snarled and dropped onto me, stopping me dead with his weight.

His huge wolf head was level with my waist, and I was pinned to the floor by his sheer size. I was naked, of course, in front of a crowd of staring betas. That alone would be my worst nightmare...if I wasn't already inside an even worse one.

Leif placed a padded paw over one of my wrists, holding me in place. His long wet tongue flicked out, and he dragged it up from my waist, roughly up my sternum between my breasts, and back up to my neck.

He moved his entire body up, and I felt his wolf cock hard against my leg while he licked my neck, then grazed it with his sharp teeth.

Thank Gaia, he was being more careful now I was in fae form. So obviously, he wasn't planning on killing me. But his growling was so fierce I didn't dare to move a muscle in case he changed his mind.

He was trying to mark me, marking his territory and making me his possession. He wanted to show everyone that he was in charge. His heavy paws pressed into the floor on either side of me, and his massive chest covered my entire body. His weight was a crushing force, pinning me down.

I didn't know what to do. I couldn't breathe, and my heart was thumping in my chest. I couldn't move.

A sob from over Leif's shoulder made me turn my head. Selene stared at me with wide eyes, and I gave her a slight smile to reassure her and whatever nod I could manage while my neck was still inside the giant wolf's jaws.

The alpha released his grip slightly, and I struggled to take a breath. But then he bit my neck again, a little harder, and I yelped in pain.

With a sharp nip on my ear, he shifted back into human form and pinned both my wrists with a single hand. His cock pressed hard against my stomach.

"There's no escape, Alara. You're my prisoner, and you will remain my prisoner. That's what happens to little liars." His tone was stern and commanding.

He stood up, unashamedly naked, with a raging erection. Man, you had to admire that level of confidence. But with a body like that, why wouldn't you strut? His toned muscles glistened in the moonlight, accentuating every curve and angle of his masculine frame, setting him in silvery flames.

He moved closer and took my hands as he pulled me up from the floor, pressing my body against him as if he couldn't wait to be close again. His erection was hard against my stomach, a reminder of what was yet to come.

He barked an order to one of the staring betas, "Take her down to the dungeon and tie her up."

Without hesitation, they did as they were told. Again, it was difficult to hate that level of respect; it wasn't something I'd ever experienced.

"Where are you taking her?" Selene asked. Brave and stupid, just my kind of girl.

"To hell," Leif growled. The beta shoved me roughly out the door and along the corridor, back down to my next round of punishment.

Leif

I gave Nikita and Alara a head start so I could catch my breath and rein in my anger, then I followed them down to the playroom.

Low lighting flickered off the stone arches. Entering the playroom always set my skin tingling, the whips and paddles were promises of pleasure. Especially today.

Alara stood in the middle of the room, completely naked and vulnerable. Her light brown skin contrasted against her wild orange hair, which hung to her shoulders. Her wrists were bound with a velvet rope, but she was otherwise unrestrained.

Nikita stood beside her, his hand resting on her shoulder as if to protect her from me. His face was expressionless as he watched me approach. With a single glance from me, he stepped away so I had full access to Alara.

"Leave us," I commanded, and my beta scurried from the room. Nikita and I used to share a room, both betas of almost equal standing, and I thought I'd never change, never become a monster like my father. But that was before I understood the effect of power, how a single act of disobedience could bring down an army.

The attack on my family's den, which killed one-fourth of the pack, was due to two moments of insubordination.

Two shifters who should have been on duty. Two fae whose moments of inattention caused countless deaths. Now that I was Alpha, I couldn't let anything slide. The weight of responsibility for my pack was a concrete vest I couldn't remove.

So, although the tiny cub inside me whined at seeing my beta scurry off so fearfully, the alpha I had to be preened in pride.

As soon as Nikita left, I moved closer to Alara, my eyes never leaving hers as I took in every detail of her body; the curves of her hips and breasts, the graceful arch of her neck, even the way she held herself with a hint of defiance despite being so vulnerable. It made my heart beat faster and my wolf stir within me.

"You disobeyed me, Alara," I said in a low voice, circling her slowly. "Again. You know the consequences of such actions." I was pleased that I sounded ruthless, sounded like the tough alpha I needed to be.

She didn't flinch or look away from me but lifted her chin as if daring me to punish her. "You don't own me, city dick," she said, her voice steady.

Her voice was liquid, and the word *dick* on her tongue reminded me of my cock in her mouth. I was bare-chested, wearing just my light gray sweatpants, and they tented, my cock already rigid.

"Yes, I do," I corrected her. I stopped behind her, and my hand came down hard on her bare backside. "You're mine." This shifter from the ass-end of nowhere was becoming my personal battlefield, a trial more important than any that Gaia could send me. If I could force her to submit to me, I could keep my entire pack in line and protect every shifter in the realm. She was a test of my fitness to be Alpha.

But still, the reckless cub inside me, who used to play pranks on his friends and flip the bird at authority, admired her resistance.

Alara gasped in pain but didn't move from her position.

I moved closer to her, my hands reaching to touch her skin. I traced my fingers down her spine, eliciting a shiver from her. I liked how responsive she was to my touch, and I planned to use that to my advantage.

"I'll make sure you remember this lesson," I growled, my other hand trailing down her spine and between her legs, feeling the wetness already forming there.

Alara moaned softly at my touch, her body betraying her defiance. I leaned in to whisper in her ear. "You're going to beg for mercy before I'm done with you."

Heat built between us, the tension thick in the air. I ran a finger along the inside of her thigh, relishing how she shuddered at my touch.

Without warning, I grabbed her by the hair and pulled her head back, exposing her neck. I leaned in, my lips brushing against the column of her throat. She moaned, the fragrance of her arousal stronger.

"I'll never beg, Leif," she said, her voice husky. She arched into me, offering herself.

"You will," I promised her, "You're mine, Alara. You're mine to do whatever I want with."

I bit her firmly on the shoulder, marking her. She whimpered.

"You belong to me, and I will treat you as I see fit." I bit her again, right above her collarbone, and she cried out. I thought that if she hated this, I'd stop...but I was half-monster on my father's side, so maybe I wouldn't.

In any case, her arousal was crystal clear. I pulled back her head so I could look into her eyes. Her pupils were dilated, her lips slightly parted, and her breathing shaky. The look in her eyes made my cock throb, and I felt a bead of pre-cum ooze from the tip. She was mine, even if she didn't know it yet.

I released her suddenly, letting her fall to her knees and rise to her feet, watching her carefully as she struggled to keep her balance with her hands restrained.

My alpha wolf was in control, angry and ready to dominate, but my fae side was intrigued by the way she was so determined to be defiant. She stood with her head high and shoulders back, almost as if daring me to take her. I'd never encountered a shifter who stood up to me like she did. It turned me on more than I liked to admit.

"I'm going to show you what happens when you try to fight your alpha."

She held my gaze as I stalked toward her, not backing away, not looking away. I smiled, liking her courage. I could smell her arousal, strong and musky. Would she scream when I finally claimed her? I was tempted to do it now. Damn tempted.

I pulled her into me, my hand tangled in her hair again. I brought her to my lips, kissing her hard. I felt her body go rigid, but she didn't pull away. I held her tightly, my body pressed against hers, before pushing her away again.

"The way you respond to me is delicious," I said, my voice low. And it was true. She was tastier than one of D's dishes. "You like the way I touch you, don't you?"

She looked away, refusing to answer, but I could see that it was true from how her hands clenched and unclenched in their velvet binding.

I took a step back and lowered myself onto a wooden bench.

My cock was hard and throbbing to be inside of her. With a quick jerk of my hips, I freed it from my sweat pants, heavy and full. I let the sweats drop to the floor and beckoned her to come, but she didn't move.

"Come on, Alara. You can't resist me. Show me how much you want me." My voice was rough and low.

I watched her, waiting for her to move, my wolf desperate for her to take the bait, but she stood still. I growled angrily and reached for a riding crop on the floor behind me, then smacked my own thigh with it. She moaned unexpectedly, and I felt myself grow even harder.

"Fuck me," I said, my voice thick and heavy. I whipped the riding crop on my other thigh, drawing a thin line of red blood along my skin.

Alara gasped and instinctively moved forward but then caught herself and stopped. I saw the conflict in her eyes and felt my wolf grow even more eager. Then, she couldn't hold herself back any longer. She lunged at me and straddled me on the bench, final proof that she wanted me.

As the heat of her pussy touched my cock, I used every ounce of self-control I possessed and pushed her off, not wanting to give her the satisfaction of release.

"No, bumpkin," I growled, holding her by the neck. "You haven't earned that yet. No release until you submit. Properly. Now walk over there." I pointed to the mark on the floor beneath a hook with velvet cuffs hanging down.

She stared at me, weighing up her natural defiance with my order to submit.

No submission, no orgasm. Even I was smart enough to figure that out, and I didn't doubt she was more intelligent than me. I'd caught her reading books when she should have been bonding with the pack.

She walked to the mark, and my chest swelled in victory. I snapped her wrists into the leather cuffs above her head, and her breasts pushed forward, perfect and round and large. I'd never seen tits as perfect as hers. I needed her naked and moaning under me.

Needed her to submit and prove that I would be a good alpha, but she kept fighting me.

I traced my free hand along her marvelous curves, feeling her nipples stiffen against my palm, and she moaned. I tweaked one nipple hard, and she cried out, husky and needy. I smacked her ass, and she gasped.

"Fuck," she cried, making it sound like she was begging, her voice hoarse with desire, my cock throbbing in response.

"I'm going to tell you how I'm going to punish you, Alara," I said, listening carefully to the change in her breathing, the way her breasts rose and fell quicker as I spoke.

I turned my back on her and walked to the box of toys on another table, deliberately letting her see what I was doing.

I turned to her and smiled. My cock was so hard it hurt.

"This is a wooden paddle. It's heavy, solid and meant to hurt, but I will use it to pleasure you if you ask nicely."

She looked at me, her eyes filled with defiance.

"No, Alara," I said, my voice stern, "You either say, 'Please, Alpha, may I have pleasure?' or you get to feel my hand."

No answer.

"I'm giving you one last chance, Alara. After this, there will be no pleasure."

She still didn't speak.

I smirked. Time to teach her the real lesson.

I picked up the paddle and smacked her with it. Hard. The

flesh of her ass jiggled after the satisfying thud.

Gaia, that was hot.

She whimpered. I smacked her again, and her body pushed against the restraints.

"Come, Alara," I said, my voice deep and low. "You like feeling the paddle slide across your skin, don't you?"

I was talking to her wolf. I was talking to the inner animal that craved domination, yearned for punishment and the promise of ecstasy.

She cried out, and I rewarded her with a stripe of pain across her lower back, her eyes closing at the sting.

I smacked her harder, reveling in the sensuous sound of wood against flesh, my body heating up with each stroke. I could feel her surrender, and I wanted to take it further.

Her breath came in short bursts as I pounded her ass and thighs, the paddle leaving a flush of red against her skin. She was so beautiful like this—her poise, defiance, and submission all rolled into one.

I wanted to look into her eyes as she came, wanted to see the heat and need and lust in her orange eyes, wanted to see her lose control and know that I was the one who made her lose it. I wanted to see her break.

I licked my lips as she opened her mouth to speak.

Alara

"I will never beg."

I already knew I was lying. I was naked with my wrists tied to the ceiling by a velvet rope, and everything Leif did made my pussy throb and my skin burn. Even paddling me.

I tried to think of a spell I could use to escape, perhaps something to burn through the velvet rope, or a demon-summoning incantation. But I was never any good at spellwork, and creating a flame hot enough to burn through these restraints was beyond me.

Especially while I was so distracted.

Leif stepped back and gave me a long, appraising look. His eyes were dark and endless, like the vast expanse of the night sky. "I think we need to take this up a notch."

Leif stepped away from me, and I heard him move around the room. "You won't be able to see what I'm doing," he said, his voice low and smooth like silk.

He moved closer and reached up to my face, caressing my cheek gently as his fingers trailed over my forehead, then brushing aside my hair. My breath hitched in anticipation as I felt the blindfold slip over my eyes. Everything went black, the only sensation now was Leif's hands on me. He wrapped the velvet rope around my ankles and tied it securely so I couldn't move—not even an inch.

My wrists were still bound with the rope as Leif positioned himself in front of me again. His warm hands rested on my shoulders as he spoke softly in my ear. "Focus on my touch."

Something cold and wet slid along my skin, starting from my neck and traveling slowly down over my chest. Was that ice? I shivered, hyper-focused on the sensation of the frozen cube pushing over my fevered skin. He continued his journey, tracing the outline of my curves with the ice before finally moving it up to trail along my thighs. I gasped as the coldness sent a thrill through me, and Leif chuckled softly in response.

He moved around me again, bringing various items that he used to tease and tantalize every inch of me. I felt the warmth of feathers brushing against my skin, the gentle tug of silk ribbons wound around me, and the sudden shock of pins being pressed into strategic locations on my body.

My entire body shivered as each new sensation hit me, leaving behind a trail of pleasure that made it almost impossible to keep still despite being securely bound by rope. The sensations kept coming—each more exquisite than the last—until the pleasure was almost too much to bear.

He stood before me, his chest barely touching my breasts and his cock pressing into my belly.

"Do you want this?" he murmured.

"Yes." The word was out of me before I could stop it.

He edged lower, bending his knees, and placed the tip of his cock at my entrance, resting lightly against it.

I bucked forward, trying to get onto his cock, but he just tutted and laughed.

I didn't care anymore. My pride was irrelevant; all I wanted was to ride him and find release. It was frustrating to have my hands and legs tied. If I was free, I'd run my hands all over his muscled chest and wrap my legs around his waist, riding his cock until I wept.

But all I could do was rock my hips forward, aching for friction.

"Call me Alpha."

No, I'd lasted this long without using his damn title, I could last longer. He didn't deserve the respect since he didn't show me any. But apparently, my mind and my slutty tongue didn't agree, and the words rolled from my lips. "Yes, Alpha."

"Good girl. Will you do what I tell you?"

"Yes, Alpha." I shut down my mind. For now. My body was so much more important, and it needed release. So yes, I would do anything. Anything to get his cock inside me and his hands on my breasts.

I was already on the edge of my orgasm, so close that I was gasping with need, clenching the muscles of my pussy and my ass, trying to hold onto my climax.

"Good girl."

He leaned forward, pressing his cock right against my pussy. I spread my legs as wide as I could, which wasn't very wide with my ankles tied together, just enough to allow him to push inside me.

His cock filled me, and I threw back my head and cried at the sensation.

"I'm going to move," he said, his voice shakier than I expected.

The warning had barely left his lips when he pulled out and then slammed into me, impaling me on his cock.

"Oh, Gaia. Fuck."

"You want more?"

"Yes."

He pulled out and thrust back in again, making me moan with pleasure.

"Alpha," I breathed as he began to move inside me, sliding so deep that he touched spots I didn't even know had nerves.

He leaned down and caught my nipple between his lips, tugging it gently before letting it go. "You want to come, don't you?"

"Yes," I breathed, ready to do anything to get it.

I had never been so aroused in my life.

He played with my other nipple, rolling it between his thumb and forefinger until I thought I would go mad with desire.

I wanted to kiss him, but my mouth was the one place he wouldn't touch.

He pulled out again, thrusting back in deeper, and I cried out. He did it once more and then again, this time going even deeper, my pussy tightening around his cock to encourage him. He froze. He'd buried his cock completely inside me. My pussy quivered with the sensation of being full. It was a perfect fit.

"Come for me," he commanded.

I cried out as I came, my pussy spasming around his length. He gave me another few thrusts before he came, too, roaring as his cock pulsed inside me, filling the room with noise.

I sagged against my wrist restraints, unable to hold myself up. I still couldn't see, but I could feel Leif bending down and untying my ankles, then reaching up and releasing my wrists.

I fell, and he caught me in his arms and pulled me against his chest, more tenderly than I expected. My cheek pressed against his taut pec, and I breathed him in.

His arms were tight around me, supporting my weight. "You are beautiful, bumpkin. So fucking beautiful."

I didn't expect a compliment. Didn't expect the intensity of that orgasm or the feelings rolling through me. This moment of intimacy, where he wasn't punishing me and I wasn't hating him, felt right.

"Why are you so angry?" I asked, my lips half-squashed against the hard planes of his chest. "Some of the betas say you used to be different, that you used to play games with them and joke about doing nothing once you were Alpha."

We had earned this small moment of intimacy, and I didn't want to waste it. For just this instant, I wanted to know more about him. But I didn't expect him to answer.

He sighed and brushed a strand of hair from my face. "Everything was different before Mom died. She was a wonderful alpha. Everyone thought so. She ruled for five-hundred years, and the realm has never been more peaceful. I never really believed she'd go, you know. I thought she would live forever and I'd be able to mess around with my buddies."

I ran a hand down his back and breathed him in some more. "It sounds like you have a lot to live up to."

He was quiet, and when he shifted his weight, I thought he would loosen his arms from around me and walk away, but he tightened them instead.

"I guess so. Mom would have been...disappointed in me. So I need to fix that."

His pec against my cheek was firm and warm, and his arms holding me up gave me the courage to ask. "Would she have wanted you to be ruthless with your own pack?" Swear to fucking Gaia, I meant the question legitimately, but he took it as an insult.

He released his arms and abruptly stepped away, leaving me stumbling to support myself and cold. The spell of intimacy was broken.

His silver eyes narrowed. "That's none of your business, country bumpkin."

He stepped away and quickly pulled on the gray sweatpants he'd discarded earlier, restoring the power imbalance between us, leaving me vulnerable and naked and with none of the armor of lust.

"Don't ask questions of your alpha, or next time will be pure punishment with no pleasure." His voice had lost all trace of gentleness, and the firm planes of his body seemed severe and intimidating.

I shivered at the thought of receiving a more brutal beating. I was damn sure the night would be painful, and I wouldn't be able to sit down for days, even with my shifter's speedy healing.

Leif strode to the door, and I called out. "Can I have some clothes?"

He whirled around. "You promised to do exactly as you were told."

"Oh, only during...I mean, not while..."

His jaw tightened. "You will submit to me always. And you will get clothes when I say so." He spun on his heel.

"Wait. You're not going to leave me here, are you?"

"I'll have someone return you to your room."

Did he mean the beta dormitory or my cramped cell?

He left, and the door clanged loudly behind him as he slammed it.

So much for our moment of intimacy. So much for thinking he might not be as awful as he seemed, that maybe part of his assholery was just grief at his mother's death.

So much for escape.

Leif

A few days later, I sat on a plush velvet sofa in the opulent purple room, adorned with purple-marbled walls that exuded a faint floral scent. I'd requested the enchanted walls to be turned off because I wasn't relaxed enough for soft instrumental music.

A couple of betas sat on either side of me, leaning against my arms, and a third one brushing my hair. Their touch was comforting, and I needed it, but when Bryen suggested we have sex, I brushed him aside. I couldn't get it up for anyone the past few days—at least, not unless I was thinking about Alara. Something about her defiance had etched her permanently into my thoughts. I just needed to punish her properly so I could forget about her and move on.

Lost in thoughts of Alara's defiance, I was momentarily pulled back to reality as the hallway door swung open, and two spellbirds whizzed through, their papery wings fluttering in the air and interrupting my reverie. The spellbirds landed on my lap. I tore them in two and let the paper drift to the marble floor, still twitching.

"You're not going to read it, Alpha?" Bryen asked. "It might be important."

I gave him a cold look. "It's not."

A dozen spellbirds had tried to reach me today, their enchanted origami battering against the windows to get to me. But I didn't need to read them to know what they said. The spellbirds would be nagging me about the trials.

Today was the first heir trial of the year. Each year, the five heirs to the five thrones of Verda had to sit three tests: one physical, one for spellwork, and one for inner magic.

Like all wolves, my inner magic was evident from birth. I was a Lupus, through and through. Before I ascended, I had poor control over my wolf, which only emerged when I was angry or in danger. That's how it was for all wolf cubs. Some faelings didn't shift at all until after they ascended. Some poor bastards didn't ascend into Lupus and were kicked out of the pack. Others didn't survive the Ascension.

At the first Ascension rite after my twenty-fifth birthday, I ascended, and since then, I'd had perfect control over my wolf. I could shift at will and used that to my advantage during the physical trials. There weren't many tasks a fae could do better or faster than a wolf.

So if today's trial was the physical one, I'd probably come first and score five points. My gold was on Ronan to score the four points, Gabrelle to come home with three points, Neela to earn two, and poor old D to get the measly single.

Since I ascended a few years back, I usually looked forward to the physical trial because it was where I shone. That and inner power. I sucked at spellwork.

The points determined the pecking order of the heirs. It was all very well for five Houses to rule jointly, but we needed some way to sort out disputes, and the point system was it. Once the majority of our parents died and we inherited the thrones, our points totals would be locked.

Ronan was in the lead; he'd earned the most points over the years we'd been sitting the trials. Gabrelle was a close second, and the rest of us were somewhere down the back. I always thought I'd finish ahead of Sebarah, but he was six feet under, dead as a lump of coal, and his younger sister Neela was a lot stronger than him. Maybe she'd surprise us all and come in first place.

I'd never cared about my points. Was happy to let Ronan and Gabrelle sit around feeling important and making all the boring decisions while I screwed around and played with my balls. And my other balls.

But I always turned up to the trials. It was a fun challenge, a day to jeer my buddies and take the piss out of whoever came in last.

But not today. I still didn't care about the points, but my reasons had changed. My freedom to goof off and leave the important stuff to others had disappeared, gone up in fucking flames. Mom was dead, and I was the alpha of my pack. The alpha of alphas, responsible for every damn pack in the Realm of Verda. I didn't have time for children's games.

As I stood up from the sofa, the betas scattered, sensing my mood. I couldn't keep my mind off Alara, the way she challenged me and made me feel alive. I needed to forget her, but my thoughts kept circling back to her defiance and how it made me want to dominate her. If I couldn't get one lowly rural shifter to submit to me, how could I rule my whole pack? And every other pack in the realm? How could I keep them safe?

I shook my head, trying to clear my thoughts, and went to the door.

Leaving the lounge room behind, I made my way down the

hallway. My newest friend, anger, reared inside me. Why couldn't the other heirs just leave me alone? I was a different fae now from the one they used to know.

As the spellbirds continued to peck at the windows, my frustration grew. I couldn't handle the distractions anymore. 'Fuck it,' I muttered, my mind made up. I needed to confront them at the damn Lakehouse and get them off my case, once and for all. They needed to hear it from my own lips, then maybe they'd steer clear of me.

Half an hour later, I emerged from the lake in wolf form, water sheeting off my silver fur. I bounded up the stairs to the deck and pushed open the glass door with my snout.

Inside, the aroma of freshly cut wood mingled with the crisp scent of the lake. Sunlight streamed through the floor-to-ceiling windows, casting a warm golden glow across the room.

Neela shrieked at the sight of me and leaped off Ronan's lap to come and greet me. "Leif, hey." She patted my head, and I couldn't help leaning into the feeling, enjoying the touch. A mix of surprise and amusement filled the room as I padded in.

Neela smelled fae now; when she first arrived in the realm, she'd smelled a hundo percent human. I nuzzled into her crotch, and she giggled, but Ronan gave a low growl.

There was a general air of happiness and spent adrenaline. Gabrelle lounged on her crystal sofa with her long shapely legs crossed at the ankles. Her purple jumpsuit hugged her curves, and she rose to her feet elegantly and crossed to me. Bending low to bring her face to mine, I copped a perfect view of her tits, which annoyingly reminded me of Alara. The bumpkin's boobs were even better than the beauty queen's, and that was saying something.

"I'm glad you came," Gabrelle said silkily, and when she

leaned in for a hug, my tail wagged.

I was prolonging my time as a wolf, delaying the shift into fae form that would bring my worries crashing onto my shoulders.

"But you missed the trial," the beauty heir said, stretching to standing and giving me a close-up of her curves. "Bad dog."

A whine escaped me, which was weird. I didn't care what these guys thought of me anymore—I couldn't afford to, not when all my wolves depended on me making the tough decisions.

Dion was in the kitchen, his curly hair a deep red that made me suspect he'd been drinking Dionysus wine. Something delicious-smelling wafted from him, so whatever he cooked would be good. Usually, he hated that I kept spare sweatpants and tennis balls in his kitchen drawers, but today he fished out a ball and tossed it to me. My paws skidded across the floorboards as I pounced on the ball and snatched it up. Chewing it around in my mouth was satisfying and calming, so I kept it up.

I trotted over to greet Ronan, who sat on his black leather armchair with a wide grin at seeing me. He was dressed all in black, with his T-shirt the same shade as his hair and eyes. His mood was infectious, of course, since he was of House Mentium, and when I padded closer, I felt more like my old self. I sniffed his crotch just to annoy him, and he swatted my muzzle away. "Bad mutt," he said with a smile.

I loped over to my huge white sofa, jumped on, then curled up, still in wolf form. It made no sense to stay shifted—it didn't reduce the threat of the Shadow Walkers or clear Alara from my thoughts—but I did it anyway. It gave me a few more moments of peace.

Neela came and wriggled in beside me, making me move

over to give her room, and I rested my muzzle on her lap while I chewed my ball. She smelled familiar and comforting, like friendship. Like the past. She wore a blue and green wrap top with no sleeves and sensible fae-denim pants. A far cry from the puffy blue dress she'd turned up in for last year's first trial.

"Don't you go sniffing my female," Ronan said with fake severity.

To piss him off—and to cop a feel—I raised my head and licked Neela's thigh slowly, letting the tennis ball roll off the sofa's edge. She laughed and patted my head, Ronan grizzled, and I contentedly returned my head to her lap, only slightly missing my chew toy, which had rolled across the floorboards and lodged under Gabrelle's chaise longue.

None of them pressured me to shift or asked why I hadn't, for which I was grateful. Perhaps they sensed that this was easier for me.

Neela chattered comfortably beside me, stroking my fur. "Today's trial was spellwork," she said matter-of-factly.

Gabrelle lounged on her crystal sofa. "You missed quite a show, Leif," she teased, her eyes lingering on me.

"Yeah," Neela agreed, running her hands through my fur. "We had to cast illusions to make an object disappear. Mine was a crystal flower. You know, the ones that can make wishes come true. Only I had to make it disappear. I sucked. Two bloody points for me...I guess I should thank you for not turning up, otherwise I would have scored the single."

I looked at Ronan. He grinned. "I had to cast an illusion over an Unseelie necklace. It was unfair, actually, you know how tricky Unseelie jewelry is. It jiggles all over the place."

"Don't complain, toy boy. You still got four points," Neela said.

Gabrelle interjected smoothly. "I came in first place, obviously, with five points. I made the changeling stone vanish within minutes." She flicked a strand of dusty pink hair over her perfect brown shoulder, and my tongue lolled out at the sight, which made her smile.

"Dinner's ready." Dion carried a steaming pot of something to the table, and the heirs all rose to go over.

Alara paused when I didn't follow. "Come over, wolf boy. We can put a plate on the floor for you."

I slinked off the white sofa and followed her. It seemed a step too far to eat from a bowl on the floorboards while my best friends ate dinner above me, so I shifted into my fae form.

I immediately thought of my pack and how I should be home looking after them instead of hanging out with the heirs. What if Shadow Walkers attacked the den while I was out here swinging my big dick in Gabrelle's face? What if information arrived on how to kill the Walkers, and I was here instead of being home to do something about it?

I sat slowly on the wooden dining chair, but Gabrelle placed a cold hand on the small of my back and nudged me back to standing. "No ass crack on the communal furniture." She called out to Dion, who was still in the kitchen putting the finishing touches on dessert. "Emergency sweatpant situation, Big D."

He pulled open a bottom drawer and retrieved a light-gray garment, which he tossed to Gabrelle, who shoved it at my chest.

A protest formed on my lips, a quip about how covering my perfect dick was a crime against fae-kind. But it didn't make it out of my mouth. The fear for my pack clamped my lips shut and held my tongue.

I chucked the sweatpants on the floor. "I've gotta go." Dion's food smelled amazing—he was the best Magirus I knew, and I used to joke about getting him on my staff. But I couldn't sit around and talk shit while my pack might be in danger.

I strode across the room and squeaked open the sliding glass doors onto the deck. With a ripple of energy, my silver fur receded, replaced by smooth, glowing skin. Warmth and power surged through me, and the air crackled with electricity as I completed my shift.

Maybe I could work out some of my stress on Alara's body.

Leif

A few nights later, I led my pack to a Gathering of Shifters. My wolves slunk into the sacred grove, their eyes aglow with an eerie light. The clearing was shrouded in secrecy and guarded by a powerful enchantment that kept most fae at bay.

White globes flickered atop the twisted tree trunks, casting a sinister light on our surroundings. They weren't globes of contained Lightning from the Realm of Caprice and were eerier and softer than fae-summoned globes, so they must be something else. Whatever they were, their glow barely penetrated the darkness that crept at the edges of our meeting place, where powerful nature spirits lurked in watchful silence.

This was my first time here—the different shifter packs met rarely, and when Mom had asked me to accompany her to the last Gathering, I'd made some bullshit excuse to stay home and goof off. Like a damn faeling.

I reached out to touch the rough bark of a tree but recoiled in horror as my fingers sank into its flesh like rotted meat. Its branches writhed like serpents, hissing with malevolent intent. A shiver ran down my spine as though I'd disturbed something that had been dormant for far too long. I should have paid more fucking attention when Mom spoke about this shit.

Kaida, the Lioness Queen, her hair cascading around her in a halo of gold, loomed on a small throne that her lions must have carried through the densely packed trees. The graceful form beneath her golden dress demanded reverence with every movement, and I knew she would fight tooth and claw for her pride's protection.

Graz, the High Shaman of the bears, glowered down at us with a menacing scowl on his massive brown face. He was a hulking tower of muscle and fury, looming over us all and teeming with barely contained rage that threatened to unleash at any moment. "You are late," he boomed, making his brown suit quiver.

Every fiber in my being screamed for me to flee before he could unleash his wrath, but I held my ground. I'd chosen my black suit with a silver shirt that exuded power, and I knew I looked badass, so I straightened my shoulders and held my ground. "Yes," I said simply, and my frankness seemed enough to appease him.

The fiercely independent eagles were gathered, too, as were the gentle deers, probably here to protect the spirits in the grove. The final group of shifters represented were the snakes, who slithered over one another near the glade's perimeter. Each leader had several shifters in support, so the small grove was packed with fae, either clothed in finery or standing in animal form.

Kaida the Lioness spoke first, her voice elegant and commanding. "The Shadow Walkers present the greatest threat we shifters have ever faced. They are attacking shifters and not other types of fae, so we shifters must decide how to deal with them." She crossed her legs gracefully, and her golden gown flowed around her like water.

It was rare for so many different shifters to gather in one place. Usually, we held each other in contempt. I respected the bears, but the lions had their heads too far up their own asses to smell anything other than shit, and the others were all lazy or stupid.

Talon, the Sky King, flew down from his perch on a branch and landed silently, retracting his wings and timing his shift perfectly to land seamlessly on the forest floor in fae form. He wore a feathered shirt without sleeves, so he could partially shift and remain clothed. His partial shift looked kinda cool, but I'd never admit it out loud. "There is no decision to be made. If the Shadow Walkers set foot near my nests, I will destroy them." His eagles in the trees around us squawked in agreement, the red mottling on their feathers dancing under the eerie light.

Viper, the Trickster Queen, hissed in annoyance. "And how do you propose to do that, you fool?" The snake on her right flicked out a forked tongue while she continued. "We have no idea how to kill them."

Talon twisted his neck around, looking almost behind directly behind him to fix his angry stare on the snake leader. "You don't know how to slay them, but it wouldn't take long for my flock to figure it out."

Tension bubbled through the fae. This meeting was going to shit, fast. I glanced at Jet, who stood on my left, and he smirked. He'd bet on the first fight breaking out within ten minutes, and he was on track to win. Thank Gaia I'd instructed a few of my shifters to remain in wolf form so we would be ready to defend ourselves if this turned physical. I wasn't worried about the deer, snakes, or eagles, but you couldn't get lazy around lions or bears.

Viper slithered forward, flanked by her serpents. "We are the Shadow Walkers' primary target, and we have information that might be useful in defeating them," she said, holding up a hand to silence the squabbling among the fae.

Kaida raised an eyebrow, one hand caressing her golden throne. "Why should we trust you?" Her golden gaze was piercing.

"Because we have nothing to lose and everything to gain by stopping them." Viper's diamondback rattled in warning, and several snakes hissed.

Graz growled in agreement, his powerful ursine voice echoing through the trees. "She's right. We can't afford to let our differences divide us. The Shadow Walkers are the real enemy here."

Kaida uncrossed her legs, drawing every eye in the glade. Her golden mane of hair hovered about her head. "Fine. What do you know about the Walkers, Trickster Queen?"

The snake took a deep breath. "They're led by a fae who calls himself the Night King. He's as old as the trees. He has been amassing an army of undead soldiers and plans to attack all the shifter clans."

It was time to put an end to this parade of crap. With determination, I picked some invisible dirt from my nails and projected my voice. "Bullshit." Viper hissed at me, but I swiped away her objections with a hand through the air. "That's just a rumor. There's a million rumors about the Walkers. That they're ghosts of long-dead fae. Or followers of the Father of Death. My favorite is hot, though, you've gotta hear it: A faeling in Brume was trying to make shadow cookies and his spell went wrong. Imagine his fucking surprise when a bunch of zombies walked out of his oven." I looked around, drawing out the silence. "It's all bullshit."

Viper hissed. "My sources are reliable, cub."

I rounded on the Trickster Queen, heat rising to the surface of my skin. "It doesn't matter anyway because we don't know how to kill them. Everything we do, every single damn thing, should be trying to find that out. How. Can. We. Kill. Them? Everything else is a waste of time."

Sable, the Guardian of the Forest and leader of the deer shifters, trotted forward. The filtered light from the canopy landed on her skin with a magical glow, and the air filled with the hum of ancient magic. "We must remain respectful of each other if we want to find a solution."

Kaida scoffed. "Trust the deer to avoid conflict. Better to talk around issues than to speak clearly, am I right, Sable?"

Sable bristled at the lioness's comment. She countered in a firm yet composed voice, "We are not avoiding direct conversation. On the contrary, we are simply trying to keep the peace so we can work together to defeat the Shadow Walkers. After all, they threaten all of us, not just one clan or another."

Graz nodded his big head. "Sable is right. We need to work together if we are going to succeed." He punched a hand into the flat of his palm, and the sound echoed loudly. I took a mental note never to underestimate a bear.

Talon snorted. "Fine, we'll work together. But we need a plan. We can't just keep throwing mud at the Shadow Walkers, hoping that something sticks." He scraped a boot through the dirt like a chicken pawing at the ground. Like an overgrown fucking pigeon.

Viper slithered forward. "I have an idea. It's risky, but it might be our best shot."

The fae quietened, eager to hear what she had to say. Meanwhile, I hung back, positioning myself at the grove's edge and observing their reactions. I didn't trust the Trickster Queen, but I didn't trust any of them, really.

She flicked her tongue as she spat out her words. "We must find the Night King and destroy—"

"Oh, shut up," Talon bellowed, still scraping at the dirt with his boot. "We can't keep throwing shifters down the toilet, death after death after death. You're talking about a suicide mission."

"We gotta find a way to do this," I roared, smacking my fist against a tree, then yanking it out when it sank beneath the bark.

"We need an exit plan in case we can't defeat them," Sable said, a hint of desperation in her voice.

Talon sneered at the fear in Sable's tone. He partially shifted, revealing just his wings, then flew up to an overhanging branch. "Let's take to the skies and be gone!"

"It's time to end the Night King," Viper yelled, her voice blasting like an anthem.

This was chaos, getting worse every time any of these dickheads opened their mouths. I was done with this.

What would Mom do?

My heart sank at a familiar pang of longing as I yearned for her guidance. If Mom were here, she'd know what to do. How to soothe the anger between the factions and convince them to listen. Show them what idiots they were being.

But Mom was dead, and I was alone, feeling more useless than ever without her.

My pack needed an experienced leader who could unite us and point us in the right direction. Someone brave enough to face the Shadow Walkers head-on and lead us into battle.

Someone we could trust. Thoughts of my mother flooded my mind. She had always been that fae for me. But now, she was gone, and I was left with these strangers, each with their own agendas, bickering like animals in a cage.

I clenched my jaw and stood up straighter, feeling the weight of determination harden my bones. I reminded myself that I had been trained since birth by one of the greatest warriors the shifters had ever seen. Now, it was time to prove that I was worthy of her legacy.

Now was the time for strength. Dominance. Decisions.

"I'm going to find out how to kill them," I growled, and something in my voice snagged the glade's attention. "Then I'll gather you again to figure out the next step." Honestly, I'd only send word if I could be bothered and thought they'd be able to help.

"But—"

"No, we—"

"That's a terri—"

I roared until the trees around us shook and leaves rained from the sky. I roared out my guilt at my mom's death, my anger at being made Alpha before my time, my hatred of this stupid bickering.

When I finally shut my mouth, every objection had been silenced, and the other shifters stared at me.

"I'm doing this," I growled, familiar hot anger filling me again, helping me decide what to do. "And there's nothing you can do to stop me."

Graz, the High Shaman of the bears, growled, his brown suit quivering. His attention shifted to me. "Little cub, you are just a pup—you know nothing of Shadow Walkers and death."

A fierce grin spread across my face as I bared my teeth. "I

know more than you, old fae."

"We're not here to fight each other," Sable said, her voice calm.

"Then stay out of my way," I snarled at her, stalking past the fae to the border of the grove.

My hand clenched into a fist, ready to punch through any fae's face that got in my way. These other shifter clans were worse than useless. I had to find out how the Shadow Walkers could be killed. Had to find their weakness. Had to prove myself. For Mom.

Alara

Now that I was a good little submissive, Leif allowed me to sleep and eat with his personal guards. Settling between Selene, who briefly rubbed against me, and Kellan, who offered a friendly smile, I balanced a plate of food in my hands. But, despite the comfort and food, the thought of escape nagged at me.

"Who could have slipped me that key?" I leaned in closer to Selene, my voice filled with curiosity and a touch of anxiety. "I told you about the key, right? It just appeared outside my cell, as if someone was trying to help me escape."

Selene chewed on a bagel. "Yeah, you mentioned it once or twice," she teased.

"Maybe it was a guardian angel?" Kellan suggested. We were becoming friends, and I didn't mind him joining the conversation. Three heads were better than two.

I swallowed my steak. "I still reckon it was Leif."

Selene sighed. "Why the fuck would he do that? Lock you up, then sneak you the key."

Kellan chuckled. "You don't know him very well. He probably wanted to catch her so he could punish her."

I pointed at Kellan. "Yes! Exactly that!"

Selene shook her head. "No way, hon. He was already

punishing you. Besides, he doesn't need an excuse..."

Kellan paused with a bread roll halfway to his mouth. "Maybe our alpha likes the chase." He winked.

"Yeah, I wouldn't put anything past him," I grumbled.

No matter how many times I turned it around in my mind, I couldn't get any closer to figuring out if it was Leif who sent me the key or somebody else. Could I trust whoever it was, or were they just leading me into a trap?

Kellan and Selene were discussing the day's training, which would apparently involve learning to shift while running. Not for me, though, because I was Unascended and could only shift when my life was in danger or I was really, really angry.

Also because our alpha wouldn't let me train with his precious War wielders.

I put down my fork with a clatter. "Why the hell did the prince bring us here just to learn how to shift? What kind of arrogant asshole tears fae away from their families just to play running games?"

Fear for my father always circled in my mind, and it came to the forefront now. Was he okay without me? He could barely stand up unassisted, let alone hunt for himself.

My mood must have shown on my face because Selene put an arm around my shoulder, and I nuzzled into her warmth. "Your dad'll be fine. The rest of the village will take care of him."

"The rest of the village are dickheads," I muttered, and she laughed.

"Not all of them. My parents are okay."

"Your parents are the worst," I joked, feeling slightly better under her caress. Selene's mom was a good fae, she would make sure Pa ate every day, so that was something.

Kellan snorted through a mouthful of food. "It's not the other shifters you have to worry about back East. It's the Shadow Walkers. That's why Alpha brought us here."

Selene frowned, still running her soft hand down my bare arm. "That makes no sense. Why would he take away the best warriors and leave our families defenseless?"

The outrage in her tone made me glad, made me feel less alone among all these wolves who were so far up Leif's ass they could suckle his intestines.

Kellan looked at us like we were wild, his bronze eyebrows knitted together. "Leif's building an army to protect the whole realm from the Walkers."

Selene's hand paused on my arm, and my skin rose in goosebumps. "What?"

"Of course he is. That's why he gathered Wars from all over Verda. He wants to stop the Shadow threat, and nobody else is doing anything, so he has to do it all on his own."

My mouth fell open, and a "Nooo" popped out.

"Yes," Kellan said.

"But...I thought he was just a selfish prick who wanted the best fighters in his personal guard to protect his royal ass."

Kellan snorted. "Hardly. He's the only one doing anything. All the other royals are too busy protecting their precious backsides, and the other heirs are off partying or whatever they do. Alpha is the only one working for us."

My knife clattered to my plate. "So, he's not a total asshole."

Kellan shrugged. "I never said that. Although, apparently, he used to be a total prankster, pulling shit left and right."

I had this all wrong. I'd assumed Leif was selfishly recruiting War shifters to protect himself, but he was doing so much more. Building an army to protect the whole realm.

"Holy crap on a hell stick," Selene muttered. "Why didn't we know about this?"

"Because you're idiots?" Kellan offered cheerfully, munching on a breadstick.

Selene nodded thoughtfully, then looked at me. "We're idiots."

I might act like a submissive when I was being pleasure-tortured by Leif, but outside of his playroom, I was an independent bitch. "No. Leif is still an arrogant prick who is terrible at communication. I can't underline that enough—he is truly awful at communicating. He could have cleared this up with a single word. His guards could have told us back in Sylverclyff instead of dragging us against our will. They would have had more volunteers! Nah, we're not idiots. Leif is still the idiot."

Selene grinned. "Oh, good. I hate being made a fool."

Kellan watched us closely with a slight grin, then shook his head. "You guys are weird."

My best friend and I exchanged a glance and then replied in unison. "Thank you."

I leaned back in my chair and stretched my arms above my head, feeling relief flood through me. It was good to know Leif wasn't just doing this for selfish reasons. But it didn't mean that I trusted him any more than I did before.

As we finished our meal and the conversation turned to lighter topics, my mind lingered on the idea of Leif building an army. Could he truly be doing something good for the realm? Or was this just another scheme of his to increase his power and control?

I wandered outside to the back lawn with the other War conscripts, even though I didn't have to. Pretty good for someone who hated joining in. I settled down to watch their training, listening to Leif's instructions on how to shift mid-lunge. I could barely summon my inner wolf, but hopefully, one day, I'd be just as graceful as he was, leaping through the air as a fae and landing gracefully on four paws.

He was naked, of course, as were all the others. Thank Gaia I didn't have to join in because, other than when Leif had me panting with desire, I hated being nude in front of others. Honestly, I would make a terrible Ascended shifter when the time came.

I admired Leif's naked body. Even compared with all the other nudes, his beauty stood out. In the sea of flesh, all of them hard, hot, and toned, Leif towered above them all, his muscles more defined and his body in perfect proportion. When would our next training session be? My panties got wet as the question formed in my head.

But there were bigger issues to worry about. The Shadow Walkers. Oddly, I hadn't given them much thought before. We always kept the lights on, which seemed enough to prevent attacks. But a nagging question began to gnaw at my consciousness: How long could this fragile protection last? A couple of globes of light seemed shitty protection against such evil creatures. And what dangers would arise if the Shadow Walkers kept multiplying?

As Leif gave the signal to shift and the War wielders leaped into the air to transform, unease settled over me. The Shadow Walkers were a real threat that could wipe out our entire realm if we didn't do something about it soon. And as much as I hated to admit it, Leif might be our best bet in defeating them.

But trusting him wasn't going to be easy. Not when he had me leaping at his command, manipulating me into becoming his submissive. Not when he had a reputation for being a ruthless ruler who would do whatever it took to maintain power and control.

I watched as the Wars shifted mid-air, their bodies transforming into powerful wolves in a blur of fur and teeth. After several attempts, most of them could begin their shift in the air, stumbling onto four paws as they hit the ground. Without exception, their eyes were trained on Leif as they waited for his next command.

Envy swept through me. I wanted to be able to shift like that, to be able to run free and wild with my pack. But I was still Unascended, still trapped in my fae form.

Leif turned to me, his piercing silver eyes locking onto mine. "Enjoying the show?"

I refused to lower my eyes. In the dungeon, maybe, but not out here. I jutted out my jaw. "It is adequate."

He chuckled and didn't challenge me further but turned back to his wolves, who all stared at him with perfect attention. Honestly, if I could get an ounce of the respect that male had, I'd be set for life. It dawned on me that maybe, just maybe, his tough-guy act was a show to keep the pack's respect. If it was, it was working.

I kept watching the show. And yes, I was enjoying it. Especially how Leif moved with effortless grace, his muscles bunching and his huge cock slapping against his thigh. I would never get tired of seeing that.

As I watched the intensity of their training, a new sense of determination built within me. I might not be much of a joiner, but these were my fae. My pack. I owed it to them to do everything I could to stop the Shadow Walkers. I owed it to myself. Owed it to Pa.

My wolf curled deep within me, adding her strength to mine.

Leif

After a long training session with the War betas, I dozed in bed in wolf form, curled up beside Jet, who had taken to sharing my sheets. It was all platonic, which was weird. I hadn't slept a night through without screwing somebody in years—at least, not until lately.

Now, I only got hard for defiant country bumpkins with too much backbone and not enough respect. And I only got to sleep when I was shifted in wolf form and my worries filtered to the back of my mind.

A tap at the door jolted me awake, my hackles rising and ears on high alert. Relief washed over me as one of the shifters on night duty cautiously poked his head around the wooden door.

I tilted my head in question, and he held out a spellbird, which wriggled in his grasp, trying to get free. "A message arrived for you, Alpha. It seems pretty urgent, I hope you don't mind me waking you?"

He sounded frightened of me, and a pulse of guilt stabbed my gut. Fae weren't scared of Mom when she was Alpha. They respected her, almost worshipped her, but they didn't fear her.

I lowered my large head in a brief nod, and my beta flattened out the spellbird and read. "I have information. Come quickly. Krand."

Krand was one of the Secret Keepers I'd sent to gather information on the Shadow Walkers, with specific instructions to find out how to kill them. I had sent shifters to every corner of the realm and even some to the neighboring kingdoms. No other rulers seemed bothered by the shifter deaths, and even the other shifting communities couldn't stop squabbling long enough to put together a plan. So it landed on me to figure it out.

It sounded like Krand had learned something valuable. I shifted quickly, feeling the tension creep through my limbs as I found my fae form and dressed in one of my many gray sweatpants.

"Where did we send Krand?" I asked Jet, who was awake and attentive to my movements.

Jet was almost invisible in the dark room. "Krand went to Sylverclyff."

I stretched out my muscles, trying to wake myself up completely. "What do we know about Sylverclyff?" I noticed the beta still standing in the doorway, and I barked at him to go away. He scurried out the door like a mouse. A submissive rodent without an ounce of sass; he wouldn't be getting me horny anytime soon.

Jet sucked his teeth. "That's where some of the latest batch of Wars came from." He paused as though reluctant to go on.

"Spit it out," I growled.

"It's where Alara's from."

I stood up and cricked my neck. "I see." Her naked body formed perfectly in my mind, and for an instant, I could see her curves and hollows as clearly as if she stood before me.

I shook away the vision. "Then I guess she's coming with me."

Because I was an all-around stand-up good guy, I was allowing Alara to sleep upstairs instead of in the filthy dungeon. The fact was, I couldn't bear the thought of her shivering and dirty and alone. I hated the idea of any wolf being forced to sleep alone. So her bed wasn't far from mine—which was one of the things that kept me awake at night.

I burst into the beta room that contained my baby army. It smelled of sweat and cum. Most wolves were asleep, a few were screwing, and there, nestled between her friend Selene and the wall in the room's far corner, was Alara.

A reveler spotted me and walked over, his erection swaying with each step. "Fancy joining in, Alpha?"

"Not tonight." I crossed to where Alara slept, her orange hair floating loose around her face. She looked more peaceful than I'd ever seen her. Probably because she was usually receiving punishment...well, she should learn some respect, and then she could live in peace.

I shook her awake. She rolled over, opened her eyes briefly, then mumbled, "Piss off, city dick."

I growled and pinched her arm. "Show me some respect. And call me Alpha."

"Piss off, Alpha," she mumbled, and my cock twitched. But I didn't have time for that.

"Get up and get dressed, we're leaving."

She swatted me away sleepily. "Can't. I'm busy."

Jet moved forward to intervene and shake her awake, but I growled at him fiercely, and he backed away. I didn't want him touching her.

I ran a hand down her bare arm, a gentler touch than we usually shared. That was enough to alarm her, and she opened her eyes. "What's going on?"

"I need your help with something."

She rolled away from me, pulled the covers off her body, and wiggled her naked ass in my direction. "Help yourself," she said, and I scented a slight hint of her musky arousal mixed in with her citrus tang as I stared at the curve of her cheeks in the steel moonlight.

My cock jumped. Did we have time for a quick fuck? I could lie down behind her, jam myself into her wet warm pussy and reach one hand around to her clit while her hot back pressed against my chest. She was rotating her ass in small circles, inviting me in.

"I'm not here to screw you," I growled, sounding angrier than I intended. "Get dressed. We're going to Sylverclyff."

Her eyes flew open at the name of her hometown, and she sat up, her nightgown sadly falling down to cover her body. "We're going back East? Really?"

"I'm not joking, for Gaia's sake!"

She stood and crossed to the massive bank of drawers to the one marked with her name, then pulled on a simple circle skirt and a fitted singlet top. "Hell, Leif, you could have led with that. You know I want to go home."

My lips thinned. "You're not going home. Not permanently, at least. I'm going on a work trip, and I need someone who knows the place."

Her beautiful friend with the startling blue hair, Selene, who'd caught my eye when I'd first welcomed the new Wars, piped up. "I'm from Sylverclyff too. I know it like the back of my hand. I know everybody and every place. Much better than Alara does. Can I come too?"

Alara scowled at her friend, but there wasn't much anger in it. I could give her a lesson on proper rage.

"No, Alara is coming," I growled. "You're staying here. Don't question my decisions again."

Selene ducked her head and sat down on her mattress. "Yes, Alpha." She had none of Alara's spunk, and she left my mind as soon as she left my sight. "Meet me downstairs in five minutes, bumpkin," I said, then I left to gather a few items for the journey.

Six minutes later, I waited for Alara in the hall, my fingers drumming on the wall. I wasn't sure why I was in such a rush, but I wanted to get this over with as quickly as possible. I wanted to be out on the road and away before the Shadow Walkers struck again.

Alara appeared a few minutes later, looking much more like the spitfire she normally was. Her hair was still a tangled mess, and her face was pale and haggard, but she walked with purpose, and I was relieved to see her.

"Are you ready?"

She nodded. "Right behind you."

We walked outside, and I felt the magic in my blood tingle and my wolf stir. The moonway that led to the East wasn't far from my den, and we were soon striding along it, the grass cold beneath my bare feet and the stars above us blurring with motion as we covered yards with every step.

"What business do you have in Sylverclyff?" Alara asked.

I sighed. "I'm not in the habit of sharing information with wolf cubs."

She ignored my dig at her being Unascended and kept pressing her point. "I'm not just any old pup. You selected me for this critical mission, and I don't want to mess it up. So you'd better tell me what the hell we're going for."

Annoyingly, she was right. I didn't want her screwing up the mission by running off her sassy mouth to the wrong fae.

I shot her a glance. "I sent shifters all over the realm, all over Arathay actually, looking for information about how to kill the Shadow Walkers."

"You sent spies? Really?"

"I guess you could call them that."

"Even to Fen? Spies wouldn't last five minutes in Fen. Someone would be like, 'Hey, are you a spy?' and they'd be all, 'Yep.'" Nobody could voice a lie within the Realm of Fen.

I chuckled. "There are ways around telling the flat truth, you know. You can talk around the facts, if you know what I mean."

She rubbed against me for an instant, her warmth seeping through my arm. "I know exactly what you mean. I get the sense your angry-male thing is more of an act than your real self."

Her skin against mine felt wonderful, exactly the balm my wolf needed to stay calm.

But that didn't mean I could let her get away with talking to me that way. "Don't talk about things above your pay grade," I snarled.

I strode out ahead of her to put some distance between us and didn't let her catch up until we spilled out of the moonway in the Far East of Verda.

"Shift," I said to Alara. "It's a long run to the village, and you'll make better time if you shift into wolf form."

She chewed her lip. "I'm Unascended, remember. I can't shift unless my wolf thinks my life is in danger."

I prowled closer and snarled in her face, pinning her arms to her side. "Who says it isn't?"

Desire sparked through her, I could smell it on the cool night air, but I didn't have time to act on it. I couldn't relax until I found Krand and learned what he had discovered.

Undressing quickly, I put my sweatpants into a backpack and shoved it at Alara's chest. "You'll have to ride me."

She spluttered. "What? No way."

I rounded on her. "Do you think the alpha of alphas, heir to the Verdan throne, Prince of House Caro, wants to be ridden like a mule? Now hold my bag and climb onto my damn back."

I shifted into wolf form and crouched so she could climb on. Her light circle skirt fluttered around my back, and a few minutes after she settled on my back, her wet pussy soaked through my fur. I growled, and she weaved her fingers tight to hold on, clinging to me with her thighs. Despite the urgency of our mission, it took every bit of self-control not to rub against her and drive her crazy.

Eventually, we reached the village outskirts, and I crouched to let her off my back. She didn't get off me immediately; she held onto me tightly for a few moments longer than necessary before finally releasing me with a sigh.

Alara

I slid off Alpha's back and shook out my arms and shoulders, which were tense from having held on tight for hours while he loped through the countryside. I rubbed my upper arms to get some warmth into them.

My thighs ached too, so I shook them out to get blood flowing.

We were at the village outskirts, where the scrubby grassland met the sparkling sea. The tang of salt in the air brushed against my lips, carried on a gentle breeze, a brutal reminder of what I was missing being stuck in Verda City.

Leif shifted into fae form and stood with his big dick swinging in the breeze and his long silver hair rippling. He looked at me briefly before growling, "Pass me the damn bag, will you?"

"So polite, as always," I grumbled, then shrugged the pack off my back and tossed it to him.

He slipped into his light gray sweatpants that would do little to protect him from the cool wind coming off the ocean. Especially since his chest remained bare.

"An alpha doesn't have to be fucking polite," he spat.

I bristled. "Nobody has to be polite, it's a choice."

He glanced up at me like I'd just insulted his dead mom but

didn't say any more on the subject. "So this is your home?"

I looked around, trying to see it through his eyes. It was super basic compared to his opulent marble palace. Little more than a one-room hut with ancient wooden beams, but it had a kickass view.

"Yes, it is," I said with my chin up. Though the truth was, my Pa was the only tie I had to the place. If he was gone, I'd have no reason to be here. Maybe I'd travel to the truth-telling Realm of Fen and try my hand at being honest. Or to the mountains of Ourea or the Realm of Caprice, where the weather reflected the king's mood. That sounded kinda cool. I'd give Brume with its Dread King and the Unseelie realm a miss.

Leif nodded, then pointed to a small path that led further into the village. "Krand is down there," he said. "Let's go and see what news he has."

As far as I knew, the prince had never been to Sylverclyff before, but all fae could navigate through unknown lands if the details had been passed to them from another fae who knew it. It was a helpful skill that would serve me well when I finally got the chance to explore Verda City.

We followed the path, winding between the dense foliage of trees until it opened onto a small clearing with a den in the center. The stone structure was bordered by a neat garden, where I could make out carrots and cabbage, which flourished despite the cool weather. Thick smoke curled from the chimney of the den, carrying with it an inviting smell of stew and herbs.

Krand must have heard us coming because he stepped out onto the porch before we reached it. He was way older than I expected for a spy, with wrinkled skin and watery eyes, his round face framed by wispy blue-gray hair and silver-rimmed spectacles perched on top of an ever-broadening nose.

I knew this den. And I knew it didn't belong to this old fae. "What are you doing in Shenti's den?" I demanded, coming closer and keeping my gaze on his watery eyes. "What have you done with her?"

I didn't have much time for Shenti, a middle-aged shifter with a permanent scowl and whose natural go-to response was a derisive tutt, but I still didn't like spies from the big city coming in and taking over dens without permission.

Krand fixed me in his pale gaze. "The owner of the den was happy to share. Besides, she joined Alpha's army."

"Unwillingly, I bet," I muttered.

Krand shrugged. "That is of no consequence. We are here to discuss far more troubling news. Come inside."

We followed him into the small kitchen at the heart of the den, the scent of wood and hearth enveloping me. I instantly relaxed inside the comforting stone structure, my wolf alertness unwinding.

A large cauldron hung over the crackling fire, its dancing flames casting a warm glow in the cozy kitchen. The stew was bubbling and rich with meat, carrots, and potatoes, the scent wafting into the room and making my mouth water.

Krand passed a bowl of steaming stew to Leif, serving his alpha first, of course. Then he gave himself a bowl and, finally, slid one to me across the wooden kitchen table. Clearly, he thought he ranked higher than me in the hierarchy, and I supposed he was right. Just another reason to hate it.

"Eat," Krand said, "while I talk."

We sat and ate, my wolf almost howling at the taste of the stew.

"I have been traveling around the region, talking to everybody who wants to share, and many who don't, gathering information. Listening to rumors, listening to facts, and studying the evidence. My investigations suggest that the Shadow Walkers are particularly targeting wolf shifters, as they can increase their numbers more easily when they possess a shapeshifter."

He paused for a moment and looked at us both with his watery eyes.

I stared at Leif, wanting him to disagree, but Alpha nodded. "Yes, I thought that might be the case. Shifters are a source of...food for the Walkers. They multiply when they feed on us."

Krand nodded, his wispy hair floating above his round face. "That much is a fact. Stealing the souls of shifters allows the Shadow Walkers to breed. Beyond that, I have only rumors."

My blood ran cold, and my spoon clattered to the table. This was an orchestrated attack, not just mindless hordes roaming the realm, but a strategic approach. Attack the shifters first to multiply, then what? It meant the Walkers had some kind of agenda, even if we didn't know exactly what it was yet.

"I have no use for rumors," Leif said, his voice low but firm. "We need to know how to kill the Shadow Walkers."

Krand nodded, his spectacles sliding down his nose. "I agree. The Walkers are becoming more organized and more aggressive. They are no longer just a nuisance, they are a threat."

Dread washed through me. I'd become so caught up in my capture and pleasure-torture that I failed to see the big picture. Shadow Walkers were coming for us. Now we knew why—they fed from our souls so they could breed—but we still didn't know how to stop them.

Leif's anger erupted, his fist crashing against the table,

splashing stew across the worn wood. "How can I kill them, Krand?" he demanded. "I traveled all this way on your word, and you still haven't told me what I need to know."

The old shifter shivered and dropped his gaze to the floor like a good submissive. But being a good submissive didn't get you anywhere when you needed cold, hard facts.

"Find out how to kill them, Krand. Don't send me for me again until you figure it out." He turned to me. "We will rest for an hour, then return to Verda City."

"No, I have to see Pa while we're here."

"No. This isn't a social visit, we're trying to save the fucking pack."

He stalked off to a corner which was lined with thick furs and lay down.

A slight whine escaped me, and I padded closer to him, breathing in the animal scent of the furs, needing physical comfort. Being a shifter was damn annoying at times, like when your inner wolf demanded a cuddle, and the only one nearby was an asshole alpha.

I lay beside Leif and wriggled into the hollow formed by his body. He sighed and reluctantly draped an arm around my shoulders, and the warmth of his touch instantly drew out some of my anxiety.

I closed my eyes, allowing myself to indulge in the comfort of Leif's embrace. We rarely had these moments of closeness, at least not without whips and paddles being in the mix. I cherished this small intimacy more than I should. The warmth of his body against mine, the faint scent of spice and leather cologne mixed with the musky scent of the furs, was all so familiar and comforting. It was easy to forget about the dangers we faced as wolf shifters.

But we couldn't stay here forever. We had to face the reality that we were in the middle of a war, and we needed to be prepared. I moved slightly, feeling the urge to stretch.

"Stop wriggling," Leif demanded in my ear. "I'm trying to rest, and I don't need your big round ass rubbing against my dick."

"Big?" I asked. "Round?"

"It is big and round and fucking perfect. Keep it away from me."

Leif

This was supposed to be a power nap so I could get up enough energy to piggyback the lying Unascended whelp back to Verda City. Instead, I was on full alert with a raging erection, and my thoughts weren't on the Walkers but on Alara's damn dad.

"Leif," she said softly, "I know we're in a hurry, but I really need to see Pa. It won't take long, I promise. I just...I don't know if he'll live long enough for me to wait until the next time I'm back here. He's the only family I have."

I breathed deeply. "No," I growled, harsh and low. I was being such a dick, but I couldn't afford the time. As an alpha, I couldn't choose the feelings of one shifter ahead of the safety of the whole pack.

I rolled away from her, and she whimpered slightly, like she was trying really fucking hard to keep it in.

Dammit. I got to my feet and stepped over Alara's prone body, accidentally (not accidentally) kicking her as I did.

"On your feet, bumpkin."

Oh, miracle of miracles, she did as I requested without any backchat.

"You can visit your dad. But make it quick."

The Shadow Walkers posed a severe threat to our pack, to our entire realm. We needed to act fast if we were going to have any chance of stopping them, and our trip to Sylverclyff wasn't a damn social visit. But every time Alara whimpered, I felt bad. I couldn't concentrate on the Walkers or keeping the pack safe if I was swimming in guilt. So we might as well check on her father, as long as we kept the visit short.

Alara's eyes glinted, the same exact shade as the flames in the fireplace. "Thank you!" She leaped to her feet and threw her arms around me, beaming. This was the happiest I'd ever seen her, and the light in her face lifted my mood too.

"Do you have any ancestors from Mentium?" I asked, figuring she must have some mood magic, given how her joy was infecting me.

"What? No, of course not," she said dismissively, but even her light tone eased some of the burden on my back.

Krand saw us out the door and bowed low before me in a sign of respect.

"Find out how to kill them," I said, and he nodded. "Then drop everything and tell me how."

* * *

Half an hour later, we arrived at Alara's den. It was small and shabby, even more run-down than I expected. The den was made of cobbled stone, and the walls were rocks of all shades of brown with the occasional streak of black. Wind whistled through gaps in the walls; the winters here must feel long and cold.

I liked silks and marble, fine fae threads and luxe furnishings. I'd often joked about the wild wolves of the countryside who were more like animals than fae, and yet I'd let my own packs live in the mud.

Familiar anger rumbled through me, and my heat rose, but I figured I could do better than just scream and shout. I could make their lives better. Give them a Gaia-be-fucked door without holes, for a start.

Alara took a deep breath before heading inside. I was becoming attuned to her moods, and she seemed wary. Odd. I thought she wanted to be here, so why was she reluctant to go inside?

She pushed open the door, and I saw a frail fae sitting beyond it. Her father's eyes misted at the sight of her, but instead of giving her a warm hug, he stayed seated and scolded her. "What do you think you were doing, Alara? Running off to join the alpha's army, pretending to be Ascended? You could have gotten yourself killed! When I said you should join in more, I didn't mean you should volunteer to get yourself sliced open. If the alpha of alphas finds out you lied, you'll be flogged and probably outcast."

Alara stepped aside so her father could see me. He was frail, lined with wrinkles, and as scrawny as a Seelor. I realized he'd stayed in his seat because he couldn't stand up.

"Pa, let me introduce Leif, Prince of House Caro, heir to the throne, and Alpha of Alphas. Leif, this is my father, Rooni."

The old fae paled, and he glanced between his prince and his daughter, quickly calculating whether he'd just sentenced her to death.

I nodded and offered him a brief smile. "Howdy, old dude." Hmm, that sounded less princely than I planned, but something about this den put me at ease.

Rooni bent double, getting as close to the floor as his old body would go. "Your Highness."

Alara dropped a kiss on her father's brow and gently nuzzled her nose against his. He leaned into the physicality of her greeting, and after she pulled back, she kept a warm hand on his shoulder. "Have you been eating, Pa? You look thin."

That was an understatement. The old bugger looked like he hadn't seen food in a week.

"Yes, yes, the pack has been looking after me."

"Not well enough," Alara grumbled as she began rummaging through the kitchen cupboards and muttering "Ignis ardeat" to start a cooking fire in the hearth. It took her three tries to get it started, and I took a mental note to give her some spellwork tutoring. She might be smarter than me and spend her spare time reading books, but I was better at spells.

I had never seen her like this, so full of caring. So heartfelt. I'd begun to see her like a cartoon, just a mouthy bitch who never did as she was told, but she was clearly a lot more than that. She was a daughter who loved her dad fiercely and would do anything for him.

Including lying about being Ascended so he wouldn't have to go to war. I had demanded one Ascended wolf from each family, convinced that was the least my shifters could do to fight the Shadow Walkers, but maybe I'd been wrong. I didn't view the issue from all angles. Didn't seek advice or take it when it was offered.

That sounded a lot like what Gabrelle and the other heirs kept telling me. I'd never been good at listening.

But I could start.

Alara fussed over her dad, piling blankets on his lap and filling the small kitchen with sizzling onions, garlic, and mushrooms.

Rooni fended her off. "You didn't bring the prince here to discuss my diet," he scolded. "Why are you here?"

He looked me squarely in the eyes, which most wolves never dared to do. I could see where his daughter got her rebellious streak from.

Alara stopped mid-stir and looked at me, leaving it to me to decide how much information to share.

I felt a flicker of unease, trying to decide how much information to share. But if anybody knew how to kill the Walkers, it was probably someone with a lot of years under their belt. I took a gamble. "We're looking for ways to defeat the Shadow Walkers," I explained. "At the moment, all we can do is switch on the lights and make them run away. But that's not enough. They're multiplying, breeding, growing stronger every day. We need to be able to destroy them."

Alara's eyes widened when I outlined the situation so baldly. I could almost see her shoulders sag as the weight of the task sank in.

The old male blinked his watery eyes, and for a moment, I thought he'd forgotten the question. Perhaps his mind was cracked. But then he spoke. "You should talk to Valann Croft. She knows a thing or two."

Alara spluttered. "Old Croft is as crazy as a cub with its tail on fire. We won't get any sense out of her."

Her father shook his head. "Don't judge crazy, or someone might judge you."

I barked a laugh. "You know your daughter well. She's crazy, all right."

Alara scolded me with a look, and her dad just smiled. "The wild ones are the best." He landed his gaze on his daughter. "Don't discount Valann, she's lived a long time. Heard a lot of stories."

"Made up a lot of stories, you mean."

"There's truth in fiction, Al."

As the tantalizing aroma of cooked vegetables filled the den, the bumpkin made a show of passing the fried vegetables to her father before me. He raised his eyebrows, while I couldn't suppress a growl of irritation. I'd only just eaten but never refused an opportunity for more food, so I sat on a rickety chair by the fire and accepted a plate when it was finally offered.

"Not exactly at Magirus standard," I muttered, "but not bad."

"Wow, thanks," Alara deadpanned. She pulled her chair close to her father's so their arms touched while they ate. Living alone wasn't good for a shifter.

Rooni watched the interaction between us closely, and I wondered what the hell he thought about his daughter bringing home the alpha of alphas and giving him sass.

I wanted to know more about her. More about her dad and her whole family. "What happened to your mom?" I asked, trying to keep my tone sensitive.

Alara and her father shared a look. "She died when I was a cub," Alara said. "She was out hunting when a lion ripped out her neck."

"Oh, shit, I'm so sorry," I said, feeling something other than rage, though my old pal anger was laced through the empathy. "Was it a shifter?" If one of Kaida's lions had killed one of my wolves, I would have to do something about it, and an inter-clan war was the last thing I needed.

"Not a shifter, a true lion. She was...there one moment, then not. You know?"

Fae births were rare, and deaths were a major blow to any fae family. Especially shifter families, who lost some faelings during the Ascension rite because any who didn't ascend to

Lupus had to be outcast from the pack. Any wolf who died before their time was a tragedy. Although I was glad to hear it was a true lion who did the killing.

"I'm sorry." I watched them carefully, trying to judge the room. "So it was just you two against the world?"

"Everly power," Alara said, and she and her dad made fists against their hearts and then punched the air in some kind of in-joke.

Alara laughed, her face so relaxed and happy, and she looked like a completely different fae than when I usually saw her. Her orange eyes shone as she looked at her father. "Do you remember when we tried to catch fireflies in the meadows?"

Rooni chuckled. "I remember it well. We were covered in glowing bugs, and your mother scolded us for tracking mud inside the den."

Alara leaned back in her chair, a wistful smile on her face. "I miss her."

I didn't know how to respond, so I ate my vegetables and listened to their reminiscing. It was strange seeing Alara so vulnerable and open with her father. It made me wonder what kind of person she would be if she let her guard down more often.

"Don't forget the time I convinced you to let me make a fruit cake made of meat."

Her father chuckled. "I remember it like it was yesterday. We ate it anyway, didn't we?"

Alara grinned. "And we both got sick for a week."

They both laughed, and I couldn't help but smile. It was a rare moment of genuine happiness, and it made me feel... something. Warmth, maybe. I couldn't remember the last time I had felt that way.

"Is this why you…" I turned to Alara, who sat opposite me with the right side of her flaming orange hair glowing in the firelight beside her. "Is this why you lied about being Ascended? To protect your pop?" I already knew that was the reason, but meeting him and seeing them together made me finally understand it.

She shrugged and averted her eyes. "It's us against the world. And he isn't exactly fit to fight."

"Hey!" he said. "I could take down a thousand Unseelie and still be back in time for breakfast."

Alara smiled grimly. "Well, we're not battling Unseelie this time, but Shadow Walkers."

It was hard to fault the country bumpkin for wanting to protect her father, but I was still within my rights to be pissed at her for lying. Fuck it, I'd have to sort through that mess of ethics and emotions later.

For now, there was work to do. Something inside me had moved. Transformed my rage. The anger that had been coursing through me since Mom died had a purpose now. To learn about the Walkers. And to conquer the bastards.

I wiped my face with the back of my hand and reached for a mug of water that Alara had set on the floor by my chair. "So," I said, turning to Alara's father. "Valann Croft."

He nodded. "She may be old, but she still knows more than most about this part of the woods. She could have information about how to kill the Shadow Walkers."

Alara seemed dubious, but I nodded thoughtfully. It was worth a try—after all, what did we have to lose?

Alara

Old Croft lived about ten minutes from my den, so Leif and I had time to chat.

I waited for the barrage of insults about my shitty den, but they never came. So, like a little bitch, I goaded him.

"Did you like my den?"

"It was awful," he said. "It needs repairs. You should fix it."

My cheeks flamed. "Not all of us are rolling in gold, you know. Not everyone has a Crafter on staff to grow us new walls and furniture. We're all shifters here in Sylverclyff. Every single one of us ascends into Lupus. We don't have fae with other powers to help out, like you city folk."

The arrogant prince kept staring ahead, seemingly engrossed in the perfectly ordinary purple leaves of the Brayson trees. After a moment of silence, he turned to me, a flicker of understanding in his silver eyes. "I never thought of it that way," he admitted. "I figured all packs had access to stuff, but...I guess not."

He pulled off a broad shiny leaf from a tree, crushed it in his fingers and handed it to me. "For the stress," he said.

I narrowed my eyes. "Very pretty."

"You don't look at it, you eat it," he said with a snort.

I accepted the offering and sniffed it suspiciously.

"It's not poison," he said. "I promise."

I wasn't sure what a promise from Leif was worth, but I didn't think he was trying to kill me. I popped the crushed purple leaves into my mouth and chewed. They tasted like raspberry licorice but crunchier. As soon as I swallowed, my worries slipped away, sliding off my back like I was made of ice. "What is this?"

"Brayson leaf. Don't tell me you've never used this before? It's one of the best natural drugs in the realm. And the Realm of Greed and Excess is pretty well off for drugs."

Man, there was so much I didn't know. Having been born and raised in a small rural town, my knowledge of the world was limited to what the fae around me knew, or would tell me.

"Haven't you and your friends chowed down on Brayson and gotten high? It's the best high there is, but it doesn't last long," Leif said, pulling another leaf from the next tree with a pop and munching on it.

"I, er...I don't exactly have many friends. Apart from Selene, but she's never mentioned eating Brayson leaves."

As I chewed on the crushed purple leaves, a magical sensation spread through me, relaxing me and loosening my tongue. Which explained why I admitted to the realm's chief asshole that I had no friends.

"But you're a wolf," he said. "All wolves have friends. That's kind of our thing."

I shrugged. "Not me. I'm different."

He glanced at me. "Yeah, I noticed."

"What's that supposed to mean?" My eyebrows knitted together, but the frown was only half-hearted—this leaf was good.

Leif hesitated. "It's just...you're unlike any other wolf I've met. You don't act like them. You don't fit in. Even if I was watching you from the moon, I could figure that out."

His words stung, but they weren't strictly untrue. I had always been an outsider in my own pack. I never understood their fascination with hunting or their obsession with dominance. I just wanted to live my life without anyone telling me what to do.

"You don't fit in with the others," he observed. "But that doesn't mean you can't make friends. You just need to find the right pack."

I scoffed. "Easier said than done." But hearing the idea from Leif made it resonate differently from the times I'd considered it. As we continued walking, my mind swirled with thoughts of finding my place and possibly belonging to a pack that truly understood me.

"Trust me, I know," Leif said with a light grin. "But there's a pack out there for everyone. Even a lone wolf like you."

I rolled my eyes, ducking under an overhanging branch. "I'm not a lone wolf. I have a den, remember?"

Leif snorted. "That den is a sorry excuse for a home. You need something better than that. Something that screams, 'I'm a badass wolf, hear me howl.'" He jumped over a patch of mud that I skirted, trying to keep my boots clean.

"I'll bear that in mind. Maybe I can sign Valann up to your army and take her den?"

Instead of scowling, my alpha grinned, and I figured this leaf was like magic. I yanked one off a tree and pocketed it for later.

Valann's den was as crazy as she was. A mess. Old, dented cans of food lay strewn over the floor, and it smelled of wet dog. Dirt and leaves covered everything, and the hide-of-some-dead-animal blankets made it difficult to tell what was and wasn't supposed to be there. The only thing that wasn't filthy was the large, round table in the center of the room. If I didn't know any better, I'd say she had a thing for pizza.

A ragged old wolf lunged at us as we walked through the door, and Leif pushed me to the ground out of the way. Her brown fur tumbled across the den, stopping in a big pile by the wall.

"Valann, it's me, Alara Everly. And this is Alpha Caro. We just want to talk."

The brown pile of fur let out a half howl, half whimper sound, and she shifted into fae form, curled on the floor and naked with matted brown hair hanging past her shoulders. She clambered to her feet nimbly for such an old fae. Her breasts hung long and flat down her chest, and her belly sagged down over her pubic hair. Everything except her bones were dragged down by gravity, and she looked at us defiantly, not giving a damn.

"Well, then, talk," she said, staring at us, completely unabashed.

"Pa said you might be able to help," I began carefully. Valann Croft was renowned for being a mad old coot with a bad temper, and I didn't want to set her off.

"Of course I can help," Valann said dismissively. "It's just that nobody ever understands. It's all about the woondah, you see. The woondah in the belly-brig minds. I blame the bears." She shook her head sadly.

I huffed a breath. She was already starting off on her wild talk. We wouldn't get a word of sense out of her, we were just wasting our time.

Leif nodded briefly, a small sign of respect that I was sure he didn't feel. He must be desperate. "Please, Valann, we need information about the Shadow Walkers."

She turned her beady eyes on his. "What information, cub? Out with it."

Either she didn't recognize the title "Alpha Caro," or she was more rebellious than me. Either way, I enjoyed hearing her dismiss the prince of the realm with a single barb.

Leif's Adam's apple bobbed, but he kept his cool. "We need to know how to kill them."

Valann started pacing the small room, showing us her saggy ass, then her saggy boobs, then her wild matted hair. I envied her self-confidence. "Ask the bears, ask the bears about the woondah in the Temple of the Briar. The bears know all about the shadows and the dust."

She kept pacing, her footsteps light on the dirt floor. I threw an I-told-you-so glance at Leif, then checked her cupboards to ensure the pack was still feeding her. I sliced some cheese and bread and put them on a plate on the round table, while Leif kept watching Valann pace up and down, up and down, muttering about the temple and the bears.

"Help me here, would you," I said to Leif, then shoved a broom into his hands. He looked at it like he'd never seen such a thing before. "It's for sweeping," I muttered, and he had the decency to swallow his shock and make small back-and-forth movements on the trash-strewn floor.

"Oh, give me that," I growled, snatching the broom from his grip and hastily sweeping the trash out the front door. It didn't remove the scent of wet dog, but at least the rotting smell lessened.

It didn't seem like Valann would ever stop pacing and muttering, so I walked up and placed my hands on her shoulders.

She was cold, so I grabbed a sweater and a blanket and helped her dress. I led her to the table and, with gentle pressure on her shoulders, made her sit.

She started nibbling on the bread and cheese while I collected burnable trash for a fire and tried to light it.

"No fire, no fire," Valann shrieked in alarm, and she was so agitated that I had to put it out.

"Fine, no fire," I agreed. "But you have to stay dressed, okay? Stay warm. Do you promise?"

Valann rocked a little and ate some more cheese. Leif watched the whole scene in shock, like Valann and I were stage actors and he was watching a horror play.

"Were you expecting her to hand over a scroll with detailed instructions on how to kill the Walkers?" I snapped unkindly.

"Er...kind of. Maybe like a puzzle we had to solve. Like a crossword. I like crosswords."

"You're babbling," I said, tucking the blanket around Valann's back. "Now, shall we head home?"

He looked up, his silver eyes glowing like diamonds. "Home?"

"Back to Verda City, I mean."

"Is that your home now?"

I twisted my lips. "Only because I'm a captive there." Just because my only friend in the world, Selene, was in Verda City, didn't make it my home. Or the other wolves, like Wiener or Kellan, or even the fact I played a game of ball yesterday and kind of enjoyed it.

No, my home was still here, with Pa.

"I see," Leif said, then walked out the door into the falling dusk as though he didn't have a care in the world.

Leif

I strode through the scrubby coastal forest, letting Alara trail far behind. The salty air tasted stronger as the light fell and my other senses became dominant.

The leaves cracking behind me indicated a wolf crossing the trail between Alara and me. I stopped to listen. This was her home turf, so she would be fine, but I wanted to make sure. Besides, I was curious to see how she interacted with her home pack.

The wolf's footsteps stopped at the same time as her quieter ones, and the air became laced with the scent of fear. Her fear. I knew that scent well—I'd been the cause of it many times.

But I didn't want anyone else to make her scared. My hackles rose, and I held in a growl, waiting to see what happened next.

"You've got a nerve coming back here, bitch. Did you run away from the army already? I'll escort you back there, don't worry. I'll just have a little fun with you first."

Her voice was loud, feisty. "Leave me alone, fishy."

I retraced my steps, slinking through the forest quietly until I reached Alara. She was face-to-face with a burly beta with oily black hair and a hooked nose. She looked soft and vulnerable with her loose skirt and free hair, so much smaller than the large male. Tension sizzled between them.

"Or what?" the muscular male asked, stepping closer to her. "Nobody knows you're here, right?"

I watched their interaction, knowing that intervening too early could cause more harm than good. Alara may have been scared, but she had a fire in her belly that was waiting to be ignited, and she wouldn't thank me for interfering in her business.

"Maybe not many fae know I'm here," Alara replied, her voice shaky but still defiant. "But if you lay a hand on me, I guarantee everyone will know about it."

The beta male laughed, an ugly sound that grated on my nerves. "You think you're so smart, don't you? Just because you can read books all day doesn't mean you know shit about the real world."

Alara stepped back, her eyes darting around as if searching for an escape. I knew she wouldn't find one. Not with this guy blocking her path.

But then something inside of her sparked. Maybe it was the adrenaline, maybe it was the anger, but I saw her expression change from fear to determination.

"I may not know shit about the real world," she said, her voice steady now. "But I know I don't have to take crap from someone like you."

The beta male snarled, taking a step forward. "You're going to regret talking to me like that, pup."

That insult on his tongue made me simmer. Mainly since I'd used it on her too, called her a pup, trying to belittle her. Apparently, she'd been belittled her entire life, which made me a worse monster than I realized. More like the father I'd never met.

Alara scoffed. "Yeah, I usually regret having to talk to you."

Fishy growled. "I'm going to fucking kill you, bitch. You think you're so much better than us? We'll see how much better you are when you're bleeding out in the dirt."

Alara's orange eyes blazed like fireballs in the moonlight, and her brown skin was bleached an eerie shade of bone. "You can try," she said, stepping back and baring her teeth.

"That's the spirit," the male praised, moving toward her. "Let's see what you're made of."

I remained just off the trail, watching intently. Would she fight back? Or would she submit to him? And what should I do?

My muscles tensed, and my heart beat faster. I wanted to attack—to defend her. But really, it didn't matter what I should or shouldn't do—pretty soon, my wolf would take charge and lose his shit.

A pungent odor of alcohol hung in the air as I caught a whiff of Fishy's breath, its sourness mingling with the scent of salty air. He was looking for a fight, and he had found one. Alara stood her ground, her eyes fixed on him, unafraid.

But I couldn't stay hidden any longer. I stepped out of the shadows, my large frame blocking his path. "She said to leave her alone," I growled, my voice low and menacing.

The beta male hesitated for a moment. "Are you going to protect her, mutt?" he sneered, not recognizing me. Nobody in Verda City would talk to me that way.

I bared my teeth, my eyes locked on his. "I'll do more than that if you don't back off."

"What's it to you, dumbass? She's just a weak little loner. I'm going to show her who's boss."

The hair on my body rose, and I bared my teeth. "You won't touch her," I warned.

Fishy laughed, lunging at me with a fist. I dodged his blow, snapping at his wrist with my teeth. He howled in pain, and I took the opportunity to grab him by the throat and pin him to a tree.

"You're not so tough now, are you?" I snarled, my grip tightening.

"Who the fuck are you?" the shifter spat, his eyes widening. Clearly, this dickhead wasn't used to fighting somebody bigger and stronger than him. Somebody with training.

I pressed tighter against his throat, his windpipe squishy beneath my hand. "I'm the dumbass who's going to kill you for talking shit about my female."

If I clenched my fist, the life would squeeze out of him as fast as lightning, and I was tempted. But my wolf needed a fight. This nothing-wolf had threatened Alara. White hot rage boiled through me, and I wanted to pull this bastard apart piece by piece.

I released him, and he sagged against the tree.

"Just stay out of it, buddy," Fishy said. "This bitch escaped from Leif Caro. This is the alpha of alphas' business."

I smiled creepily. "Yes, it fucking is." I stalked closer, using every ounce of my dominant nature to intimidate him. All the fury inside me, from my Mom's death to my pack's security failures, channeled into this moment. Into protecting Alara.

"Alara isn't going anywhere with you," I snarled.

"What are you going to do about it?" He undressed, preparing to shift.

Thank Gaia he didn't know who I was. Most wolves bowed their heads at my first word, and I never got to have a proper fight. But this idiot had no clue, so he was challenging me. Good. Let him challenge.

"I'm going to rip your throat out," I growled, edging toward him. I could beat him easily as a fae, but my wolf was begging for release.

"Why? She's a nothing skank who nobody wants. Just walk away, tough guy."

"Why?" I growled. "Why? Because she's mine. And you tried to hurt her." I prowled closer. "Never try to hurt what's mine."

The male's skin rippled, and he grew, hair growing sharp and spiky, his nose and mouth pulling back into a snout. When his transformation was complete, he gave a low, challenging growl. He curled his lips back over his teeth, and the scent of bloodlust and violence filled the air.

A moment later, my sweatpants were shredded, and my wolf had taken control. My muscles bulged and my fur bristled.

Our wolves clashed, our backs arching and paws skidding on the sandy dirt as we each tried to get the upper hand. We stood in the middle of the dark forest, our eyes fixed on each other as we circled around. His ears were back, and his tail was tucked low to the floor. I stepped forward, and he lunged at me with a growl. We tumbled across the forest floor, claws scratching against dirt, until he was exhausted.

I was just getting started.

With a growl, I leaped forward and clamped my jaws around my adversary's neck, biting until it bled. Fishy reared and kicked out, but all I wanted was to rip him to shreds. His blood tasted metallic as it trickled down my muzzle, and his wolf slid to the leaves. I kept biting, harder and harder, not stopping until I tasted death.

His blood was warm and salty, and I drank my fill as it poured out of the wound in his neck.

When his heart stopped pumping, and mine stopped pounding, I got to my feet and looked around for Alara.

She watched me from the shadows, her face hidden among the leaves. I couldn't tell what she thought of that performance. I didn't care, of course. That was a simple display of dominance, it had nothing to do with her...yet I found myself searching her face to try to interpret her expression.

I shifted into fae form, naked and covered in blood.

Alara's eyes widened. "Are you okay?"

She came forward and wiped the red off my body, looking for wounds but finding nothing but surface scratches. "Shit, is that all Ruben's blood?"

I looked at the wolf on the forest floor, large and black and ugly, his fur matted with oily black blood in the moonlight.

I grunted. "He shouldn't have talked shit to his alpha."

Alara's eyes narrowed, and she cocked her head. "Funny, you seemed kind of worked up before he even mentioned you. It was almost like you didn't like him talking shit about me."

I considered that for a moment. Did I dislike him talking crap about Alara? No. I fucking hated it.

But I wasn't about to admit that.

"Don't be stupid," I said. "It was a simple matter of hierarchy."

Alara pulled a water bottle from the backpack, gave me some to drink, then tipped it over me, washing away the worst of the blood. She also retrieved a purple Brayson leaf from her pocket and handed it to me. "Funny. Usually, hierarchy is sorted out by ball games and wrestling. I've never seen it go to death before."

The truth was, that was the first time I'd ever killed a wolf. Or any fae at all. An oil slick lined my gut, and I found myself staring at the black, bloody mess of fur on the ground, unable to look away. The air around the wolf's corpse was heavy with the coppery stench of blood.

Alara's voice quietened in response to my mood, and she placed a warm hand on my bicep. I whined and leaned into her touch, unable to stop the shivering that wracked my body. My wolf needed more of her affection, but I'd conditioned her never to touch me. "It's okay," she assured me. " He was a bully. He would have raped me and dumped me somewhere to die. I don't think the world will miss him."

That didn't give me the right to kill him. I was the alpha of alphas, heir to the throne of Verda, Head of House Caro, prince of the realm. And a murderer.

"Did you say his name was Ruben?" My voice was hollow. I kind of wished she'd pass me a tennis ball from the backpack or give me a full-body hug, but she just kept that warm hand on my arm, which would have to do.

"Yes. Ruben Rootswold. He tormented me for years."

"Is he why you didn't fit in with your pack?"

Please say yes, please say yes, please say yes. If that bloody corpse with his ripped-open throat had stopped the pack from uniting, I would be justified in killing him.

"No," she said. "That's on me. I just didn't fit in. Don't fit in."

"Oh."

I was rooted in place, unable to look away from the horror. Ruben's throat was wide open like a maw, his neck foaming with black blood.

"Come on," Alara said, tugging me away. "Take me home."

Leif

The following morning was the day of the second trial, when I was supposed to compete against the other heirs of the realm to sort out our rankings so that when the time came to rule, we'd have a way to solve any disputes. Until this year, I didn't care about this particular hierarchy. I was happy to let Ronan or Gabrelle rank above me so they could do all the hard work of ruling, and I could screw around and screw up and screw everything.

Before Mom died, I didn't have to work for my place in the pack hierarchy. I was technically second-in-command, though I never did any actual work. But now that she was dead and I was the alpha of my pack and every pack in Verda, I understood the true value of hierarchy.

The poor bastard I slaughtered yesterday, Ruben, understood it too.

And I was done giving away free points to the other heirs. I was done with coming in third or fourth. I wanted to win.

With one last nuzzle against Jet, I rolled out of bed and shifted into fae form. I'd already fucked up the first trial of the year by not even turning up, earning myself zero points. Today was the day I started making it up.

"Start the Wars on wolf battle training today. If someone

casts a spell that stops them from using War, I still need them to be able to fight."

"Yes, Alpha," Jet said, pulling on black sweatpants.

"Get the cubs practicing their light spells. I want every single faeling shifter across Verda able to defend themselves against the shadows."

"Yes, Alpha."

"And..." I paused, thinking back to my trip to Sylverclyff. Alara had a good reason to lie about being Ascended, but it could have cost good wolves their lives if they'd relied on her in battle and she didn't come through for them. "Find out how many conscripts have a good reason not to be here."

Jet didn't know how to take that command. He pulled on a T-shirt and looked at me, his head tilted to one side like he was trying to figure me out. "Sorry, Leif, what do you mean?"

I didn't want to explain myself. "Talk to Alara about it, get her to help you," I barked. I had to get moving to make it to Rosenia Forest in time for the trial.

When I'd filled Jet with all the orders I could think of, I trotted outside to the moonway to Rosenia Forest and bounded along it.

At the other end, I loped through the thick foliage to the clearing where the heirs met for our lessons. I hadn't set foot here since Mom died, but after all the hours I'd spent here, it was like settling into a warm bath.

Gabrelle was already there, perched on one of the ivy-covered stone ledges that surrounded the space, her long, shapely legs crossed and her brown skin sparkling in the dappled sunlight.

She smiled in her usual controlled way at seeing me. "You've deigned to join us today, Alpha? I'm glad."

The heir to the house of beauty always came across as ice-cold, but I could read the warmth between the words. I trotted closer and nuzzled her sexy legs with my muzzle, soaking up her familiar passionfruit scent, then I ran the length of my body along her, letting the warm skin of her thighs caress my fur.

Ronan and Neela were here, too, sharing the same flowering bush as a seat. It flowed around them, supporting them perfectly and sending a waft of lavender and vanilla into the air. If Neela was in Rosenia Forest, her pet snuffle tuffs were always nearby. I cast a wary glance around and spotted the two creatures at the edge of the clearing. They looked like two grassy shrubs, one slightly larger than the other, but they were fiercely protective of Neela and would transform into terrifying, large, sharp-fanged creatures if she was threatened.

Going the long way to avoid the snuffle tuffs, I crossed to Ronan and Neela and let my wolf sniff them, rubbing my nose against their skin. A slight whine escaped me, and Neela rubbed my head, misinterpreting the sound. "Good to see you too, wolf boy."

I hadn't whined because I missed them, but because of their easy intimacy, the connection between Neela and Ronan that I would never have with anyone. My strongest physical relationship was with a submissive who hated her role and would rather be home with her sick dad in her shitty den.

Ronan let me lick him. He usually hated that crap, but he put up with it since I'd been behaving so wildly recently. Might as well take advantage, so I left a long streak of slimy saliva up his forearm.

"Bad dog," he said, but he didn't bat me away.

I ducked around a vibrant green vine brimming with flowers

that hung like a decoration and trotted to my massive jasmine-bush mattress, which I flopped onto. It caught me, grew around me in support, and I relaxed into it.

The three heirs looked at me. Their stares were heavy, and I knew they were waiting for me to shift. Wondering why on earth I hadn't already.

They didn't understand.

Eventually, I shifted into fae form and instantly felt the burden and responsibilities of my role as Alpha of Alphas.

"That's better. Now we get to see your beautiful face," Neela said.

"And beautiful body," Gabrelle added with a slow smile, letting her gaze rove from my head to my toes. Maybe I should keep up this moody-wolf routine for longer if it got me compliments from the beauty queen.

Ronan jumped up and darted to the stash of gray sweatpants I kept in a basket beneath a stone lid, then tossed a pair at my chest. "Cover up, mutt," he growled. "Nobody wants to see that."

"Well..." Neela said with a smirk, eyeing me, and Ronan leaped on her, covering her in kisses to distract her.

I pulled on the sweats but kept my chest bare. It was too restrictive and uncomfortable wearing a shirt—pants were bad enough. If it was up to me, I'd walk around naked every moment of the day. In fact, everyone would. Maybe I should make that a law of the wolves...

Dion walked into the clearing from the direction of his moonway. His hair was bright blue, his irises the color of the sky, and he smelled of blueberries. His eyes lit up when he saw me, and he flopped onto the jasmine mattress beside me. "Glad you're here, Leif. I brought extra rations for you."

I rested my head on his shoulder while he unwrapped a blueberry muffin as big as my head. In my rush to get here, I'd forgotten breakfast, which was an indicator of my state of mind—the last time I'd forgotten a meal was when I was five years old and had gotten my first erection. I'd followed a poor beta around all day with my cock up and hadn't eaten a thing.

"Thanks, dude." I bit into the muffin and groaned. It tasted like lying on the beach in summer when you had no worries or cares in the world except whether to swim or screw someone.

D had really tapped into his Magirus powers with this one. And, apparently, he knew exactly what I needed. Perhaps I wasn't hiding my stress as well as I thought.

"Is it any good?" Dion asked.

I took another mouthful. "You know it is, Double D." Neela snorted at the nickname she had initially coined. If I could form a mating bond with that blueberry muffin, I would.

By the time I finished the damn thing, I felt much more like my old self. I fished out a tennis ball from my stash beneath the jasmine mattress and tossed it against a tree, snatching it out of the air when it bounced back. There was something calming about that. Therapeutic. Throw, rebound, catch. Throw, rebound, catch.

"Being Alpha sucks, guys." Throw, rebound, catch. "But I've decided to kick your asses in the trials from now on because not-being Alpha would be even worse."

Ronan snorted. "Yeah, right. You couldn't kick my ass if you had a size-twenty boot."

Throw, rebound, catch. "We'll see about that, toy boy."

Ronan had lost all his property, all his money, all his possessions. He'd made that choice—because the alternative was either he died, or Neela left the fae world. An easy decision.

Now he was supported by Neela, who had the entire Floran fortune, so he was officially her toy boy.

Neela coined that phrase too, but I loved it. And now, I felt relaxed enough to use it.

Gabrelle uncrossed and recrossed her legs. She wore a purple miniskirt which made a good show of her assets. "You may come third, Leif," she declared like she was bestowing me a gift.

I watched until her legs stopped moving, then snorted. "Hardly. It's the physical trial or the inner magic trial today, so it's between me and Double D."

Neela harrumphed. "I'm the most powerful Grower in decades, so I'm in with a chance, too, you arrogant princeling."

The banter felt good, almost as relaxing as the blueberry muffin.

Throw, rebound, catch.

"Do you still have that poor country faeling locked in a prison cell," Gabrelle asked, and I missed the catch, and the ball went sailing past me.

"That's none of your business, babe," I said, the hair on the back of my neck prickling.

"It is, actually. I rank higher than you among the heirs, and I'm telling you, you're being too harsh on your pack. They aren't to blame for your mother's death. The Shadow Walkers are."

A moment later, I was on my feet and in Gabrelle's face. "Don't talk to me about my mother. And don't ever dare to tell me how to run my wolves. I am the alpha of alphas, and you're just a pretty princess with a mommy complex." I ran a finger slowly down her cheek, watching her flinch. "Go look in a mirror or something, beauty queen, and stay the hell out of my business."

The air in the clearing crackled, and every heir stared at me. I remembered why I was here. Not to eat enchanted food and talk crap with my old friends, but to prove myself worthy to the Earth Goddess, Gaia, and to earn five points in today's trial.

"Where's the scroll?" I demanded, wanting to get on with the task so I could return to my wolves where I belonged.

Ronan produced a scroll, unfurled it, and read. "The second trial is a gauntlet. It consists of a series of obstacles crafted to challenge the heirs' physical prowess."

"Yes! Physical," Dion said, pumping the air.

Ronan continued reading. "Contenders must navigate a labyrinthine course filled with ethereal barriers and shifting paths, ending with a climb up the Crystal Cascades. The first fae to reach the waterfall's summit shall earn five points, etc., etc."

We all knew how the point system worked. It was a physical trial, and nobody came near my speed or agility in wolf form. I would race through the first section of the gauntlet and hope that gave me enough of a headstart to climb up the waterfall, which I would have to do as a fae.

I shifted, not bothering to remove my sweatpants, so they shredded into rags. Good. Hopefully that would intimidate the others. I was really getting through my clothes lately, leaving shreds of material all over the realm.

A glowing stream of light on the forest floor highlighted the path of the race, and the other heirs jostled beside me in a rough line.

Ronan stamped the ground. "Try and keep up, guys."

Neela whacked him in the chest. "Yeah, right. Eat my faerie dust, loser."

"You'll both lose," Dion said, taking a starter's crouch.

I was in wolf form, so I couldn't speak, but I wouldn't anyway. This was no time for banter. It was time to concentrate, so I shut out the sounds of their trash talk and focused on the glowing path that shimmered around a large tree and off into the distance through the forest.

Gabrelle wasn't immune to the shit talk. She exhaled loudly, which was as close to a snort as she ever gave. She patted down her purple miniskirt, then she called, "Ready. Go!"

My muscles exploded, and I loped ahead, instantly in the lead. Dion would definitely come in last place. He had ascended, but being a good cook didn't help you run, and he'd always been slow.

The other three would be jostling for position. Ronan usually beat Gabrelle on foot, but the trial would include elements of agility and balance, so she might dominate. And I had no idea how fast and strong Neela had become over the past year since she'd embraced her fae nature.

I didn't care. As long as I came in first. The glowing path led me on a winding course through Rosenia Forest, suddenly changing direction without warning, so I had to avoid tree trunks and shifting paths, dodging sparkling illusions, and leaping over moss-covered stones that materialized out of nowhere.

I didn't miss a beat, dodging, leaping, and sprinting without slowing down. When I reached the base of the Crystal Cascades, I figured I was a long way ahead of the others. Shifting into fae form, I gave myself to the count of three to catch my breath before diving into the water and swimming out to the waterfall. The stone was mossy and slippery behind the sheet of water, and I lost my grip several times and plunged back into the river.

Changing my technique, I partially shifted so my wolf claws extended from my hands and feet, and I pierced the stone with every step, fighting the powerful current of falling water, battling against nature itself.

Finally, I claimed victory. My adrenaline gradually subsided, leaving me drowning in a mix of conflicting emotions, none of which I was ready to face. As I caught my breath, my mind drifted to the intimate relationship between Ronan and Neela.

Before long, the two lovers appeared at the waterfall's base, jostling for position. I didn't want to face their emotions, or my own, so I shifted into my wolf and watched my old friends climb the waterfall. Ronan was the better climber, so he beat her up.

"I'll give you the win, just this once," he said to me with a wink. The silence between us wasn't comfortable like it used to be. He had to be wondering why I stayed shifted, and he was having trouble keeping up a conversation when I refused to answer.

Neela collapsed over the edge of the waterfall, soaking wet and panting. Ronan gloated at her, and she scowled back at him, and when he said, "Ventus siccatio," to help her dry off, she swatted his hand away and demanded that he teach her the spell instead.

Their casual intimacy made me whine again, and my damn wolf couldn't even keep it silent. Neela looked over and flung her arms around me, which helped. Being close to a friend was balm to a wolf, and my tail wagged slowly as she stroked my fur.

Gabrelle appeared at the waterfall's base, and Ronan and Neela yelled out encouragement as she climbed up. When she reached the top, she looked displeased at having been beaten by Neela—previously, she'd beaten House Flora every time. Her ranking was in real danger of collapsing.

Especially since I was taking the trials seriously too.

Finally, Dion emerged from the forest below and battled against the torrent of water to the top.

"Ventus siccatio," Neela roared, casting a massive wind that blew the Magirus right off the top of the cliff, and he plummeted back down into the lake at the waterfall's base.

"Fuck," Neela said. "I didn't mean to do that. I was just trying to dry him off."

Ronan was laughing too hard to respond, and even Gabrelle had a glowing smile.

"Sorry," Neela yelled down to Dion, making Ronan double over again and laugh even harder.

"I think you mastered the wind spell," Gabrelle said smoothly, setting Ronan off again.

But her mood soured when the shimmering number '2' appeared above Gabrelle's head. Dion finally joined us at the top of the waterfall again, fuming, his hair a pale blue from all the water he'd drunk.

"Don't you fucking dare," Dion growled when Neela lifted her hand to dry him off again. "Let someone competent do it. Like me." He dried himself off with a gentle wind, while Ronan fell about laughing and making fun of him.

Ronan was happy with his four points, and Neela looked satisfied with her three points, though she definitely muttered something about, "I'm still coming for the top spot."

And I looked at the shimmering silver '5' above my head and released a long breath.

Finally, the rank I deserved.

Gabrelle

Go look in a mirror or something. As I ran along the labyrinthine path, competing in the heirs' second trial, Leif's words cycled through my head on repeat. But it was the venom behind them that really affected me. Like he'd spilled a truth he'd been bottling up for years, like he really thought I was that superficial.

I was born to House Allura, the house of beauty, and beauty coated my skin, but that didn't mean it ran through my veins.

His barbed words put me off balance, slowed my feet, and made me slow to dodge the obstacles that appeared in my path. When I was traversing a narrow beam of light between two tree branches, a Gilded Python slithered onto the beam before me, and I hadn't been fast enough to close my eyes against its allure.

I fell under its spell.

The majestic snake was native to the Realm of Greed and Excess, Verda, and couldn't survive beyond our borders. It embodied wealth, luxury, and ostentation, and sparkling gemstones studded its sparkling scales. Its gaze lured the curious and the covetous.

I was both.

Ambition stirred within me as I stared at the spellbinding

snake, unable to look away. To steal from the Gilded Python was to doom yourself. Even so, knowing this, I leaned forward to pluck a golden scale from its body.

Thank Gaia, I lost balance and tumbled off my narrow bridge of light, falling to the forest floor below.

Hitting the dirt with a thud broke my spell, and I was able to avert my gaze until the Gilded Python slithered away.

"Get it together, Gabrelle," I told myself. "You're better than this."

Usually, I was neck-and-neck with Ronan in footraces, but he was well ahead of me today. I was in danger of being caught by Dion, of all fae.

By the time I finished the gauntlet and climbed the Crystal Cascades, Ronan and Neela were already dry.

Ronan smirked at me in victory, but at least he offered to dry me off with a basic elemental spell. None of us heirs had mastered air, but Ronan was probably the most skilled. Even so, he couldn't isolate my clothes the way a proper Air could, so being dried under his incantation was like standing in a desert storm, minus the sense of adventure.

"Thank you so much," I said glibly, then Ronan returned to trying to teach the spell to Neela.

I turned to see if Leif was ready to apologize for his outburst. The mutt was lying in wolf form, sulking like a faeling who couldn't go to the Wild Hunt of Fen.

I knew he was going through a tough time and that the world was a burden for him. But two could play at the sulking game, so I ignored him and sat quietly while Ronan and Neela chatted and giggled like idiots.

Finally, Dion finished the trial, and we could all disperse. I declined to go to the Lakehouse. Our merry little band of heirs was no longer the tight group it once was, and without Leif, the Lakehouse felt empty.

Before I left for home, Neela made me promise to meet her for a drink at the Ogre's Nose. I agreed, just to get her off my back, but I would send my apologies later. Even Ronan's happiness at coming second in the trial wasn't a strong enough emotion to cheer me up.

I approached the Mirror Palace in the late afternoon, and the deep blue sky reflected off every inch of the grand building, making it hard to see. But I'd lived there my whole life and could navigate the grounds blindfolded.

In the foyer, I had the misfortune to meet my mother.

She looked me up and down with a slow, appraising gaze. "You look terrible, Gabrelle. Go and clean yourself up at once."

My mother never greeted me with a simple hello, always with a comment on my appearance. Usually a compliment, although she was happy to cut me down when she felt it was needed.

My purple super-miniskirt was torn, and my white sleeve-less top was covered in mud and leaves from when I'd tumbled to the forest floor after almost falling prey to the Gilded Python. Even the trip up the waterfall hadn't washed away all that muck.

"Why thank you, Mother, how lovely to see you too," I quipped.

"No need to be snide, dear."

I breezed past her, hoping I stank of rhona shit. The forest mud was often mixed with a little eau-de-manure. "Au contraire, mother. There's every need in the world."

Mother wore a long gown of turquoise that made her liquid green sparkle. Her hair was up, her shoulders free, and she looked every inch the Queen of Allura. "Don't be like that, darling. Now go and change, then come downstairs looking decent. We are expecting company."

Groan. Mother's idea of company was any fae willing to fawn all over her, which was my idea of hell.

Go look in a mirror.

I painted on a happy smile, the kind that covered my emotions so perfectly that I had earned the nickname the *ice queen*. I much preferred that to the *beauty queen*.

"Sorry, Mother, I have an appointment in the city."

It looked like I'd be meeting up with Neela after all. *Ogre's Nose, here I come.*

I crossed to the quill and parchment on a side table and penned a quick note to tell the Floran Princess I would be early. I muttered, "Avem volare," and the paper folded into the shape of a bird and flew out the tiny high window that was bespoke for spellbirds.

I needed to unwind before I faced anybody else. My poor performance, compounded by my encounter with Mother, had me stressed. I pulled out my faeboe and played it, blowing gently into the reed and letting the mournful, sweet sound chase away the worst of my disappointment. I had spent countless hours playing this beautiful wind instrument and found it comforted me. The melody was enchanting but sad and matched my mood well.

When I had restored my emotional equilibrium, I packed away my faeboe and readied myself for the evening.

An hour later, I was showered and changed into a pristine white jumpsuit, with my pink hair flowing about my shoulders. I pushed open the creaking door of the Ogre's Nose and inhaled the sweet smoke that infused the bar. Jazz played from the enchanted ceiling, and the lighting was low.

As I swept past each table, fae turned to watch me pass. A male with tight purple curls and an intense violet stare stopped me with a hand on the shoulder. "Please, can I have the honor of buying you a drink?"

I sighed. Fawning fae were sometimes a nice ego boost, but they became tiresome. "No," I said simply.

Neela waved at me from a dark wood booth at the back of the bar, and I walked over. She had brought her housemaid, Liz, who watched me approach with a glare. Both females were dressed like maintenance workers, wearing loose fae denim jeans and button-up shirts with pockets and without shape. I might expect that from the housemaid, but honestly, it was as though Neela had learned nothing from me.

Neela leaped up and embraced me. "Thanks for coming. I wasn't sure you would."

I tolerated the hug and patted her gingerly on the back, but I was more comfortable after she released me, and I'd slid into my bench. I held in my comment at her appearance—that was one element of Mother's personality I didn't want to mimic.

The princess pushed a frothy pink concoction at me. "I ordered a round of Fae Fizzes."

I sighed. I would have preferred whiskey. "Okay. Now, tell me, why are we here?"

Neela chewed her lip. "Because we're good friends and we like hanging out together?"

The housemaid barked a laugh and flicked a green braid behind her shoulder. "Because we're scared of you and are here under duress, more like, biatch."

I had no idea why Neela tolerated her housemaid speaking to her that way, but I didn't care enough to intervene.

Neela sipped her drink. She mumbled something into the Floran Bracelet tattooed on her wrist before addressing me and Liz. "I'm worried about Leif. He's gone off the rails, and a bunch of wolves might pay the price. It's gone too far. What're we gonna do about it?"

Liz narrowed her eyes suspiciously. "Why didn't you ask Ronan and Dion along too?"

I appreciated her suspicion. Perhaps I'd underestimated her intelligence.

Neela shrugged. "Ronan doesn't think there's anything we can do. And D thinks we can cure him by baking him muffins. We need a proper solution, and those guys only hinder the conversation."

I considered that for a while, slowly running a finger around the rim of my glass. "That makes sense. Well done."

Neela scowled. "I'm not a puppy, I don't need praise." She watched closely as my finger kept rubbing around my glass. "And would you knock that off, Gabrelle? It's very distracting."

Liz nodded. "Yep. We already want to screw your brains out, princess. Stop making this so difficult."

I stopped immediately. I wasn't used to being called out on my behavior, least of all by a washerfae or housemaid, or whatever this fae was.

A snapped reply was on the tip of my tongue, but then I remembered the venom in Leif's voice as he snarled, *Go and look in a mirror*, and I held it in. Maybe they all thought I was superficial. Not that I cared what anybody thought.

I pushed back my shoulders. "I have already tried to intervene. I slipped a key to the country fae he had locked in his dungeon, but I haven't found out if she escaped."

Neela hiccupped, then swallowed a giggle. "Good idea. But

we need to think bigglier. Bigglier. Bigger."

I raised an eyebrow at Neela's made-up word but decided not to comment. Despite her occasional moments of flightiness, she was a true friend, and I respected her concern for Leif.

Liz, on the other hand, seemed to have a hidden agenda. I couldn't quite decipher her motive for being here, but I knew better than to underestimate anyone in the fae world.

"I agree, we need a bigger plan," I said, taking a sip of my Fae Fizz. "Leif's anger has been escalating, becoming a danger to himself and those around him. We need to find a way to help him deal with his grief and stop taking it out on others."

Neela nodded in agreement, but Liz seemed skeptical. "And how do you propose we do that? The guy's like a ticking bomb. He's gonna go full psycho any day."

I scowled at her. "Don't talk about a prince that way."

Neela intervened. "Liz can talk however she wants, Gabrelle."

I sighed. This conversation was getting out of hand. Ronan was the heir I usually discussed important issues with, leaving Dion to cook and Leif to goof around.

But all our roles within the group had changed. Leif had turned serious, Ronan had started screwing up, Neela had appeared out of nowhere, disrupting the entire balance of our group, and now this lesser fae, Liz, was sticking her nose in.

I took a deep breath and tried to refocus the conversation. "We need to find the root of Leif's anger. What's causing it? How can we help him process his grief in a healthier way?"

Neela chewed on her lower lip, deep in thought. "Maybe we could bring his mother back from the dead? I mean, if we could find a powerful enough magic spell, it's possible, right?"

Liz rolled her eyes. "That's the stupidest thing I've ever

heard. Bringing someone back from the dead always ends badly. And it's a super hard spell that we don't have a hope of pulling off. Plus, we don't even know if Leif would want that. He needs to learn to move on."

I nodded in agreement with Liz, surprising myself. "She's right. Bringing someone back from the dead is dangerous and unpredictable. And almost impossible. We need to find another way."

Neela pouted, then rubbed her hands on her jeans. "Fine. Like what?"

I lowered my voice. Half the fae in here were trying to eavesdrop. "I have an idea. It won't bring his mother back, but it might help him to find some perspective."

The other two leaned in. "Whassit?" Neela asked. "What's the idea?"

"Leif's mother had a garden that she loved. It was her sanctuary. I think if we can get Leif to spend some time there, it might help him find some peace."

Liz rolled her eyes. "Great idea, princess. Except his mother's dead, and the garden's probably overgrown and forgotten."

I ignored Liz's snarky comment and continued, flicking a strand of pink hair over my shoulder. "I know where the garden is. I can take Leif there. You never know, it might help."

"A garden?" Liz asked. "To fix his psycho mood swings?"

My sigh was bigger and more expressive than strictly necessary, but I wanted this washerfae to understand exactly how annoying she was. "A garden to give him some perspective and help him understand his mother better. It can't hurt."

Neela's eyes lit up. "It's perfect! It might bring back some good memories for him. I can help restore the garden to its former beauty." She was an excellent Grower, and I had no doubt she could do exactly as she promised.

Liz looked skeptical but, thank Gaia, held her tongue.

I ran my forefinger around my glass. "It'll be a peaceful and healing place for Leif to spend time in. At least it's a start."

Neela took another sip of her Fae Fizz, and a lock of spiky blue hair fell across her forehead. "I'm free toromow. Tomomo. Tomorrow."

Neela followed that declaration with a decisive nod that knocked her off her balance, and she had to hold onto the table for support. She really needed to work on her tolerance to Fae Fizz.

I slid to my feet and walked away. It felt good to have a plan, even if it had little chance of working.

Liz muttered to Neela, "Is she just going to take her sexy swishing ass and leave without saying goodbye?"

"Yup, that's kinda her thing," the Floran Princess replied.

I nodded at the barkeep to indicate that the drinks should go on the House Allura tab, then I took my leave.

Something had to get through to Leif eventually. Surely.

Alara

I was getting more comfortable with being naked. Other fae's nudity had never bothered me, and the longer I spent in the Verda City den, the more relaxed I became about my own.

Possibly because of all those hours tied up in Leif's sex dungeon while he inspected every inch of my body.

The sun was just beginning to rise, casting a burnt orange hue across the sky as I walked back from the hunt. Although I couldn't shift on cue because I wasn't Ascended, I'd been assigned to the hunt. Because, apparently, "everybody has to help out."

I'd even managed to shift under the strong moonlight while we were chasing down a herd of deer. As soon as Brunor, one of Leif's top betas, had determined that the herd was true deer, not deer shifters, he signaled the attack, and my adrenaline had freed my wolf. It felt amazing.

As we left the forest, the first rays of dawn broke over the marble den. The hunting group members were all panting and covered in sweat, our hair matted from exertion. The smell of blood still lingered on our skin. I was beginning to suspect I belonged in this pack, after all.

Leif had told me everybody had a pack where they belonged, and maybe he was right. Perhaps I belonged in his.

Leif was the alpha of the pack, but he was much more than that to me. The way he examined my body in his playroom was more intimate than any sexual encounter I'd ever had. He knew every inch of my body and commanded me to do things I never thought I'd enjoy. Oh, but I did, very, very much.

I imagined running my fingers over his body, feeling his skin under my fingertips. He rarely let me touch him, and after every session with him, my desire to run my fingers over his body grew. Now, it was all I could think about.

Even returning home naked, covered in the blood of true deer, with the taste of their fur still on my tongue, my thoughts were on Leif.

As I entered the vast marble den, I shook my head to clear my mind. Several pack members nodded respectfully to me. I had proven myself on the hunt, and the feeling was like the afternoon sun on my back.

But I was only interested in one person's respect. Leif's. I could hear him talking in his office as I walked down the corridor. I hesitated for a moment. I should go upstairs and shower, or at least get some damn clothes on, but I really wanted to see him. He hadn't summoned me in days, and he was hard to catch, constantly darting off to some alpha or heir business.

"Come here, Alara," he called, and the command sent a tingle through my body. I was already wet thinking about him, but the way he commanded me drove me wild.

I had to force myself to walk slowly along the corridor to his office door as if I had all the time in the world. My heart was pounding. I wanted to please him so much that I was about to explode with anticipation. Since when did I want to please my alpha without being commanded to?

I let my hair down, shaking my head so my hair fanned out behind me. When I entered the office, I was panting. Naked, streaked with blood, and panting. Leif was sitting at his desk with a glass of water.

He was bare-chested, and for a moment, I thought he was naked too, but then I saw the light gray sweatpants under the desk.

He motioned to me with his finger, indicating that I should come to him. My heart was pounding, and I took several steps toward him before I could stop myself.

"What is it?" I asked.

"Come here," he said.

He motioned to me again, and my body moved without me even thinking about it. I closed the distance between us, stopping just in front of his desk. He looked me up and down, taking in my naked form with a slight smirk.

"You look good covered in blood," he said, his voice low and husky.

A shiver ran down my spine. I wanted him so badly I could hardly stand it. I needed him to touch me, to take me, to use me.

"What do you want me to do?" I asked, my voice barely above a whisper.

Leif leaned back in his chair, his eyes never leaving mine as he slowly sipped his water. My eyes trailed down his neck, watching the muscles in his throat move as he swallowed. I couldn't tear my gaze away from him.

"I want you to let me taste you."

He set his glass down, and my eyes traveled along his arms as he leaned forward without breaking eye contact. The muscles flexed in his forearm as he reached for his glass. A drop of water trickled down his throat, and I licked my lips. He was so close I could feel his hot breath on my skin.

I wanted to run my fingers down his jawline, across his full lips, and then let them travel all over his chest.

He extended his hand and tangled his fingers in the baby curls at the nape of my neck. He grasped my hair in his fist and pulled me toward him.

"Open your mouth," he commanded.

My lips parted, and his breath fanned over my face. I could feel his hot, delicious breath in my mouth. As he leaned in closer, my heart was beating so hard I was sure he could hear it. His lips brushed over mine, and his hand in my hair tightened.

I let out a small moan, and he pulled away.

"I told you to open your mouth," he growled.

The words dripped off his tongue like liquid sin, and I wanted nothing more than to give myself to him.

"Whatever you say," I replied, my voice little more than a breath.

"Good girl," he said, and the praise sent a jolt of electricity through my pussy.

I opened my mouth wider and drank him in, tasting him. He smelled like spice and leather, a scent that never failed to turn me on.

I leaned my body into his, feeling his hard cock press into my belly, but he pulled away. "Naughty girl. Let me lick you first."

He dragged his tongue and mouth down my neck and over my breasts, licking away the blood from the hunt.

As he moved lower, tracing a path down my stomach, my muscles contracted, and I clenched my fists at my side. He wouldn't let me touch him, so I had to dig my nails into my palms to keep my hands still.

His tongue flicked over my belly button, and I shuddered.

The anticipation of what was to come was driving me crazy. I had never wanted anyone as much as I wanted Leif.

"So, wet," Leif said, his voice laced with approval. His approval sent a wave of pure energy through my body.

He pulled my left nipple into his mouth, sucking hard. I arched my back, putting my breast in his mouth. He was so good at that. He brought me to the brink of climax in so little time. It was always just a few minutes before he had me moaning in pleasure.

I couldn't help but wonder how many other fae had been in this office, on this desk. I knew there had been a lot; after all, Leif was an alpha. Wolves never felt jealous—we were pack animals who viewed sharing sex like sharing a meal. It was better in groups, and the more the merrier. But the hot feeling in my chest felt suspiciously like jealousy, and I forced the image of the other fae he'd slept with out of my head.

Leif slipped his hand between my legs, and a moan escaped my lips. He was driving me wild, and I knew it wouldn't take him long to bring me to my climax.

"What have you been thinking about, bumpkin?" he asked, his hot breath tickling my skin.

"You," I moaned.

"Good girl," he said, his voice so low and husky, the word sent shivers of pleasure through me. "I want to taste more of you," he said, standing up and moving behind me.

He trailed his tongue down my spine, and the feel of his liquid tongue on my sensitive skin made me shiver. Slowly, he licked his way over my ass and around my hips, then he pushed me forward so I was bent over his desk, exposing my pussy behind me, and he slipped his tongue inside me.

A moan escaped my lips as I pushed out my ass, trying to get more of him inside me. My hands on the desk were streaked in deer blood, which added to my animalistic pleasure.

He grabbed my ass and pulled me closer, burying his face in my pussy.

I gasped as his tongue went over my clitoris and back down. He licked me, harder and faster, and the tingling feeling in my legs became almost painful.

"Can I touch you?" I asked, my voice breathy.

"No," he replied, his voice muffled.

I groaned. I was so close to climaxing, but I didn't want to do it this way, with his mouth on my pussy.

I wanted his cock inside me. I needed to feel him, to taste him. I needed him to fill my mouth and my pussy. I needed to crawl inside of him and never be apart from him. It was more than a want. It was a need. I needed to be with him more than I needed air to breathe. It felt like my body was being torn apart. I needed to be whole, and Leif was the missing piece. He'd help me come together, and I never wanted to be apart from him again.

With a horrible realization that I was falling for the asshole alpha, I orgasmed, shuddering and crying under his expert touch.

Alara

After shuddering in climax, I sagged against Leif. His chest was now streaked in blood, and his mouth was coated in my juices. I pressed my cheek against his chest over his heart and wrapped my arms around him.

He was the alpha of alphas, the heir to the throne, the Head of House Caro, the fae who had torn me from my sick father against my will. And I was fucking falling for him. Thank Gaia he was such an uptight prick; otherwise, my heart would be in real trouble.

I breathed him in, listened to his heart beating in his chest, then smiled slyly against his skin. "Now it's my turn to take care of you."

I ran my hands slowly over his hips and slipped them under the waistband of his gray sweatpants, but he placed his larger hands over mine, stopping the movement.

"What are you doing?" he growled.

"Returning the favor. You might have magical fingers, but my hands have some power too."

I tried to waggle my fingers, but his hands were too heavy over them.

"No." He closed his hands around my wrists and pulled my fingers out from the waistband of his pants. "This isn't a transaction."

I frowned. "What do you mean?" We were holding hands now, though his were closed like a vice around my wrists. He was firmly in control, as always.

"I give you an orgasm, so you have to give me one. This isn't like that."

I pulled my hands free and placed them gently on his chest. "I didn't say it was. I want to do this."

He picked up my hands again, throwing them away this time. "No. That was a one-time thing. A reward for joining in on the hunt. I know you don't like doing that sort of thing."

I swallowed a whine at being rejected physically and instead smiled in what I hoped was a sexy way. "Actually, I love ripping bodies apart, tasting blood, the thrill of the chase."

He crossed his arms across his broad chest, and the muscles of his forearms stood out. "I meant joining in. You aren't much of a team player, which is weird for a wolf. So I was just rewarding you for being a good pack member."

A streak of true deer blood ran along his forearm, and I traced the line of red. "Well, let me reward you for being a good alpha."

He stepped away from me, snatching away his leather scent and his body heat. "I'm not a good alpha."

I stood before him, naked, vulnerable, exposed. "Leif, you're a great alpha. You have an amazing pack, and they'd do anything for you."

"I have a good pack. That doesn't mean I'm a good alpha."

"What? Of course you are. The amount those shifters respect you..." I shook my head. I'd love an ounce of that respect.

Leif's erection had gone down, which was disappointing. He walked away from me and thumped a fist on his desk. "I've lost fifteen wolves since I became Alpha. That's fifteen lives gone. One of them by my own hand."

"Fishy had it coming," I snarled. I took a step toward him, and he jerked backward as if I'd try to touch him. "And you're doing your best. You're working on a way to defeat the Shadow Walkers. You're doing a shitload more than any other leader in the whole damn fae world."

He shook his head. "Maybe, but my best isn't good enough. We still don't know how to kill them. We don't know shit." He slumped in his desk chair. "Mom would have known what to do."

There was no answer to that. Stella Caro was famously brilliant, an insightful and charismatic leader who was renowned for her strategic talent. Nobody could live up to that.

Leif stripped and used his sweatpants to clean off the blood, then tossed them to me to do the same while slipping into a fresh pair. "I have to go. See yourself out, okay?"

Rubbing the soiled sweatpants over my body and between my legs to clean off, I smiled coyly. "Is the alpha of alphas actually asking me a question instead of commanding me?"

He narrowed his eyes at me. "Let me rephrase that. I'm leaving now. So are you."

"Great, thanks for the invitation. I'll come with you. Where are we going?"

"We're not going anywhere. I am going to meet the other heirs. You are going upstairs to get changed."

I pouted. "Do you really want me to shower upstairs and end up screwing a bunch of the other betas?"

Leif snapped his head around to look at me. He looked me up and down, then trotted over to a laundry bin and fished out a fresh white shirt with thin blue stripes, which he tossed to me. "Put that on. We're going to my mom's garden."

I slipped the shirt on over my head. Its hem hung at least a foot below my hips, and the sleeves dangled down past my elbows. We went outside, him wearing only pants and me wearing only a shirt. At least together, we made one sensibly dressed fae.

We dived into the forest, greeted by a tapestry of moss-covered trunks, towering evergreens, and low-hanging branches. The sun filtering through the canopy cast patches of warm light across our path, and the air was filled with chirping birds and buzzing insects, the occasional animal rustling in the undergrowth.

"The garden was Mom's special place. The place she liked to go to unwind, away from prying eyes."

"Sounds like your Lakehouse," I said, and he glanced at me curiously, so I rushed to explain. "Everybody knows the heirs go to some special private Lakehouse nobody else has ever seen. And I noticed that when you go there, you're stressed out, and when you come back, you're a bit calmer. I guess I figured that was because you can decompress, get away from the responsibilities of being an heir and an alpha."

Leif tugged me off the forest path between two large stones. "Yeah, that's exactly how I feel about the Lakehouse. Well, less so these days. But I suppose you're right. Mom's garden was like her Lakehouse."

We entered the garden through a small gap in some thick foliage. It was like a birthday party thrown by Gaia herself. Luminescent flowers of every color were lit by a soft, ethereal glow. Grasses by my feet danced to my footsteps, responding to my every movement. The air was filled with the sweet scent of honeysuckle, lavender, and jasmine, and it shifted between earthy and floral tones as we weaved through different sections of the garden.

"It's beautiful," I breathed, skipping along a stepping-stone path between two large mossy stones. I passed some orchids that sang a glorious tune as I walked by, then fell silent when I moved on to the next wonder.

"Yes," he said, looking around in as much wonder as I was. "It's beautiful."

"Do you come here often?"

He shook his head. "No, I've never been here before. Mom never let me come. She never even let Dad come here when he was alive. She said this was the one place she could be herself."

A glowing white plant drew my eye, and I wandered closer, holding its brilliant petals gently. "What's this?"

Leif shrugged, and just as my curiosity peaked, a voice from behind us startled me. "Ah, that's a celestial starflower," the voice said. "The petals open at night on the full moon, and they say they're as bright as a star."

I shrank at the fae who was talking, and at the second fae who appeared at her side. They were Neela Flora and Gabrelle Allura. Princess Flora wore fae denim overalls over a bright pink singlet top, and with her bright blue hair and flashing blue eyes, she looked like a life-sized doll. Princess Allura looked more like a sex doll, with her curves squished into a purple jumpsuit that left little to the imagination, and her plum lips slightly parted. She really was beauty personified.

I wanted to sink to my knees before them, but I'd had enough of submission. I also wanted to go over and run my tongue up the long arms of the beauty princess, but I somehow managed to keep my feet in place, with just a slightly moronic expression on my face.

Princess Allura looked at Leif with a slight smile. "This one has remarkable restraint."

Leif grinned like a puppy and trotted over to the other heirs, rubbing his face against each of their heads in turn. Princess Flora ruffled his hair and smacked his ass, and Princess Allura tolerated his physical intimacy and called him a "good dog."

My jaw must have hit the soil because I had never seen anybody treat the alpha of alphas like that. Like he was a friend and an equal, not the domineering prince I always saw.

He looked young and carefree, and I saw a joy in him that made me like him more. It also made my heart clench at seeing how much of himself he'd given up to become Alpha.

He'd had to give up this easy affection with his peers, the ease of being accepted into a group. His only reward was the respect of his pack, but he needed somewhere he could just be himself.

"I can see why your mom liked this garden, Leif. It's beautiful." Neela Flora's musical voice made the garden even lovelier in the soft light of early morning.

He turned to his friend. "Did you help restore it? I thought it would be overgrown for sure."

The Floran Princess smiled. "I tidied it up a bit yesterday and added a few touches," she said, gesturing toward the garden. "But only to the parts your mother's Growers made. I didn't touch anything she grew herself. I thought you might like to see her patch."

Princess Flora pulled us aside, away from the vibrant maze of flowering bushes and dazzling topiaries. The small garden patch she showed us was far from glamorous; struggling weeds had taken over patches of cracked soil, and withered stalks lay scattered about. The few vegetables growing in the beds were wilted and pale.

Leif's brow creased. "Are you sure this is it, dude? This place looks like shit. Mom's patch would have had more pizazz."

Princess Allura inspected her fingernails. "I'm sure the queen of sensuality's patch was glorious," she said smoothly.

Leif's expression turned serious, and he gently swatted the princess's arm. "Cut it out. We are not talking about my dead Mom's vajayjay. A bit of respect, ice queen."

The princess wasn't fazed. "Oh, I'm sure it had a lot of respect."

I snorted. This was the best interaction I'd ever seen. I'd imagined the heirs to be uppity dicks with their heads so far up their asses they could see out their own mouths, but these guys were entertaining. Hilarious.

Even Leif couldn't hold onto his anger. He grinned and gave the princess the bird.

I shook my head, trying to take it in. The heir to the Alluran throne talked shit about my alpha's mom's vagina, and he responded by flipping her off. My mind was spinning.

"I certainly respected it," I said, joining in for once—who said I didn't play nicely with others? All three heads snapped my way. "Your mother's rule," I explained hastily, but they all kept staring at me, and I didn't want to appear rude, so I clarified, "And, I suppose, her vagina."

Princess Flora chuckled, and the other female smiled coolly. But I monitored Leif's reaction the most closely—he barked a laugh, and his silver eyes shone with mirth. I had the feeling this was the true male, the fae beneath the crown. One he'd been hiding for a long time.

He looked back at the pathetic excuse for a garden at his feet. "So why was Mom's garden so shitty? I mean, I could literally take a dump here and improve it."

I laughed loud enough to make Princess Flora jump, and Leif shot me a grin of pure joy.

"I guess that's the point," I said.

The two princesses tilted their heads, and Leif said what they were all thinking. "What point? She could have anything she wanted, she was awesome at everything. Why would she pour time and energy into this crapbox?"

"To prove to herself that she wasn't great at everything," I said.

Leif scoffed. "Well, that's dumb."

Gabrelle Allura looked at me closely, and I sensed that she was weighing my soul somehow, that her gaze understood more about me than I wanted it to. She lifted a purple-clad shoulder a fraction in a perfectly orchestrated movement that exuded grace. "Actually, I think your little project might be onto something."

Defensiveness coursed through me, and my hackles rose. "His little project?" My voice rose dangerously. "I am nobody's project."

Neela Flora acknowledged me with a nod of approval, wiping her dirty hands on her fae denim overalls. "Good." She looked at the others. "I like this one, let's keep her."

Leif let out a low, commanding growl, drawing the attention of everyone present. "Let's refocus," he urged, his gaze fixed on me. "What was your point, bumpkin?"

Princess Allura looked at me closely. "Bumpkin? That's cute."

Straightening my posture and summoning confidence, I projected my voice. These guys might be heirs to the throne, but they were fae, just like me. "I think your mother came here to remind herself of her weaknesses. To keep herself humble. To remember that she wasn't perfect."

Princess Flora nodded gravely. "And that only Growers are actually perfect."

Leif whacked his friend lightly across the nose as if she were a house dog instead of a princess. With a mischievous smile, he refocused his attention on me.

"Mom wasn't perfect," he said, as though he was just realizing that for the first time.

"And she made a damn good alpha anyway," I agreed.

.

Leif

My gaze kept returning to Mom's awful little garden, with the undersized vegetables and sickly soil. It was such a contrast from the magical gardens around. A reminder that she wasn't perfect.

"Is wolf boy still keeping you locked up in the dungeons?" Gabrelle asked.

Alara blanched and fidgeted with her fingers. "Oh, er, no, not anymore, Princess Allura."

The beauty queen sat elegantly on a riddleberry bush which caught her gracefully. "Oh, I think we're beyond the princessing and fawning, don't you? You may call me Gabrelle."

The bumpkin smiled, and soft sunlight caressed the curve of her cheek. "Really?"

Gabrelle adjusted her purple jumpsuit and crossed her legs. "Yes. I have a rule. After I have discussed a monarch's vagina with somebody, they may address me by my first name."

Alara laughed, a free and wild sound that made me smile. "That seems fair."

The breeze picked up, catching the tendrils of Alara's hair as they danced around her face and neck. She brushed them away from her eyes with one hand while Gabrelle and Neela continued to chat.

When Alara called Neela "Your Highness," the Floran Princess practically snarled. "Call me Neela. I hate that hierarchical crap." I could see why Ronan called his lover a tomcat—she definitely had a feral side.

I'd often wondered what Neela would be like in bed. Pretty wild, I bet. But now I only thought about Alara that way, which was probably tied up with anger about Mom dying and me suddenly becoming Alpha before I was ready. Waaaaay before I was ready—I only wanted to mess around and have fun, not save the damn realm from the Shadow Walkers.

But looking at my mom's plot of crappy land, I felt better about feeling unprepared. Like maybe Mom had felt the same way when she became Alpha, and she'd ended up doing a kickass job of it.

"Neela it is," Alara said with a smile that made her whole face glow. It also made my cock twitch, and not because I wanted to punish her, but for some other reason I couldn't figure out.

Maybe my mojo was coming back.

I smirked. "Alara hates that 'hierarchy crap' too, Neela, so you're in good company."

Gabrelle moved her head slightly, an indicator of interest in the conversation. "Is that so? A wolf who fights the hierarchy? How uncommon."

Neela winked at the bumpkin. "When I'm first-ranked queen," she ignored my scoff and Gabrelle's eye-roll, "I'll take you on as an advisor, and we'll bring down the Man."

"Babe, you'll be the Man," I told her. "But if you need to go down on anyone, I'll volunteer."

Neela waved me away, flicking dirt from her hands dismissively. "Bring down, not go down," she clarified with a wry smile. "Get your head out of the bed, mutt."

I grinned. It felt good to relax. Like my old self was emerging from the shitstorm. Perhaps, just perhaps, I could find a way to strike a balance between my responsibilities as an alpha, an heir, and a friend. I fished a tennis ball out of my pocket and started playing with it, squeezing it between my fists, then tossing it in a low arc from hand to hand.

Neela trailed her finger along the tops of some azaleas, and they pulled toward her as though drawn by some invisible force. I supposed they were, since she was a Grower and had unknowable connections with every plant around her. She certainly looked the part in her fae denim overalls. "I'd better get going. Liz has promised to find the most outrageous and ridiculous frock in the realm for me to wear to the party tonight."

"What party? Dude, is there a party I haven't been invited to?" I asked. The ball felt so light and right in my hands, drawing perfect arcs through the air.

Neela withdrew her hand from the azaleas, and they wilted in displeasure. "Tonight is the pre-Ascension party, Leif. Not only are you invited, but you are expected. If you don't turn up, it will be considered a snub against every other realm, so you'd better be there." She turned to Alara. "Make sure he comes."

I let the tennis ball fall to the grass, not bothering to catch it. "I don't have time for parties. I'm the al—"

"The alpha of alphas, we know," Neela said with a dismissive wave of her hand, which made Alara's eyebrows shoot upward. "You're also the heir to the Caro throne and one of the five future monarchs of the realm. You know very well that the representatives of the other realms are visiting for our

Ascension rite, and it would be discourteous if you didn't greet them."

I scowled and folded my arms across my bare chest. "Discourteous? I think I'll be able to live with myself." I nodded to Alara. "Let's go."

"Look, buddy," Neela said, "I'm not exactly into all this diplomacy shit. But apparently, it's the best way to stop all the fae wars that kept happening centuries ago. Plus, I *am* into rockstar parties and getting drunk, so, you know, it's not all bad."

How could I get these princesses to understand that I had more on my plate than just picking a killer outfit for an Ascension party? I opened my mouth to speak, but the beauty queen got there first.

Gabrelle looked up at me through her lashes, then rose gracefully to her feet with a gentle push from the riddleberry bush. Her purple jumpsuit fell into exactly the right position without needing any adjustment. "Leif, it's just one night. You're coming."

I sighed. There was something so damn persuasive about Gabrelle, something to do with how closely linked our Houses were—the house of beauty had a lot of influence over the house of sensuality.

"Sex," I said aloud, thinking about my House.

"That's my boy," Gabrelle said without missing a beat. "I'll see you there at seven. Don't be late."

I followed the swish of her ass as she walked away. "Where is it?"

"At the Temple of the Briar."

Alara and I exchanged a glance, the anticipation quickening my heartbeat. I'd only heard one person mention the Temple of the Briar—that crazy shifter from Sylverclyff. When we'd asked how to kill the Shadow Walkers, she'd muttered about the bears and the woondah and the Temple of the Briar. I'd thought she was out of her mind, but if this Briar place was real, maybe there was some truth in her wild ramblings.

Alara stepped forward, shoving the too-long sleeves of my workshirt up her forearms. "I'll make sure Leif is there."

As always, the bumpkin's boldness stirred something inside me. Usually, it was just something in my pants, but the warmth felt more diffuse this time.

Still, I was her alpha, so I had to take control. "I am not a cub, Alara. I don't need a babysitter," I growled.

The three females ignored me, and Gabrelle looked Alara up and down. "You can't wear that."

My shifter was half-naked in just one of my T-shirts. She patted down her hips and thighs like she was hoping her clothes would turn into a dress. "Oh, well..."

"Come with me," the beauty queen said. "I'll have a Dresser fix you up. The wolf doesn't keep skilled Dressers on staff."

"No," I agreed. "I prefer my pack to be naked."

Neela snorted a laugh and held out a hand for Alara to take. The three females walked before me, winding through the magical garden, diving through the thick foliage, and into the forest.

I watched them go. The slight form of Neela in her gardener's overalls, with all her wiry strength and determination, and her spiky blue hair; the alluring beauty of Gabrelle in that purple jumpsuit, who was born to attract the gaze of every fae she met, with her perfect curves and swishing ass.

But I couldn't drag my eyes from Alara's form, the way her hips swayed with every step, and how the fabric of my T-shirt clung to her curves and exposed her shapely legs. Her hair fell in waves around her shoulders like flames, a reflection of her fiery nature and independence. Even beside the princess of beauty, she shone like a star.

Alara

Gabrelle Allura wasn't kidding about lending me a gown. I was wearing the most beautiful dress I'd ever seen, worthy of a fae princess. It was a deep sapphire blue, glittering like stars on a clear night. Silver embroidered patterns adorned the bodice and skirt, and it was cut in a low V at the neck.

"Isn't a bit low cut?" I asked, hitching the dress up at the front.

"Nonsense," Gabrelle said. "Your breasts are beautiful, and they should be celebrated."

"Maybe I'll throw them a party," I snorted. It wasn't an elegant sound, but nothing seemed graceful compared to the heir of House Allura.

The princess's mouth moved in a tiny smile. "Every gathering is an opportunity to celebrate your beauty, faeling. You've been sheltered in your tiny village for too long, I can see you have a lot to learn."

She was seated on a white chaise longue in the foyer of the Mirror Palace. The space was airy, with high ceilings and looming windows that stretched from one corner to the other. Mirrored mosaics lined the walls, each tiny piece crafted in intricate detail. Glowing orbs hung from the ceilings, casting their soft light across the floor like a shower of diamonds.

I released the neckline of my dress, letting it fall to its natural position, highlighting the curve of my cleavage. "Well, we didn't have Dressers in Sylverclyff. Or fashion. Or any fae apart from shifters, who really don't care about that stuff."

Gabrelle moved smoothly to her feet, and my eyes were glued to her form. She wore a dark brown dress that matched her skin tone and hugged her curves so closely that she looked naked. Jaw-droppingly, mesmerizingly naked. A large pink brooch on her chest held the dress together...how many fae would attempt to unclasp it during the party?

"You look amazing," I said.

She brushed me away. "Of course." She assessed me. "You look passable."

That was a massive compliment from the princess of beauty, who I was already figuring out was understated in her words and actions.

I went full smug, grinning from ear to ear. I even did a little spin, and the hem of my midnight gown fluttered around my knees, the little gemstones picking up the light from the foyer's glowing orbs. It felt like being caressed by a cloud.

Walking alongside the princess, we traversed a private moonway, its ethereal glow guiding our steps. Soon, we transitioned onto a bustling public path, leading us to the grand entrance of the Temple of the Briar. I took a deep breath and followed her inside.

It was overwhelming. Like, flick-me-and-I'll-fall-over intimidating.

From the outside, the temple was all crumbling stone and moss-covered brickwork, and it looked like it would fall over if you farted too loudly.

But inside was a dream. The temple was carpeted with moss

and wildflowers, cutting a yellow and blue garden path to the heart of the hall. The walls were draped with white and silver cloth, and the columns were wrapped in garlands of tiny silver and purple flowers.

Tinkling laughter, music, and conversation.

Gabrelle led me through the sea of fae, each more beautiful than the next. Some wore masks, adding an air of mystery to their already alluring presence. Others seemed to be glowing, their skin shimmering in the light of the orbs. I felt like a pebble among diamonds.

Gabrelle must have sensed my unease because she leaned in and whispered in my ear, "You belong here as much as anyone else. Much more than you belonged in that dungeon."

My jaw dropped. "You gave me the key so I could escape? You're my mystery savior!"

Gabrelle's eyes twinkled. "Perhaps," she said with a sly smile.

"Oh, Gaia, sorry I fucked up the escape. I went to see if my friend Selene was okay, and Leif caught me."

I wished Selene was at the party. She would have loved checking out all the dolled-up fae in their fancy frocks and bringing them down a peg or two.

"Caught by the big, bad wolf," Leif said as he grabbed my waist from behind, pulling me close before twirling me around.

His tailored silver suit fit his athletic physique perfectly, glistening in the temple like a beacon.

His eyes were hooded with desire as he licked me with his gaze. "You look fucking gorgeous, bumpkin."

Desire swept through me like a raging wildfire—my pulse raced, and my pussy throbbed with need. "Hardly. Not compared to Gabrelle."

Leif didn't even glance toward the beauty heir. "I can't even see her, babe."

That was the first time he'd called me babe, and I shivered in delight, hoping he didn't pick up on my reaction. I knew he called his friends that, and I wasn't excited by the intimacy of the word but by its normalness. It was a sign that Leif was relaxing.

"I'm so glad you decided to come tonight. Jet will be able to take care of things back at the den," I said.

"You can be very convincing," he said in a gravelly voice. "Besides, this is a good opportunity to poke around the back rooms of the temple and see if anything sticks out."

I snorted. "Yeah. Hopefully, we'll find a sign with an arrow that says 'Shadow Walker poison here.'"

Leif threw back his head and laughed, and it was such a delightful and contagious joy that I joined in, and so did a few nearby fae. If I thought my alpha was powerful when he was dominating me, he was even more powerful as a star that lit the whole room.

"Here, catch!" A loud voice called from across the room.

Out of nowhere, Leif snuck up a hand and snatched a tennis ball from midair with a massive grin. "Can't get one past me, Colzan. I'm the ball king."

A fae sauntered closer. I assumed he was Colzan Blunt. As in the heir to the throne in the Realm of Ourea, the mountainous region in the West, as far from my home as it was possible to get and still stay within the borders of Arathay. Another prince.

He had vibrant blue hair, tanned skin and a square jaw, but his most noticeable trait was his mischievous, cheeky smirk.

Leif rocketed the ball at Colzan and got him square in the

chest. The mountain prince ooffed out a breath and grinned. "OK, fair play. But I'll catch you out one day."

Leif turned at a call from across the room, and Colzan took the opportunity to peg the ball at the side of his head, but a wolf shifter's senses were unbeatable, and my alpha snatched the ball out of the air before it whacked his ear. I'd never been more proud to be a wolf.

Leif feinted up high, then threw the ball at Colzan's groin, and the Prince of Ourea doubled over in pain.

"You've got a very short memory, Blunt," Leif said, grinning. "But I'm happy to teach you over and over until you get it. I'm the ball king."

These two clearly had some history with the tennis ball thing. I could almost picture them trying to catch each other out every time they met up—probably at these fancy parties. And I knew for a fact that my alpha would win every single time. I grinned at him, and when he caught me looking, he returned it. He stalked closer, like I was a true deer, and snaked an arm around my waist, one of the most tender physical interactions we'd ever had. He pulled me close and whispered in my ear. "Tell me your safe word, Alara. I never want to hurt you more than you can take."

His arm around my waist was heavy and warm, and I melted against him. "What, so now you want it to be consensual?" I teased.

He pulled away, suddenly on edge. "Wasn't it always?" His demeanor changed from jocular to flat and earnest. "Oh, bumpkin, if I—"

I put a hand to his lips, his perfect soft lips. "No, I'm only joking. Well, I never consented to being locked in your filthy cells..." I let the pause lengthen because I didn't want to let him off too easy. "But I always wanted the sex."

Saying the word with my finger still pressed against his lips, surrounded by all these fae, sent electricity through my blood. I moved my fingers to the left and along the ridgeline of his jaw, then cupped his cheek. He never let me touch him. Ever. This was the most I ever had, and I wanted more.

"My safe word is…" I thought about how he made me feel. How his laughter lit up the entire temple. How he filled the world with light and safety and warmth. "Moonlight."

His jaw moved as he grinned. "Every wolf's favorite time of the day."

I smiled wickedly. "My favorite time of the night."

A severe-looking fae with straight gray hair pulled back into a tight bun tapped Leif on the shoulder. She wore a pristine white suit that was probably a bespoke design, but it hung from her bones like clean laundry. "Prince Caro, I am duty-bound to greet you. Please accept my congratulations on the upcoming Ascension of fae from your realm and my best wishes for their success and safety. Particularly the Ascending wolves from your pack, Luna and Grolenya."

The female's manner was very direct, but I couldn't fault her words.

"Thank you, Arrow. Let me introduce you to Alara Everly, one of my wolves."

It clicked. This must be Princess Arrow Sanctus of the Realm of Fen. She cast her sharp gray gaze on me. "Is she one of your top betas? Next in line for Alpha?"

"No," Leif said.

She turned her gaze away from me. "Then I don't need to meet her."

Ok, bitch, that was quite enough. I stuck out a hand and

said loudly, "Pleased to meet you, Arrow." I should call her Princess Sanctus, but I was not into the hierarchy at the best of times, and she was being rude, so I didn't owe her any politeness.

Arrow looked at Leif. "Your junior is addressing me. Please make her stop."

Leif tried to hold back his smirk but failed. "I can't make Alara do anything. Believe me, I've tried."

The stick-up-her-ass princess looked Leif up and down, slowly. "That makes you a poor alpha."

What a complete bitch. Leif already felt like a crappy alpha—even though he wasn't—he didn't need this uppity heir from Fen spouting her opinions. Heat grew inside me, and I bounced on my toes. "Just a minute, Arrow, I don't care who you are, but you don't talk about my alpha like that."

She finally deigned to look at me again. "Why are you defending him? He is controlling you poorly, and I merely pointed it out. Why do you let your emotions interfere with the truth?"

Gabrelle swanned in to the rescue, interjecting herself into our little circle as smoothly as if she'd always been there. "Arrow, how pleasant to see you."

The arrow-shaped and arrow-named princess looked at Gabrelle. "Princess Allura, I am duty bound to greet you, though calling it pleasant is unnecessary. Please accept my congratulations on the upcoming Ascension of fae from your realm and my best wishes for their success and safety. Particularly the Ascending fae from your House, Willia and Tomas."

Gabrelle nodded slightly. "Thank you. Would you like to join me and the other heirs for a drink?" She indicated a raised dais where Neela sat on a lounge with Prince Mentium, Prince Dionysus, Prince Colzan Blunt, and several fae I didn't recognize. Above the dais hung a magnificent tapestry depicting a Gilded Python wrapped around trees of gold. The snake was supposed to bring fortune and favor to those who were generous, so hopefully, it would rub off on the rich fae sitting beneath it. And to the Princess of Fen, if she wanted to join us for a drink.

As Princess Arrow followed Gabrelle's gaze, her expression remained unchanged. With an air of disinterest, she dismissed the invitation. "No, I wouldn't like that. Goodbye," she replied curtly and slowly drifted away.

I watched her departing back and exhaled. "Holy Gaia, she was charming."

Leif snorted. "A barrel of laughs. Honestly, she's the life of the party."

"Such a shame she couldn't stay and have a drink with us," I said.

Gabrelle said coolly, "If you think she's bad, you should meet her brother. Apparently, he is ten times worse."

I recoiled. "Does she have a brother? But she's heir to the throne of Fen. Aren't they worried about..." I lowered my voice to a whisper. "Gaia's curse?"

Gabrelle shrugged, and Leif said, "I know, right? That's what I'm always saying. One of those siblings is going to die for sure, and whenever I mention it, these assholes just shrug and look all superior."

Gabrelle gave him a withering stare.

"Exactly!" he said. "Just like that."

The beauty queen took one step toward the dais, then turned and looked over her perfect brown shoulder. "I assume you two will join us for a drink? D assures me that tonight's vintage of white wine is one of his best."

Leif snatches up my hand. "No, we have to go exploring in the ruins first."

Gabrelle looks between us. "Fine. But when you're finished screwing, come back to the party. I don't want Alara's look wasted in filthy corridors when it should be admired by everyone."

Leif's grip tightened around my hand possessively. "She gets enough admiring from me."

"Is that a spark of jealousy, wolf boy?" Gabrelle asked with a flicker of curiosity behind her pink eyes. "Isn't that a sign of a mating bond?"

She was right, actually. A mating bond between two wolves usually started with unusual jealousy. Any jealousy was unusual, so even a tiny amount could indicate a bond. Mates weren't monogamous, but they had all sorts of agreements with each other that made their sex lives complicated, and I didn't want any part of that.

But I also didn't want Leif screwing anybody else.

"Wishful thinking, beauty queen," Leif said with a grin. "You just want me to stop propositioning you for sex." He tugged me away, and my belly soured and squirmed at the idea of him licking Gabrelle's perfect curves and thrusting his cock inside her.

Would he let her touch his body?

Leif

I ducked aside to swipe us a couple of drinks while Alara wandered over to the corridor that led to the main part of the temple. When I joined her, she was irritated and having words with a bouncer who wouldn't let her through.

His demeanor did a one-eighty when he saw me, and he bowed his head. "Good evening, Prince Caro."

"What's going on here?" I asked.

Alara curled her hands into fists. "This idiot won't let me through."

The bouncer looked exasperated. "Like I told you, nobody's allowed into the back part of the temple."

"Well, make an exception for me." She stamped a midnight blue heel.

The large male shook his head. "I'm sorry, King Dionysus's orders. I can't make any exceptions."

I looked between the muscled male and the fiery female, loving her discomfort. Finally, she'd found a situation she couldn't talk her way out of.

But time was of the essence, so I stepped in. "She's with me," I said smoothly.

The bouncer darted aside. "Oh, sorry, prince, I didn't realize." The poor male almost bent over and licked my boots, but I let him off and breezed past him with Alara at my side.

As we ventured beyond the ornate decorations, the temple revealed its true state: crumbling stone and debris. Alara and I carefully made our way along the ancient corridor, stepping over fallen remnants.

"Is it safe here?" Alara asked, ducking around a fallen rock.

"You're never safe with me," I growled. At the flirty smile she tossed me over her shoulder, my cock jumped.

She looked so good in that dress. So fucking good. Like a goddess of the night, swathed in deep blue and sparkling with stars. Her boobs were out and proud in a super low-cut V, and I could barely tear my gaze away from them. Her hair was piled on her head using some kind of anti-gravity magic and dotted with sapphires that matched her gown.

"Never fucking safe," I said.

We crept through the dark hallway of the aged temple, navigating around fallen pillars and cracked limestone tiles. The air was thick and musty, and centuries-old dust coated every surface in a fine sheen.

I summoned a globe of light, and we shuffled ever deeper within the temple's walls. Around a corner, we came to an alcove illuminated by the faint glimmer of moonlight that filtered through a crack above. There lay a forgotten book buried beneath layers of dust and debris. Its leather-bound cover was stained and cracked, but it seemed intact.

Dust came away under my finger as I revealed the title, but it was in an ancient language I couldn't read.

"Shit," I said.

"A Secret History of the Shadow Isles," Alara read.

I turned to her. "You can read this?"

She lifted a shoulder. "I'm not just a country bumpkin, you

know."

I leaned down and kissed the skin on her shoulder, inhaling her citrus scent. "I never said 'just.'"

She gingerly flipped open the book and read haltingly, her lips mouthing the words as she grappled for understanding. "It's Eldralith," she told me, her eyes never leaving the page. "The ancient written language of Arathay."

"A written language?"

"Yeah," she nodded, her eyebrows knitting together. "It was never spoken aloud. It was only written and used to store the most important secrets of the fae world. I've been studying the language for years. That's why fishy—er, Ruben—called me word-girl. He always teased me about it."

"Why?"

"Because he liked ball sports and hunting and stuff," she sighed, looking away wistfully. "My pack doesn't exactly value literacy."

"No, I mean why did you study the dead language?"

Her lips slowly curved into a smile. "I've always been attracted to secrets." She looked at me with an amused glint in her eye. "I think that's why I'm so fascinated by you."

"Fascinated?" That was a powerful word, and I felt honored that she used it to describe me.

I'd been called many things. Powerful, sexy, sex-crazed—by my pack. Foolish, loyal, sex-crazed—by the heirs. Good at sports, fast, physical, good with a sword, strong...but never fascinating.

"Yes," she said matter-of-factly, then found an entry and flipped a few pages with an excited gleam in her glowing orange eyes. "The Birth of the Shadows," she read. "That sounds like what we're looking for, right?"

Watching her full lips move was mesmerizing, and I had to resist darting in and kissing her. I needed to focus. "Yes. Can you translate it for me?"

"Of course." She cleared her throat and then began reading.

In the realm of legends and whispers, a tale is told of the Shadow Walkers, ancient fae who emerged from the depths of darkness. Their origin is steeped in mystique, tracing back to a forgotten time when an arcane ritual gone awry birthed a cursed land known as the Shadow Isles.

Long ago, a coven of sorcerers sought to harness the potent energies of the Shadow Realm, a world bridging the boundaries of light and darkness. Fueled by ambition and blinded by their hunger for power, they conducted a forbidden ritual within a hidden temple, invoking incantations that tore open a sinister portal.

Yet their grasp on the dark arts was inadequate, and the ritual spiraled out of control. The unleashed energies consumed the coven, shattering their bodies and binding their essence to the newly formed Shadow Isles. Thus, the first Shadow Walkers were born, cursed to forever dwell in the realm they inadvertently forged.

Shrouded in perpetual twilight, the Shadow Isles became a cursed and desolate land where the boundaries between the living and the dead grew thin. The Shadow Walkers, now trapped in this ethereal realm, discovered the eerie gifts bestowed upon them. They could traverse the realms by stepping into and merging with the very shadows that danced along the land.

With each passing century, the Shadow Walkers honed their abilities, mastering the art of shadow manipulation and traversing between worlds undetected. They became skilled hunters, preying upon unsuspecting wanderers who dared to tread upon their forsaken domain. Consuming the souls of their victims, the Shadow Walkers found sustenance and eternal youth, their own life force forever entwined with the twisted magic of the Shadow Isles.

But their curse bore a sinister twist. The souls devoured by the Shadow Walkers were not extinguished but transformed, trapped in an undead state between life and death. These unfortunate souls became mindless puppets to the will of their captors.

And so, the Shadow Walkers, born from a cataclysmic ritual, haunted the shadowed depths of the realm they called home. Their existence was perpetuated by their insatiable hunger for souls, their mastery over shadows, and their macabre ability to twist the very fabric of life and death. They remained a nightmarish reminder of the consequences of delving too deeply into the realm of darkness, forever trapped within the eternal dusk of the Shadow Isles.

May Gaia curse whomsoever frees these monsters from their prison home.

"Fuck Gaia," I said. "That must have been a long time ago. I mean, the dead dude who wrote this book was going on about how ancient the Shadow Walkers were, so they must be really ancient. Like, really, really dead."

Alara nodded. "Yep. Super dead."

"Keep reading," I urged.

Suddenly, a deafening boom reverberated through the corridor, so I instinctively positioned myself between Alara and the source of the noise. All this talk of Shadow Walkers was creepy as fuck, so I summoned a brilliant globe of light to banish all shadows from the dim alcove.

Alara's eyes widened, and a tang of fear washed off her. "Was that...?" she whispered.

I met her gaze, my expression grave. "I don't know," I replied grimly, my mind conjuring images of the Shadow Walkers that had attacked our den not too long ago. A chill ran through me as I power-walked back to the main section of the temple. "Make a light globe and stay close," I barked, clamping down on a primal urge to run in the opposite direction.

Alara followed close behind as I expanded my light globe so that we could find our way safely. As we approached the main temple, the music and laughter were replaced by shrill cries of terror and wet gurgles of pain. The air was thick with fear and death. We held our breath as a dark figure glided past us, dragging off a helpless faerie by her wings before disappearing into the night.

My stomach churned at the sight, and I almost threw up. We had no choice but to carry on into the chaotic scene inside the grand hall.

The lights had been extinguished in an orchestrated attack, and most guests were screaming in terror, running around half-blind. Dark silhouettes slithered through the blackness like greasy oil, and an acrid scent of blood hung heavily in the air.

Pockets of fae tightly huddled together in misery, using their summoning magic to create small light sources to protect against the darkness. Outside these feeble barriers, the remaining fae frantically cast spells at any shadow creatures they saw or heard near them, but with no effect.

The soft perfumes of the well-dressed fae were mingled with the salty-iron stench of blood.

"Summon globes of light," I roared, but my voice couldn't be heard above the mayhem.

A Shadow Walker attacked a winged faerie on my left, pouncing and dragging her out of the sky. She lay on the ground, frozen, as still as a corpse, but her eyes locked on mine in panic.

I moved toward her instinctively, determined to rescue her, casting spell after spell at the shadow beast, but nothing stuck.

Eventually, blood oozed out of slashes on her small body, and the dark shadow slid away, sated.

Amidst the chaos and carnage, Alara's voice broke through, a calm and gentle presence beside me. "They're moving on from shifters." My wolf roared inside my head, and the pressure of her weight against my arm was the only thing that kept me grounded and stopped me from going feral and leaping on the nearest Shadow Walker with my fangs bared.

I hardened myself against my fear, stood tall, and shouted desperately for everyone else to summon globes of light to fight back against these damn Shadow Walkers.

And I knew that shifting wasn't the answer. My pack had already paid a heavy price, learning that lesson the hard way.

Suddenly, a male at my side shifted into a majestic lion, his black tuxedo ripping into tatters in mid-leap as he pounced. The chaos intensified as fae around us screamed and scattered in every direction, some resorting to shifting into their animal forms in a desperate attempt to escape.

"No! Don't shift! Light! Summon light."

Too late.

The dark shape simply slinked around the lion like oil,

coating its golden fur in black until it slumped lifelessly to the ground.

"Summon light," I roared again and saw the other heirs barking orders, too, bathed in their own magical light.

Ronan and I leaped into action, shouting commands as we summoned light with every ounce of energy we possessed. Neela grabbed several sap-rich plants and ignited them, creating makeshift torches. Gabrelle and Dion moved through the panicked crowd, pushing their streaks

of light into the darkest corners and trying to protect as many fae as possible.

But most of the fae didn't understand what was happening—they had never encountered Shadow Walkers before, and many still believed them to be nothing more than a myth. We worked desperately to keep them safe even as they screamed in terror.

But this wasn't enough—we were still outnumbered, and most fae didn't even know how to defend themselves against Shadow Walkers.

My every nerve felt like it was wired with electricity, screaming desperately at me to fight against the looming threat. But no matter how much I wanted to take action, I was utterly helpless in the face of this evil. Fear gripped me, its icy claws sinking deep into my veins, sending shivers of terror coursing through my body.

Alara

I was paralyzed with fear in the middle of the battle. Leif had barked at me to never let my light go out and then bounded into the darkness, leaving me alone.

As the chaos of battle surrounded me, one of Leif's wolves, Fenrys, materialized at my side. He had been slashed open from cheek to shoulder, adding to the sickening coppery smell in the air, and his eyes were wide with terror. "Go and protect the heirs from the other realms," he said urgently. "If any of them die, it will start a war."

My stomach dropped. "I can't—"

"You're the only War wielder we have," he snapped. "Go now!" Then he disappeared back into the fray.

Oh, crap. Everyone still assumed I had War magic based on my association with Leif—an assumption I'd done nothing to correct. I still slept and ate with Leif's personal guards. In fact, I'd loved the idea of shifters looking at me with fear and respect, so I'd let them keep believing my lie.

My chest tightened. I might be unable to use War magic, but I could summon light to protect the visiting heirs.

Spinning on my heel, I frantically searched for anyone who might be an heir. Names and faces flashed through my mind as I ran through the chaos, desperately trying to find them before it was too late.

Colzan Blunt, the Prince of Ourea, was in the central dais near Ronan and Neela; they must have told him to summon light because he was bathed in a wide yellow glow.

I found Bastian and Bree Athar, the King and Queen of Caprice, standing at the temple doors, ushering fae outside to safety. They, too, were in a warm pool of light, a shield that the king must have summoned to protect himself and his mortal queen.

King Mala Draylar from the Unseelie Realm of Dust hadn't sent any representatives to the soiree, and neither had the Dread King of Brume. So that left Princess Arrow Sanctus from Fen.

With growing panic, I darted through the shadows, safe in my pool of light, until I found Arrow.

She was near the back of the room, backed up against a pillar and surrounded by Shadow Walkers. Arrow bravely fought off the creatures with a long ceremonial blade, but it had little impact on them.

Desperate, I shouted, "Summon light!" as I strained to reach her in time. Arrow screamed in pain as one of the creatures slashed at her arm with a dark claw before finally overcoming her, coating her body in shadow, and leaving her slumped against the wall. I watched in horror as she slowly sank to the ground, lifeless eyes staring into nothingness, and two of the nightmare creatures slunk around her body, feasting on her soul.

Slowly, the madness muted as more and more fae summoned light until the whole room was bright and the shadows had been banished.

The fae around me had been screaming in terror throughout

this conflict, but all fell silent when they saw the bodies strewn around the temple's stone floor. Sobs rang through the space, and Arrow's name was whispered from every corner of that room until it eventually reached my lips too.

One by one, the dead bodies of fallen fae started to twitch and rise, their colorful eyes turned milky white and their faces blank. The stench of death was thick in the air as they stumbled toward us. Many looked wounded and ravaged, but one female looked pristine in a floor-length turquoise gown with cutouts over the hips and her blue hair tied back in a bun. She lurched toward me, and I backed away.

Seeing your friends and loved ones rise against you was a savage kind of hell. But slicing off their heads and salting their lifeless bodies was even worse.

But this, at least, we could deal with.

We raised our swords and swung them with dull thuds as we chopped off the heads of our once-vibrant friends. I helped to scatter salt over their bodies, watching silently as the tears streaking down my face mixed with the remnants of this brutal ritual. With each headless body, a wave of guilt crashed over me.

Arrow was brave and courageous, willing to fight for her beliefs. Now she was gone, her life snuffed out by my own inaction. If only I hadn't lied about being able to wield War; if only I had actually been Ascended... all these 'if onlys' reverberated through my mind, and guilt surged through my veins.

"Enough," whispered Fenrys into my ear. He had appeared beside me without a sound and placed his hand on my shoulder. "It's over."

Reluctantly, I trailed after him, stepping out of the temple into a scene of grieving fae milling about, seeking solace and casting sorrowful gazes at the entrance. The sun was rising, dispelling the darkness once and for all, but an icy rain began to fall.

I scanned the crowd, frantically searching for Leif. I needed to know he was okay, that he had survived the battle.

I needed him to tell me everything would be okay and that the guilt of Arrow's death wasn't mine alone to bear.

Everywhere I looked was a blur. Finally, I spotted him and, without thinking, sprinted across the grass and threw myself into his soaking wet arms.

He pushed me away. "Not now," he said with a sternness that chilled me to the core.

Guilt slammed into me. "Do you blame me for Arrow's death?"

He narrowed his eyes. "You told me to leave the pack under Jet's care. You convinced me to take the night off and party with my friends. You made me believe that everything would be alright."

The accusation in his voice made my eyes prick with tears."But—"

"But nothing, Alara. I can't talk to you right now."

"But—"

"But nothing," he shouted.

Desperation consumed me as he turned to leave, and I couldn't bear the thought of him slipping away. Clutching onto his arm, I pleaded, "Don't go." But he continued walking. "I'm sorry," I begged. "Punish me."

I didn't mean it sexually. I just wanted to keep him in the conversation, to keep him near, because if he left me now, I would fall apart.

He whirled around, his face pure rage and his silver hair slick with rain and sweat. "Fae under my protection have just been fucking killed, and you want to have sex?"

My throat dried up like sandpaper, every word of protest dying. I could feel the heat radiating from his body, see the anger flaring up in his eyes—and then there was nothing but the sound of my racing heart. "I need you. I—"

He stepped closer. "Get out of here." His voice was low and dangerous.

Without another thought, I broke into a run. Fear clung to my steps as I ran away from him, my gaze fixated on the path ahead, never daring to look back.

I would have run all the way back to the den if I could have, but I didn't have the energy. I was exhausted, not just physically but also mentally and emotionally.

I just wanted to be alone. I wanted to be in my bed, with the covers over my head, until I could breathe again.

I darted between the trees, trying to shield myself from the lashing rain and the forest's icy fingers.

By the time I reached the den, I was shaking with cold. Water dripped from my drenched sapphire dress, leaving a trail of puddles with every weary step.

I stepped cautiously into the den, eyes scanning for signs of destruction. The foyer was untouched—the low leather chairs still arranged around thick fur rugs, and the black marble floors still spotless—and I breathed a sigh of relief that the Shadow Walkers hadn't made their way here as well.

My steps were slow and heavy as I crept upstairs. Every inch of me tensed, hoping like hell the bedroom would be empty of fae. No such luck.

Selene rushed over to me as soon as she saw me. "You look

awful, hon! What happened to you? Did that alpha fucker make you walk home in the rain?"

Hot tears ran down my cheeks, and I couldn't talk. She pulled me gently to the bathroom and ran a hot shower, then she peeled my sodden clothes off me and kept me company while I washed away the death and horror with steam.

"Can you tell me what happened, honey?" she asked gently while she wrapped me in a soft white towel.

"The Shadow Walkers attacked. A bunch of fae died. Including Princess Arrow Sanctus from Fen."

"Oh, fuck."

I forced myself to meet my best friend's gaze. "It was my fault, Selene. Fenrys thought I had War, and he tasked me with protecting Arrow and, and, I couldn't."

"It wasn't your fault, hon," Selene said. "Leif knows you don't wield War. If Arrow's death is on anyone, it's on him. He's the alpha." She pulled me close, and I rested my chin on her shoulder, sagging against her.

I shook my head, nudging her cheek with my wet hair and talking into her powder-blue hair. "No, I let everyone believe I was Ascended. I should have told them, then Fenrys would have sent someone else to protect her. Or gone himself. I just wanted everyone to respect me, so I kept up the fucking lie."

I felt apart on Selene's shoulder, sagging so heavily she had to support both our weights. "Where's Leif now?" she asked.

"He's still at the temple. I only left because...he sent me away." The words make me shatter even harder, like a razor-thin mirror smashing over an iron spike. "He couldn't even fucking look at me, Selene. He hates me."

We both knew what my friend was thinking...that I was supposed to hate him too.

But I didn't, not anymore. I hadn't despised him in a long time. Now, I only hated myself.

Selene guided me to the bed and held up the blankets while I crawled under them. "I can't say anything about Leif because I don't know what the hell he's thinking, but the only thing you should feel fucking guilty about is not calling him out again for being an asshole." She shook her head. "He's treated you like crap since the moment he saw you. If he can't even look at you without wanting to rip your head off your shoulders, he's not worth a second of your time. That's not love, hon. You deserve someone who'll accept you for the glorious Unascended female you are, who won't make you feel like shit all the time."

I chuckled hollowly. "Who said anything about love? He's never claimed to feel anything about me except contempt."

She tucked the blanket around me. "Well, like I said, that's not good enough. You deserve better."

I closed my eyes and tried to believe her. I really fucking tried. But my mind kept returning to the look in Arrow's eyes the instant they'd sprung open after death, how the stern gray color was replaced by milky white. That was on me.

I didn't deserve better than Leif's contempt. I didn't even deserve that.

Leif

My fists clenched tight with rage, and my heart thumped like a war drum against my ribcage. How could I have been so stupid to let Alara manipulate me? Betrayal surged through me, burning like fire in my veins, as I realized I'd dropped my guard for someone undeserving of my trust. Someone who didn't understand the first thing about ruling.

As soon as I'd let my guard down, the Shadow Walkers had attacked. I should have been home monitoring the situation, taking reports from my patrols, and I could have picked up on the attack and prevented it. My negligence had cost me, allowing the Walkers to launch a devastating attack without warning.

I should have bathed the temple in light. I should have known better. Instead, I'd let Alara distract me from what was important.

My den was spared from the attack, thank Gaia. So I stuck around at the temple and supervised the cleanup, forcing myself to watch as the bodies were salted and burned. The crackling and popping of the burning bodies like sizzling bacon fat sent a chill down my spine. Maybe I would never get the stench of charred flesh out of my hair.

Gabrelle attempted to start a conversation, but I cut her

off tersely. "Not now," I snapped before turning away. All I wanted to do was fucking destroy something. Alara, mostly.

Neela looked at me with pity in her sky-blue eyes, and I bared my teeth so forcefully that she recoiled. Ronan lunged forward, positioning himself between us, his lips pulled back to reveal a terrifying snarl. "Get a hold of yourself, Leif," he ordered. I supposed I should be glad she hadn't brought her pet snuffle tuffs, or I'd be dead by now.

Hot anger boiled inside me, but I took a deep breath and released it slowly. I had to get out of there before I destroyed the remaining tatters of my friendships.

I released my inner wolf, letting it shred my clothes. I howled at the sky and then bounded into the forest. My sharp claws carved through the fallen leaves on the forest floor as I sprinted effortlessly through the misty pines, caring little for obstacles as I took the long way home.

Usually, when I stepped inside the comforting stone den, my wariness disappeared, but not today. I was fucking pissed at Alara. And myself.

I pulled on a pair of sweatpants from the stash near the front door. Before I knew it, I was headed upstairs and pushing open the door to the betas' bedroom. It looked disheveled, sheets and blankets twisted all over the four massive mattresses and clothes flung on the floor. The betas must have had a good time last night.

Alara was tucked in her corner under the blankets, her chest rising and falling slowly. Her friend, Selene, with the blue hair and long legs, was sitting beside her reading a book, watching over her.

Selene looked up at me, then lowered her eyes immediately. My silver hair was mussed, and I probably stank of blood and salt and fury, so she was right to be afraid of me.

I stalked closer, and Alara woke up, somehow sensing my presence.

She rolled over and opened her eyes, locking her gaze onto mine. She blinked up at me slowly, her orange eyes not dropping from mine. But I didn't find it arousing, just fucking disrespectful.

Alara sat up, pulling the blanket around her chin and leaning against the stone wall. "Can we talk, Leif?"

My hands were balled into fists, my jaw clenched as she spoke. And when she used my first name instead of calling me Alpha, all I could do was grit my teeth and fight the urge to scream.

"I'm not here to talk. I'm here to fuck. I'm here to punish you."

Alara's jaw twitched, and I could tell I'd surprised her. If that thick blanket wasn't covering her pussy, I was sure I'd be able to smell her arousal. But I wasn't here to punish her like that.

I turned slowly to Selene, and from the corner of my eye, I watched the desire slip from Alara's face and turn to anger. "Selene," I barked, "on your feet."

The powder-blue-haired female complied immediately, standing before me with her head lowered in perfect submission to her alpha. "I'm going to take you down to the dungeon, Selene, and then I will punish you for your friend's mistakes. I'm going to fuck you brutally. Then I'll let you run your hands all over my body and do whatever you want to me."

I knew I was hurting Alara. I knew she wanted to splay her fingers over my body and explore every inch of my skin. I burned for it, too, I longed to feel her hands on my muscles.

But we both deserved punishment tonight, real fucking punishment, not the pleasure of each others' bodies. So I took her friend instead.

I stalked toward Selene, slowly grinding my teeth together as I advanced. The air around us became heavy and cold. When I was mere inches away from her ear, I snarled, "Go." My voice echoed off the walls like thunder, lingering in the dead silence that followed.

With an apologetic glance at her friend but not even a peep of disrespect to me, Selene walked out of the room and downstairs.

I followed, trying to work up an appetite for the beautiful female, watching her ass sway and the elegant tilt of her head. But the truth was, I hadn't worked up energy for anyone except Alara in weeks. That country bumpkin had gotten far too deep inside my head, and it was time to evict her.

Selene's footsteps echoed off the damp stone walls as she descended into the depths of the playroom. She paused just inside, taking in the stale air and hovering globes of light that fluttered, casting a dim light over the cramped space. Her shoulders slumped, her fear growing like an unwelcome houseguest.

Her submissiveness annoyed me instead of turning me on like it would have a few months ago. Fuck, that Alara female really had gotten to me.

"Move to the wall," I barked.

Selene walked to the stone wall and stood right beneath a studded collar. I approached her slowly, waiting for my cock to respond. It didn't.

A shiver ran across her skin, but I didn't feel like touching her, so I said, "Strip." I watched as she removed her shirt, then wriggled out of her pants, but my body didn't respond.

What the fuck was going on? My thoughts lingered on Alara, even as this beautiful shifter revealed more and more of her skin.

I snapped the collar around Selene's pale neck, trying not to touch her skin. She was objectively sexy, and she'd caught my eye when she first turned up at the den, but I couldn't concentrate on her now. All I could think about was Alara.

My cock didn't respond to Selene, even as I paddled her white ass, and her whole body jiggled. As she quivered in pain and anticipation, my guilt just grew. I kept thinking about how much I had fucked up. How I should have kept my mind on being an alpha. How I should have focused on the Shadow Walkers instead of how hot Alara looked in that dress. With my fists tightly balled, I felt nothing but impotent rage.

"Call me Alpha," I snarled.

"Yes, Alpha."

Nothing. Zero cock action. Usually, my pack calling me Alpha made me hard as steel, but my dick had forgotten how to rise. I had to try again.

"Tell me what you want me to do to you, Selene."

"Fuck me, Alpha," she said. I paddled her again, and her ass wobbled. She held in a moan, and I could smell the musk wafting from her pussy, but my cock didn't even twitch.

"More," I growled.

"Please, Alpha, fuck me hard. Spear me with your cock. Make me scream. Let me come all over you, Alpha. Please."

Selene whimpered and moaned and pleaded.

Still nothing.

With a firm stroke, I landed the paddle on her thigh, watching her reaction from side on. Her breasts jumped, and her leg quivered, and her breathing reached a full pant.

"Please, Alpha," Selene begged, her voice wavering. "Fuck me, claim me. I want your cock."

I knew she wasn't lying—her arousal filled the dungeon with a heady musk that should have me salivating on the stone floor.

"Please," she moaned.

What the fuck? No matter how desperately Selene begged, I couldn't get hard. When she tried again, this time in a softer voice, I almost laughed out loud.

"Please, Alpha," Selene said. "Fuck me, claim me. I want your cock."

This time I couldn't stop the laughter. What kind of a fucking alpha couldn't get hard after hearing that?

After my eerie laughter died out, Selene spoke timidly. "Did I do something wrong? I'm sorry."

"Don't apologize," I snarled.

Selene's powder-blue eyes narrowed, and her nostrils flared. I could sense her anger growing, which reminded me of Alara's sass for a moment. Maybe I could fuck Selene after all.

But when I tried paddling her ass again, all I could think about was Alara's sweet pussy. Her hair. Her smile. Her fiery orange eyes. And the way she raised a sassy eyebrow when she wanted to call me out on my shit. I just couldn't focus on Selene.

I let go of the paddle.

"Please, Alpha. Please don't stop. Please."

I was no good for any of the shifters in my pack tonight. I couldn't even punish Selene and get hard. I was a fucking failure.

With a heavy sigh, I stepped away from Selene, still collared to the wall. She was trembling, her eyes wide and pleading with me to come back to her, but I could not. I had already failed once tonight, and I wasn't about to fail again. There was too much guilt churning in my gut for that.

I stormed out of the dungeon and took the stairs three-by-three. I went outside into the bright sunshine, and the weight of my failure pressed down on me like an anvil. The icy rain had stopped, but the glorious day just made me feel worse.

I shifted, destroying another pair of sweatpants. So much for the moderation and care my Mom was always trying to instill in me. My paws moved faster and faster as I ran away from it all—away from the sexy shifter in the dungeon who wanted me, away from the broken shifter in the bedroom who I'd wounded, away from the guilt that was threatening to swallow me whole.

But no matter how fast I ran or how far I got, the guilt followed close behind me like a dark cloud of shame. It hung on my shoulders, reminding me of what kind of Alpha I was—an inadequate one too distracted by his desires to be a true leader and protector of his pack. Let alone a future king of the entire damn realm.

Alara

Red-hot anger bubbled inside me as I watched Leif take Selene away, out of the betas' bedroom and into the dim corridor. And then, I knew, down to his playroom.

Selene. He fucking took Selene. He was supposed to take me.

The familiar heat of jealousy flooded my veins, and I blinked back tears as I imagined what they were doing downstairs, her naked and vulnerable and him torturing her with pleasure while his giant cock filled the space between them.

All the ways he would be dominating her and making her squirm.

I could almost hear the clanking of chains and the deep rumble of Leif's voice as he instructed her on what to do. His deep, authoritative tone would intoxicate her, and I knew she wouldn't stand a chance against his will. And then I thought about how she must feel—the sensation of his fingers over her skin, exploring each curve and crevice, igniting a fire within her that only he could feed.

His lips would explore every inch of her body—suckling on her nipples before dipping lower to taste between her legs while his strong hands explored her curves. She'd moan in pleasure as he pressed into her with more force than she was used to—penetrating deeper and deeper until they both reached their peak. His breathing would become ragged as he pushed harder against her and moaned into the crook of her neck.

The idea of Leif taking Selene into his dungeon felt like a violation, like I was being replaced and forgotten. But I couldn't deny the spark of desire in my chest when I thought about what might be happening down there, what kind of wild passion they were exploring together. Would she scream as he entered her? Pleasure from pain? Or would she whimper as his tongue caressed her most sensitive areas?

He'd told her she would be allowed to touch him. I'd never been permitted that luxury, and I knew he was doing it to punish me, letting her run her hands all over his velvet skin while mine were clutching this stiff damn blanket. He said it to punish me, but he would forget me as soon as he had her naked.

I ached to join them, to experience the same pleasure Selene was feeling, and yet at the same time, I felt a deep shame as if I was betraying my friend by wanting something that belonged to her.

It was her turn for our alpha. He wasn't mine alone, he belonged to all of us, and Selene had never had a moment's intimacy with him. So this time was hers. She deserved it.

But that didn't stop the spike of vile jealousy that snagged me whenever I thought of them. Wolves shouldn't feel jealous. Never, ever, ever, except for the first few months of a new mating bond.

I certainly couldn't be mated to Leif. He was the alpha, and I was just a nobody country bumpkin from the far distant coast who'd never even left my village until a few weeks ago. He was powerful and destined for greatness, and I just wanted to take care of my Pa.

Anyway, he obviously didn't feel the jealousy too, and mating bonds couldn't be one-sided. No, I was just fucked in the head. I'd always been a lousy wolf, excluded from the fun and games because I was a loner, not a pack animal. This was just more evidence of how I didn't belong.

The scent of leather and sex filled my senses, and a wave of arousal washed over me. No matter how hard I tried to push the thoughts of Leif and Selene away, they kept coming back.

"Fuck it," I muttered, flinging aside the blanket and getting out of bed. No matter how exhausted I was after a night of such ecstasy and murderous misery, I wouldn't get back to sleep, not while Leif was screwing someone else.

I might as well turn my mind to something I could be useful at. Arrow was dead because I'd lied about being Ascended and wielding War, but I could help in other ways.

I lugged the ancient book onto my lap that I'd nabbed from the alcove in the temple. I'd already tried to decipher more information about the Shadow Walkers, but the section titled Defying Death, which I thought might have clues on how to defeat them, was encrypted. It seemed to be written in some form of Eldralith, but I was missing the key to unlocking the code.

My fingers ran over the delicate parchment, and I allowed myself to be lost in the ancient language until a voice startled me back to reality.

"Leif? Are you there? Are you okay?" Gabrelle appeared in the doorway, her pink eyes blazing with concern and intensity.

I felt a twinge of jealousy as she called his name, but I quickly pushed it aside in favor of relief that someone else cared for him too.

"He isn't here." My voice sounded flat even to my own ears.

Gabrelle studied me, making me feel like a loose thread in tapestry class. "What did he do to you?"

I twisted my lips, trying for a smile. "So, I don't look as cool, calm, and collected as I hope."

She blinked slowly. "You look like you've been torn into seven pieces and sewn back together. Badly."

I snorted. "That's pretty accurate, actually."

"Anything I can do to help?"

Princess Allura had the reputation of being an ice-cold bitch, but I could see through it. Her heart was less frozen than she wanted everybody to believe.

Still, there was nothing she could do to make Leif forgive me. Or love me. Or even tolerate being in my presence.

I moved slightly, and the heavy book almost slid off my lap. I caught it gently before it hit the floor—it would probably crumble into dust, and then we'd really be screwed.

"I need help deciphering this." I held up the book.

Gabrelle tilted her head. "I can't help you with your homework, wolf girl. I meant, is there anything I can help you with regarding our mutual psychotic alpha friend."

He was the last thing I wanted to think about. Instead, I wanted to focus on the book, which might hold clues about how to defeat the Shadow Walkers. "It isn't homework. It's an ancient tome with information about our mutual zombie-making darkness friends."

The princess's lips curved slightly. "Well, why didn't you say so. I know just where to go for help."

She stared me down while I dressed, making me feel like she was studying every aspect of me. If I didn't know she was the fae who slipped me the key and was therefore on my side, I'd find her attention very unsettling.

No, even with her previous help, her gaze was still unsettling.

So I dressed quickly, pulled on some jeans and a yellow T-shirt, then followed her out the back and down a narrow, overgrown path in the forest behind the den, still well inside pack land.

"You know your way around here," I noted.

She gave me a withering look. "I'm a princess."

That didn't explain anything. Unless she was the Earth Goddess herself, I couldn't understand how she knew the pack lands better than I did.

The path ended at a moonway that was obscured by a scrubby bush with thorns. "This leads directly to the Sensory Quarter, which is a short stroll to the Rose Palace."

"Are we paying a social visit to Princess Flora?" The Rose Palace was Neela's home, and although I would love to check it out, I hoped there was more to Gabrelle's plan than a cup of tea and a scone.

She didn't bother to respond, so I kept my mouth shut and followed on her heels. Her exquisite heels, ankle strap pumps in a sheen that landed somewhere between cream and gold and perfectly accented her cream micro-shorts and long, brown legs.

"Did you go home and change? Like, your first thoughts after experiencing a party that turned into a slaughter were to shower and make yourself pretty?"

My old buddy jealousy was appearing again. Maybe if I looked like Gabrelle, Leif would want me.

"There's always time for beauty," the princess said dismissively. "Here we are."

We spilled out into the Sensory Quarter of Verda City, which was lined with busy storefronts and had a buzz of excitement.

"I thought this place would be dead after what happened last night."

Gabrelle sighed. "We minimized the damage. There's no point in alarming the common fae until we have a workable solution." She pointed out some fae lights being constructed. "We're doing everything we can to protect them. But if we let the fae become vigilantes, more will die."

That didn't sound right to me. Surely all fae had a right to know the truth about the danger they faced, whether they were common or not. I opened my mouth to speak, but Gabrelle got there first.

"We're here."

We stood outside a tall, wide hedge dotted with small white flowers that turned into lotus flowers as we stepped closer, broad white petals that faded to pink at the edges and would have been more at home in a lily pond.

"The lotus represents mystery and truth," Gabrelle remarked as the hedge opened before us.

"Um," I said eloquently, unsure of what we were discussing.

"The flowers change to represent the visitor's intent. Our intent is to pull truth from mystery, isn't it?"

"Cool."

She gave that asinine remark the look it deserved and plunged into the hedge, which was deep and opened up before us with each step. Finally, it revealed an exquisite palace that looked like a giant pink rose but somehow maintained its elegance.

"Cool," I said again and got another withering glance from the princess.

We stepped up to the entrance and climbed the stairs to the

front door, where a tall fae with gray eyes and an expression of bored detachment greeted us.

"Good morning, Princess Allura and companion," he said in a deep voice. "Please come through to the reception hall, and I will inform Princess Flora of your presence." He opened the doors with a flourish, revealing an impressive hall. Vases overflowed with flowers that seemed to grow across the parquetry floor, hitting us with a breathtaking floral scent.

Princess Flora appeared in a wide doorway. She wore black jeans and a slouchy sweater, looking very unroyal. She ran across the foyer, her bare feet silent on the parquetry floor, and pulled Gabrelle into a bear hug.

"Are you okay, Gab? Fuck, last night was awful." She released Gabrelle and put a hand on my shoulder. "How are you, honey? And how's Leif? He looked fucking awful this morning."

"Yeah," I nodded. "He's fucking awful."

Neela's lips set in a grim smile. "Come and have a cup of tea. Or coffee. Or whiskey."

Impatience churned in my gut, fueling the restless energy coursing through my veins. I couldn't handle a quiet conversation now. My inner wolf wanted to roar, and if I had any decent control over it, I'd shift and then run and run until I fell over. A tea party wasn't what I had in mind.

Thankfully, Gabrelle kept us on track. "We need to see the Library of Whispers," she said imperiously. "Alara needs help with a translation."

Neela accepted the swerve without a second's hesitation. "Sure thing. I'm still scared to death of that place, it's always giving me creepy visions. Once, it made me throw Herb out the second-floor window, but luckily he was okay."

245

"Herb?" I asked as we climbed the grand stairs.

"Herb is one of Neela's pet snuffle tuffs."

Adrenaline dumped into my bloodstream, and I looked around. "You have snuffle tuffs?" My voice rose in a shriek. "As pets?" Those things could kill you faster than a true bear and were twice as mean. They looked like large tufts of grass, but their grassy fur hid sharp teeth and a nasty nature.

"No," Neela said, laughing, "She's just joking."

I relaxed. Obviously the princess wouldn't keep a pair of the most fearsome creatures in Verda as pets. Or anywhere near her. My shoulders eased until Neela clarified.

"They're not pets. They're more like friends."

"Shit." My shoulders crept up again, and I scanned the fancy floors for rogue grass tufts but, thank Gaia, found none.

As we approached the library, a stern-looking fae stood at the entrance, opening the door for us with a formal nod. "I see you've hired some more staff," Gabrelle said.

Neela waited until the door closed behind us before answering. "Yep. It's so creepy having staff, but Ronan's parents insisted. We got a Magirus, of course, and a Healer." She lowered her voice. "Plus a couple of sinister weirdos whose only job is to creep me out, as far as I can tell."

Gabrelle chuckled, but I was distracted by the library. The whole room was shaped like a giant rose petal, gently curving to a point at the far end. Every wall was lined with shelves upon shelves, which housed thousands of books. Millions, maybe. Soft sunlight filtered in from large windows.

"When can I move in?" I muttered, wandering to the nearest shelf.

Neela laughed. "It's not as harmless as it looks. You couldn't pay me a million bucks to sleep the night in here."

"We don't have bucks in Arathay, darling. We aren't primitives," Gabrelle said.

I stepped forward, drawn to the books. "Where do I start?"

"Wherever feels right," Neela said.

"Very helpful," I muttered, and the Floran Princess chuckled.

Tracing my finger along the spines of the books, my gaze landed on one with a captivating gold title. Intrigued, I pulled it off the shelf, feeling a spark of electricity when I touched it.

It was filled with ancient text and faded illustrations, but I could make out enough to know that this was exactly what I had been looking for—a key to deciphering the code in the ancient book from the Temple of the Briar.

Clutching the book with white knuckles, I looked around for a desk where I could work. An inkpot with a quill called to me, and when I approached it, every book in the library began to whisper.

"Not here," Gabrelle said, speaking more abruptly than I'd ever heard her.

"Agreed," Neela said. "This place is creepy as fuck. Let's go to the Lakehouse. We won't have any dodgy-ass serving fae following us around. I need a swim anyway."

"It's their job to follow you," Gabrelle sighed. "And if you don't like it, you can instruct them otherwise."

The two princesses led me outside and across the lawn, then through a confusing purple hedge maze that ended in yet another private moonway. I could see the perks of being royalty. The moonway ended inside a huge tree, as a secret Floran passageway should, and from there, to a magnificent house nestled on the side of a vast lake.

It was modern and architectural and magnificent, balancing

on the edge of a crystal clear lake. It stood out from its surroundings but complemented them perfectly.

A garbled mess of syllables poured from me. "That...it's... wow...I...have?"

Neela grinned and side-bumped me with her shoulder. "It's impressive, huh? The best thing about it is how it grows and changes to suit our needs. It's grown me some perfect furniture that I just love."

As we walked closer, I saw that the house seemed to grow directly from the ground, part of nature itself. "Sweet Gaia," I exclaimed.

We walked in through a front door covered in soft fur, and Neela pushed through first. "All clear," she called out. "No pricks or dicks in sight."

I was worried Leif would be here, and even more worried he wouldn't. So hearing that no males were at the Lakehouse left me unsettled, but probably better able to focus on the translation.

"Do you want a glass of water?" Neela asked. "Double D's not here, so that's about all I can offer."

"Yes, thanks."

Gabrelle showed me to a study off one of the upstairs hallways. It had a vast window overlooking the lake, and bright sunlight illuminated the rich mahogany desk. "This will do," she said, and I agreed. It was much fancier than any place I'd ever worked before. Usually, I crouched beside the fire in my den, keeping Pa informed of any interesting findings and keeping half an eye on whatever stew I was cooking.

I settled down at the desk and heaved both books out of my satchel. The ancient, leather-bound tome from the temple and the mysterious gold-embossed book from the Library of

Whispers.

After several hours of work, my back was sore and my neck was strained, and my stomach was beginning to growl. But I had finished.

Claws raked my gut as I read over my translation.

Defying Death

Deep within the lore surrounding the enigmatic Shadow Walkers, an ancient prophecy foretells of a mystical artifact known as the Stone of Veritas, whispered to be their ultimate bane. It is said that this precious relic, forged in the fires of truth, possesses the power to unravel the dark enchantments that bind the Shadow Walkers to their cursed existence.

As the tale goes, the Stone of Veritas is no ordinary stone. It is a crystalline embodiment of truth and purity, shimmering with a radiant glow that holds the very essence of light. This ethereal gem, hewn from the heart of a star, is said to possess the power to dispel the intricate web of shadowy enchantments woven around the Shadow Walkers.

The origins of the Stone are veiled in mystery, its creation attributed to an ancient alliance between benevolent spirits and enlightened beings who sought to safeguard the realms from the encroaching darkness. Imbued with the essence of divine truth, the Stone was bestowed upon the fae as a beacon of hope and a tool of redemption.

According to the prophecies, only by harnessing the unique energy radiating from the Stone of Veritas can one hope to pierce the shrouded defenses of the Shadow Walkers. When the Stone is brought into their midst, its luminescence flares with an intensity that unravels the dark bindings enslaving these malevolent beings. Their ethereal forms, stripped of their sinister powers, become vulnerable to the forces of light and justice.

But the Stone is not easily wielded. It is a relic of immense power and requires a heart untainted by darkness to unlock its true potential. Those seeking to confront the Shadow Walkers must possess unwavering conviction, purity of purpose, and an unyielding determination to uphold the balance between light and shadow.

Thus, the Stone of Veritas stands as the key to unraveling the curse that plagues the Shadow Walkers. It represents the flickering hope that the darkness they embody can be banished, that redemption and liberation are possible even in the face of the most insidious forces. Only through the convergence of truth, courage, and the radiant power of the Stone can the Shadow Walkers be confronted and the realms be set free from their menacing grasp.

Leif

Exhaustion finally won out over rage, and I stumbled to a stop and fell to the forest floor, panting, my fur coated in leaves and dirt.

I hadn't slept in over a day, and those waking hours had been a nightmare. Death, destruction, murder, guilt, impotence, and wild fucking fury.

I just lay there for hours, my breath gradually slowing as I exhausted even my capacity for anger, my breathing gradually evening out until the only sound was the chirping of crickets and an occasional hoot from a faraway owl.

I never should have blamed Alara. She was innocent, a bystander to my own failings. If anything, she gave me strength, she didn't contribute to my weakness. My weakness was all my own.

My dreamless sleep was interrupted by a glowing light, a beacon that grew brighter as it descended from the night sky. It was the full moon, rising majestically over the treetops and casting its silver sheen into a glowing pathway through the forest. A tiny jeweled bird, like the one I'd seen on my patrol with Jet, glittered from the trees and flew along the path cast by the moon.

Something stirred in me, something primal and urgent. It

compelled me to stand up and follow the jewelwing along the moonlit path. My limbs felt heavy at first but grew stronger as I walked through the shadows of trees, down the path illuminated by silvery moonlight.

The moon penetrated deep into my soul and whispered to me, calling me out of my stupor and luring me onward.

Eventually, I stumbled to the edge of a clearing bathed in moonlight. It was breathtaking. Hundreds of fireflies danced around me like a thousand flickering stars, and the jewelwing flew up and joined them in their trees. The sweet scent of wildflowers and dew hung in the air, and a warm breeze rustled through the surrounding trees.

The clearing crackled with the convergence of energy, like the threads of fate had led me here.

In the center of the clearing, a solitary figure stood silhouetted against the trees, her arms shimmering in the moonlight. As I drew closer, I caught her citrus scent: it was intoxicating and laced with an erotic musk that made my heart race. A scent I would recognize anywhere.

I lurked in the trees, not daring to set foot in the glade.

She turned anyway, somehow aware of my presence, and set her burning orange eyes on me. "You! Did you bring me here?"

The hurt in her gaze was like a physical blow to my body. "No, bumpkin. I just...it felt right to come here."

She watched me for a few moments. She wore a yellow T-shirt that glowed under the flickering fireflies and jeans that outlined the curve of her hips and thighs. "Me too," she whispered. "The full moon, it...it pulled me here, I..."

"You felt it too."

I couldn't stay away from her any longer. As soon as I set

foot in the clearing, the moon vanished behind a shadow, and the fireflies went dark, leaving us in complete black. Then they reignited in a mesmerizing display of vibrant colors; the whole sky turned into a light show starring the bright moon that shone an unearthly shade of yellow.

A sharp pain pierced my chest, followed by a warmth that spread throughout my body as if a fire had been lit within me.

Alara shuddered too, and I felt the fire in her body as though it was in my own, the wave of exhilaration that washed through her, electrifying her senses. I could hear her heart thudding in her chest as if it were my own, could sense the wonder she felt as she looked at me. An explosive fusion of emotions and desires.

Every nerve tingled, attuned to Alara's presence. The moment lasted forever. I was acutely aware of every inch of Alara, her citrus scent, her aura, and the way her hair floated around her face like a halo of fire. Everything else disappeared in that moment, even the frenzied fireflies and the display of lights in the sky. The world was only her.

I stepped forward, drawn to her, and she did likewise. As our hands met, my body came alive for her, pleasure sparking along my nerves.

"You are my mate," she said simply, and the words fused the mating bond into place, forever entwining my life with hers.

Most wolves went their whole, long lives without finding the second half of their soul, and I had never imagined I would find mine. I hadn't even known it was missing until that moment.

"Yes, and you are mine," I said, and an overwhelming sense of belonging settled over me and around me, pulling me closer to her.

She put her hands to my face and ran them over my skin, sending shivers of pleasure down my spine. Her touch was like fire, burning through me. I closed my eyes and reveled in the sensation, unable to do anything but surrender to the need that coursed through me. I had waited too long for her touch on my body, which made this moment even sweeter.

Our lips met in an unstoppable passion, and we moved together as one. The energy between us crackled with electricity, as if we were connected by an invisible string that transcended time and space. I could feel Alara's heart beating against mine, and it felt like we were home; this was where we belonged.

With a gentle tug, Alara drew me closer, taking control. I was already completely naked, shivering in anticipation as her hands roved across my body, tracing patterns of pleasure with her fingertips. She kissed me in all the places she touched, leaving a trail of desire in her wake. With each kiss, something opened up within me that had been closed for too long.

My mate's hands were like fire on my skin, and I was helpless against the bliss coursing through me. As her fingertips brushed over my chest and abdomen, the pleasure intensified until it was too much to bear.

"I love you, Alara," I whispered.

My cock was hard and yearning, aching for her, needing her touch, finally fucking alive again, but it was the one place she avoided. This was sexual torture of the worst and best kind. Payback was a bitch.

I could have stayed in that sexual torment forever, feeling her hands trail around my hard planes, tracing the outlines of my muscles, moving with expert ease.

But Alara moved on quickly, driven by the urgency of our mating bond.

I reached out a hand to her belly and slid it up under her T-shirt, but she slapped it away with a smirk. "No. It's my turn to touch you."

"But—"

"But nothing." She walked behind me, leaving me standing with my cock saluting the full moon and her hands trailing around my hips and over my ass. I heard her remove her top and bra, then she pressed her cold breasts against my hot back, and I moaned.

"Fuck, Alara…"

She moaned too, and I could feel what it cost her to hold back. Her emotions were mine now, forever connected by the mating bond. When she admired the muscles in my ass, I felt her desire. When she pressed her aching nipples against my back, I felt her relief. And when she finally reached around and grasped my cock, I couldn't separate who was feeling the fireworks and the bliss of her skin over mine, up and down, up and down, our bodies connected more closely than ever.

She stopped, and I cried out, but she smacked my ass, so I shut up. I heard the unzipping of her fly and the swish of fae denim over soft, soft skin as she wriggled out of her jeans.

"Fuck," I breathed, imagining the moonlight caressing her naked legs, her wet, wet pussy. And when she pressed her entire nude body against my back, I almost burst.

"I love you, Alara," I said again, moaning in desire.

She went onto tiptoe, her breasts squishing against my back, her pussy dragging my ass cheeks up, and she whispered into my ear. "I know."

"Tell me you love me too," I begged.

She went to the soles of her feet again, and the motion of her breasts and belly and pussy against my back was maddening.

I wanted nothing more than to spin around and hold her down while I forced her to confess her love, but we were equal partners now. We always had been.

"Let me see," she said, toying with me while she ran a hand up my belly and tweaked my nipple. "I want you, Alpha."

"Yes," I breathed.

"I ache for you, Alpha."

"Tell me you love me."

She trembled, and I couldn't hold myself back a moment longer. I spun around and pulled her naked body against mine, my hand splayed against her lower back, and my cock pressed against her belly. Her breasts tugged on my gaze, but all my attention was on her soul. "Say it. And don't you dare call me Alpha."

She smiled, the sexiest fucking thing I'd ever seen. Her full lips were so kissable, her teeth shone white under the moon, her skin was so perfect, and her expression was so infuriatingly disrespectful that I wanted to bottle it. "I love you, Leif."

Alara

The words left my lips, and Leif kissed me, deep and hard. That crackling energy passed between us again, and I wondered if we would feel it every time our lips met, that wild passion of the mating bond.

Now that I'd said the words, I didn't want to stop saying them. "I love you, Leif."

He smiled, and an innocent joy shone from his face. "I love you, Alara."

Those words made me shiver, and I kissed him again. It didn't matter that he was an alpha and I was a lowly shifter, or that he was a city slicker and I was a country bumpkin. The only thing that mattered was the bond between us, unbreakable and undeniable.

It seemed so right, so perfect, like Gaia herself created this path for us. So few shifters ever experienced the wonder of a mating bond, and I felt honored to be among them.

I ran my hand down Leif's chest, exploring it like I'd wanted to since I first saw it. It felt just as good as I'd hoped. Better, even. He was all ridges and valleys, smooth skin over perfect muscle, and he was all mine. I'd never have to hold myself back from touching him again.

He grabbed my ass and lifted me off the ground, holding me

against his belly.

I wrapped my legs around him, feeling the heat between us grow with every second that passed. Leif's hands roamed across my back, tracing the curves of my hips and ass, sending shivers down my spine. I moaned into his mouth, wanting more of him, all of him.

Leif broke the kiss, planting hot, open-mouthed kisses along my jawline and down my neck. His teeth grazed my skin, making me whimper with pleasure.

"I want you, Alara," he murmured against my skin. "I want to feel you, all of you."

I nodded, unable to form words. He kept one hand under my ass to support me, then moved his other hand up my body, cupping my breast in his palms. His thumbs circled around my nipple, teasing it until it hardened under his touch.

I arched my back with my legs still clamped around his waist, and he supported the shift in my weight, planting his legs wide. He bent forward and licked my breast, teasing and sucking. My head fell back, and I moaned with pleasure, the sensations blending into an electrifying bliss that was all Leif's doing.

He shifted my ass away from his body and let his cock flip up between us, then rocked me close to him again. He was standing with his legs planted wide, and I was leaning away from him with my thighs clenched around his waist and my ankles hooked together behind him. The tip of his cock was sandwiched between my pussy and his stomach, and the knowledge that it was there had desire swirling through me.

"Fuck," he groaned, looking down at me like I was a platter laid before him to feast on. His gaze traveled from my face, over my breasts, down my belly, to the point where my pussy pressed the tip of his cock against his hard stomach. His desire swirled along our mating bond and through my body as though it was my own. And it was.

"You're it, babe. You're fucking it."

A laugh spilled from me, making the muscles in my pussy clench and squeeze his cock. My chuckle was short-lived because although I loved the lighter side of Leif that was shining through, I also loved the feel of his cock on my hot, wet pussy, and I could barely think of anything else.

I moved my hips up and down in a subtle movement, sliding my pussy along the side of his cock, hoping he didn't drop me as he shuddered with pleasure. The sensation of his dick sliding along my pussy and then rubbing my clit, up and down, up and down, was intoxicating.

My view was fucking spectacular, too. The fireflies surrounded us like worshippers, and the honey-colored moon reflected off Leif's silver hair like a celestial event just for us. His broad chest was perfectly muscled, and his biceps were thick and clenched from supporting my weight. Looking down my belly, past my breasts, to where my soft tangle of orange hair was pressed against my alpha's perfect V, with the tip of his cock poking up...the sight alone almost made me come.

"Closer, Leif. I need you closer." I could barely form the words, but it didn't matter. Desire flooded down the new bond between us, telling him exactly what I needed.

He flipped me up so my chest was pressed against his, and the tip of his cock found a whole new angle to press against me, making me moan. His lips found my breasts and suckled, and I almost cried in ecstasy and need.

His hair was warm and soft where it tickled my cheek, and I planted kisses on every part of him I could reach while he continued to lick and suck my breasts, flicking my nipples with his tongue, drawing ever louder and more desperate moans from me.

"Lower. Put me lower." I needed to slide down his cock and have him inside me, part of me, joined physically and emotionally. Our bond was growing desperate, yearning for full completion, and I knew he could feel it too. Like two powerful magnets drawn together, pulling and screaming for each other.

"How can you stand it?" I groaned, and he knew what I meant. How was he resisting the pull? All I wanted was for him to be inside me, for me to ride his cock, for us to be joined at the hip and the mouth, meeting our future together.

The intensity of it had me gasping for air and clinging to him as if I was afraid he would leave me. But he wouldn't. He would never leave me again.

Leif looked up at me with a smirk, his eyes almost level with mine. He knew exactly what he was doing, and he loved every second of it. "Every moment we're apart makes our union even sweeter," he said.

I scraped my fingernails up his back, hard, making sure I got every ounce of his attention. "Don't you dare stay away from me. Even if it's just to make our reunion better."

He grinned wolfishly. "I'll be by your side forever, bump-kin."

"Promise?"

"Promise."

"Good. So give in to the bond and fuck me before I kill someone."

Leif set me down on the soft grass, his silver eyes never leaving mine as he leaned over me, his eyes hooded with passion.

He lay down on me, his body pressed against me with the tip of his cock against my pussy and his mouth hovering above mine.

"Now," I moaned breathily.

He growled loudly, finally letting his inner wolf free to complete the bond. Although we stayed in fae form, we let our wild sides take over.

Leif thrust his cock inside me, filling me completely and perfectly, at the exact moment that his tongue probed deep into my mouth and mine in his.

He growled wildly into my mouth, and I moaned and cursed, lost in the sensation of our bodies uniting, his cock thrusting into me, and the taste of his lips.

Through our new bond, I felt everything he felt, tasted everything he tasted. I wasn't having sex as an individual, experiencing just one set of emotions, but as both of us. I could feel the hardness of his cock and the wetness of my pussy, the way our aching both heightened and eased with every movement, and the emotional climax that built and built as we writhed together.

I was on fire. We were both on fucking fire.

His cock was filling me up so perfectly, rubbing against my clit with every thrust and building a delicious firestorm of pleasure inside me. I was totally immersed in the sensation of his body joining with mine, his tongue in my mouth, and his hands on my sides.

I gasped as I wrapped my arms around his back and pulled him tighter against me.

"This is…"

"Amazing…"

"Incredible…"

We shared our thoughts and feelings easily, and I could sense his pleasure building and our climax fast approaching.

He slammed into me, harder and harder, and our bodies moved as one, slapping together as we fucked. His weight kept me pinned beneath him, and I loved every second of it, feeling both safe and completely owned by him.

A tidal wave of bliss crashed down on me, and I came, screaming his name, my body shaking. Leif followed, roaring into my mouth as he slammed his hips into mine. I felt the base of his cock, hard and pumping and still buried deep in my pussy, pulsing with release and filling me with every drop of his hot cum.

I moaned, my muscles still clenching, squeezing his cock in a rhythm that matched his, sucking and milking him for every ounce of his cum, and it was everything I could have dreamed of.

It wasn't just focused on one part of my body or my mind. It was everywhere, rushing through my veins, drenching and consuming my every cell. Every piece of me was filled with warm, glowing pleasure, and I'd never felt so whole.

Leif collapsed onto the grass beside me, his chest heaving.

"I love you, Leif," I said, leaning over him to kiss his lips.

"I love you too." He put a hand on my cheek and grinned. "That bond is fucking intense."

I kissed his lips again, then bit his bottom one, just to hear him growl. "That was only round one."

Leif sat up, staring down at me like I was the most beautiful thing in the world.

"Round one?"

"Hell yeah. I'm ready for round two."

My alpha wolf grinned. "I think I can handle that."

Emotion surged through me, not just passion and desire but also longing and belonging, a sense of completeness.

The fireflies settled into the trees and blinked out one by one, and the moon shifted back to its usual cool white, but the air was warm enough to keep us comfortable, and the grass beneath us was soft.

"I think I'll stay here forever," Leif mumbled, pulling me close against him so my head nestled on his arm.

Peace settled over our little clearing. A perfect harmony that nothing could penetrate. Absolute serenity.

"Me too."

Alara

I lay on the soft grass with my head resting on Leif's shoulder and my arm draped across his chest. The fireflies had gone to sleep, and the bright yellow moon and turned to its usual pale silver. The grass was soft beneath us, and the air carried enough warmth to keep us comfortable even though we were both naked.

Leif's voice broke the comfortable silence. "Have you ever been to a mating celebration?"

Mating bonds were so rare that the entire pack celebrated whenever they occurred. In my whole life, no bonds had been formed in Sylverclyff, but I had been to a celebration and was happy to share the memory.

"Just once. I was about five or six, and a couple in a nearby village felt the mating bond. Every shifter from miles around went to the celebration."

"What was it like?"

"It started with a water ceremony. The couple bathed naked in front of everyone—I always dreaded that part—and their alpha howled at the moon. I thought it was kind of scary, but I was only little."

"Why did you dread being naked?" Leif's genuine curiosity caught me off guard.

I would have been embarrassed to answer this question just a few hours ago, but now I knew I could tell Leif anything. Reflecting on my past insecurities, I realized how far I had come. Opening up wasn't as daunting anymore, especially with him. A newfound sense of trust enveloped me. "This might sound silly, but I've never been comfortable with my own nudity."

"I'm very comfortable with mine."

"I noticed."

"And with yours."

He ran a hand down my arm and squeezed my ass.

I giggled. "It was another way I felt like an outsider with my pack. But, actually, I don't feel so different from every other wolf now."

I closed my eyes for a moment and concentrated on the gentle hum reverberating along the bond. Leif's unwavering confidence radiated down the link and made my worries smaller.

Leif's voice held a hint of surprise. "You don't?"

I pushed myself up and leaned my cheek on his chest, seeking comfort in his warmth and looking up at his face. "No, not anymore. I mean, I'm not about to start chasing a ball around like a true dog, but maybe I'll strip naked more often in front of the pack."

Leif growled, and I felt his jealousy down the bond. "Whoa," I said. "That whole jealousy thing will take some getting used to, right?"

He traced light circles on the skin of my shoulder. "Yup. Apparently, it eases off after a couple of months, and mated couples start having sex with the rest of the pack again, but...I can't imagine allowing that."

"Me neither." A bolt of possessiveness struck me, and I kissed my bond's pec.

His words resonated deeply, affirming our connection. "I can't imagine desiring anyone else but you."

I gazed up at him. "Really? But you and Selene..." Just thinking about how he took her down to his dungeon made my chest feel tight, and he must have sensed my reaction.

"No, babe. We didn't do anything. I couldn't. I just kept thinking about you."

Joy lit me from the inside, bigger and brighter than the full moon in the sky. "Oh, thank Gaia. Otherwise, I was going to have to kill her, and, you know, she's my best friend, so that would've sucked."

Leif laughed, a glorious free sound that made the entire forest feel happy, I was sure. He'd been under too much pressure lately and hadn't had the freedom to be himself. I would do everything I could to take as much of his load as possible, just to hear that laugh again.

"Tell me more about the mating celebration you went to when you were a cute little faeling," he said.

I settled back into the crook of his armpit and stared up at the moon while I talked. "Like I said, it was kind of scary at first, with the massive alpha howling in wolf form and the couple dunking into the black sea. But then it got fun. We had a seafood feast and a massive bonfire on the beach."

"The crackling flames of the bonfire represent the passion and eternal flame of the mating bond," Leif said.

"Really? I didn't notice the symbolism at the time. Mostly what I remember were the drums. There was this heavy drumbeat that kept going all night." I looked over at him and watched his profile as he stared up at the moon. "Do they

266

signify anything?"

"Yep. The rhythmic beats of drums echo the pulse of the mated couple's united spirits."

"Huh. When did you get so knowledgeable about all this stuff."

Leif looked at me. "I'm a fucking alpha, wench. I know shit." He poked his tongue out at me, then yanked his arm out from under my head so I fell back onto the grass. He leaped to his feet and reached out his arms to pull me up. "We'd better get going."

"I thought we were going to stay here forever," I complained, but I accepted his hands, and he yanked me to my feet.

He held my naked body close against his, and heat began to smolder between us. "We have to do something about this," he said, indicating my naked body.

I cocked out a hip. "I thought you were comfortable with nudity?" I teased.

He growled possessively. "You are the most beautiful creature on the planet, and I can't let anybody look at you tonight. Maybe not ever."

"I'm not sure that's your decision," I said.

He growled and slapped my ass. "You're mine, bumpkin. Don't ever forget that."

I tossed my hair over a shoulder. "I might forget. And you might have to punish me." I turned sideways and bent over so my ass reached for the moon. His cock thickened and hardened, but he just gave me a gentle kiss on the ass and mumbled into my cheek. "Not now, babe. We have to go."

I straightened up. "Why? Can't we stay here all night?"

"Oh, I fucking wish we could. But the pack will have all seen the honey-colored moon. They'll know somebody mated tonight, and they'll be preparing a celebration."

"Let them celebrate. We can stay here," I insisted, unwilling to leave.

Leif's gaze held a mixture of longing and responsibility. "Babe, if I could give everything up and build a little hut in this clearing and live here with you forever, I would. Seriously. I would love nothing more. But I'm the alpha, and I have responsibilities. The pack's been through some shit lately, and they need a good celebration. Let them have this party, then tomorrow, I'm all yours."

He was right. Not five minutes ago, I'd vowed to myself to do everything I could to ease his worries, and right now, he needed me to present myself to the pack as his mate and then party hard with them.

I grabbed his hand and kissed his knuckles. "Let's go."

He started walking, tugging me along. "Wait," I said. "Let's shift."

"But you can't control your wolf."

I concentrated on the buzz of our bond. It would be fun experimenting with how it changed depending on our moods or how far away we were from each other, but right now, it was potent. And I knew I could use some of his control to harness my own wolf.

"Just try, Alpha."

His cock stirred again at my use of his title, but he didn't let it distract him. He shifted into his massive silver wolf, and I felt my wolf struggle to escape. All I had to do was let go, and the shift came naturally. My smaller red wolf trotted beside his large silver one.

He nuzzled me briefly, and I nuzzled him back, then we set off to the den at a run, diving around trees and leaping over fallen logs in perfect unison.

* * *

The pack didn't have more than a couple of hours to prepare, from when the honey-colored moon lit the sky to when Leif and I turned up, but the massive lawn behind the den was transformed, ready to celebrate our mating bond.

Softly glowing Lightning globes hung from branches, casting mesmerizing shadows over the lawn, and colorful banners fluttered in the light breeze. Decorated logs, wildflowers, and shrubs created an outdoor oasis. The smoke from the bonfire made an earthy aroma, promising a fun night.

In the center of it all was a blanket of pillows and furs arranged in a circle where Leif and I would stand to exchange our vows.

We padded into the heart of the celebration, our footsteps muffled by the grass, and gracefully transitioned into our fae forms.

Leif sat me on a fur and yelled, "Somebody bring us some clothes."

It was unusual for any wolf to care about being naked, especially Leif.

Jet's mouth hung open. "Holy fucking Gaia. It's you, Alpha? Really? The honeymoon was for you? Congratulations, dude." He shook his head. "Leif fucking Caro, a mated wolf. I never thought I'd see the day."

"Thanks, dude." Leif was grinning widely, still shielding my body with his.

The news that the yellow moon had shone for Leif and me thundered through the pack like lightning until an orchestra of howls and cheers filled the air, harmonizing with the cicadas singing in the trees.

Leif didn't relax until somebody brought out a dress for me and sweatpants for him, and then the party began. Fae slapped us on the backs and kissed our cheeks, and handed out quality Dionysus wine like it was water.

I spotted Selene's powder-blue braids in the crowd and motioned her closer. Normally, I would weave through the heaving bodies to reach her, but my yearning to stay near Leif was too intense tonight, so she had to come to me.

She screamed and pulled me into a tight hug. "Holy crap, bitch. You're mated!"

I beamed. "To the alpha of alphas."

"Oh, Gaia! How does it feel?"

Leif's hand was clasped in mine, although he was talking so some other shifters behind me. "It feels amazing, Selene. Like, like...I can't possibly explain it. It feels like the best part of myself was just lying abandoned on the street, and I found it and picked it up, and now I'm whole."

Her eyes widened with a sudden realization. "You know that he and I didn't...down in the dungeon, we didn't..."

"I know, he told me."

"Oh, thank Gaia. I wouldn't want you going newly-mated feral and slitting my throat or something."

I chuckled. "Yeah. The bond's pretty intense."

"Actually, that makes me feel much better about the whole thing. It wasn't my fault he couldn't get it up...it was yours."

Selene and I kept chatting, and a bunch of other fae joined us, their laughter and animated chatter blending with the surrounding celebration. I spoke to more shifters than ever, and it didn't even feel awkward. Leif's natural ease with fae filtered through our bond and made me more confident, and it helped that he didn't release my hand all night.

The anticipated feast finally arrived, a tantalizing blend of forest-infused flavors and Verda City's culinary delights. The air filled with the mouthwatering aroma of sizzling meats, fragrant bread, and a harmonious symphony of herbs and spices. The pack gathered around me and Leif, then fell silent.

With a regal air, Leif raised a succulent roasted chicken leg, commanding attention. "I, Leif, Alpha of Alphas in the Realm of Verda, heir to the Caro throne, and Head of that House, hereby declare Alara Everly, this extraordinary and enchanting fae, as my beloved mate."

He handed me the drumstick, letting me eat before him. A murmur rippled through the pack at that sign of respect, and when I bit into the herby meat, a great cheer erupted. One fae stripped, shifted into a small black wolf and howled at the moon.

One by one, the rest of the pack followed suit until the lawn was littered with clothing and the night air was filled with howls of joy.

From the depths of the forest, a primal drumbeat emerged, its rhythmic pulse merging with another, and then another, until we were enveloped in a symphony of tribal percussion. I felt it down to my soul, the echo of our mating bond pulsing through us both. Leif and I shared a look, then stripped down and shifted, howling as one at the glorious moon.

Leif

Gaia had a hilarious sense of humor, and she'd set the third trial for the day after my mating bond snapped into place. Well, there was zero chance of me going without Alara, so I kissed her awake, told her to get dressed and follow me, and she did as she was told for once in her life.

"Don't get used to it," she replied with a sassy little grin when I remarked on the miracle of her obedience.

I showed her the moonway that led to Rosenia Forest, and when we emerged into the leafy green forest, she breathed deeply in the mulchy scent. "I miss the sea."

"Then we'll go there. Tomorrow. Now that you can shift, everywhere is just a day trip."

She grinned. "I really don't want to leave our den, you know. Vacation days can wait."

I pulled her close and breathed her in, holding her tight against my body, then pressed a kiss on her lips. "Mine."

"Yours," she agreed.

We walked along the narrow path to the clearing where Gaia schooled the heirs on everything we would need to know about ruling the realm. It wasn't wide enough for two to walk abreast, so we mostly bush-bashed, but there was no way I was leaving her side.

Gabrelle sat on the ancient stone ledge dripping with ivy at the clearing's edge. She uncrossed and crossed her long legs when she saw us and narrowed her eyes into cat-like slits. "What is she doing here?"

"Alara's with me," I growled.

The ice queen was unfazed by my display of aggression, she just tilted her head ever so slightly. "Yes, I can see that. What is she doing here? Today is the third trial, there is no room for spectators."

A growl built in my chest, growing and growing until it filled my entire body, but it stopped as soon as Alara put a calming hand on my forearm. "I'm his mate," she said proudly, and a burst of fiery pride ran through me, chasing away my anger.

Gabrelle raised one eyebrow a fraction, which was as big a display of emotion as I'd ever seen from her. She looked at me. "Is that true?"

"Yes. The bond fired last night. Didn't you see the honeymoon?"

Gabrelle slid elegantly off the stone ledge, making the movement seem like foreplay. "Only shifters can see the moon change color, you know that. Or has all the bonded sex scrambled your brain?" She stalked closer and held out a hand for my mate to kiss. "Congratulations, Alara." Alara shook the proferred hand instead of kissing it, which made me laugh. The ice queen turned to me. "Now, aren't you glad I rescued her from that horrid dungeon you locked her in?"

"Tried to rescue me," Alara corrected. "Leif caught me and punished me, so it didn't work out as you planned."

Gabrelle looked between us, smirking. "Oh, I'd say it turned out exactly as I planned."

Neela appeared behind us out of nowhere, taking me by

273

surprise. When she'd first turned up in Verda, she sounded like a herd of rhona crashing through the jungle, even when she tried to tiptoe, but now she could even sneak up on me.

"Did you say you guys mated? Jesus! You bloody rockstars!" She pulled Alara and me into a double hug and squeezed tight, stuffing her spiky blue hair in Alara's face—I could practically feel her errant locks tickling my nose through the bond.

Neela turned to me. "What happened? Tell me? Oh my God, I love it." She jumped up and down, overflowing with excitement. "I've never met a mated shifter before. Is it true you only want to have sex with Alara now, Leif? I mean, that's not possible, right? Not for you." She turned to Gabrelle. "Gab, take your clothes off and try to seduce him. Pleeeease."

Gabrelle smiled silkily and began removing her shirt, un-buttoning an endless row of buttons and slowly exposing her glorious brown cleavage. When she was finally done, she shrugged off her cream shirt, deliberately shoving her large breasts forward and wriggling until the shirt slid off her arms and puddled on the grass. Her smile was sinful and brimming with lust. "Do you want to take me, Leif? You could lick every inch of my body or just bend me over a log and fuck me."

Alara growled and stepped between me and Gabrelle, but she needn't have bothered. My cock and my brain had zero interest in the heir of beauty.

"Not today, thanks," I said dismissively. "Raincheck."

Alara backed down, and the two princesses exchanged amazed glances.

"Holy fuck in a forest," Neela said.

"Or not," Gabrelle said, rebuttoning her shirt as Dion en-tered the clearing.

"Actually," Neela said to the half-naked fae, "Maybe just

this once, you and I could..." She shook her head. "No, never mind."

D set one foot in the clearing and then stopped, staring at Gabrelle's breasts with his jaw on the grass. We were all immune to her charms, having spent long years in her company. Fae who hadn't met her usually dropped to their knees when they first saw her, but obviously, we heirs had to battle past that initial instinct if we wanted to rule alongside her.

Immunity to her charms under normal circumstances was one thing, but when the princess of beauty, whose mom was a Lure, had her breasts out, even the strongest fae couldn't resist.

Dion crossed to Gabrelle and placed a hand over her large breast, which she swatted away. "Back off, D." The sexual tension between Neela, Gabrelle, and Dion fizzled once the beauty princess was fully clothed again.

"You got skills, girl," Neela said, shaking her head.

"Don't fucking do that," Dion complained. "Don't mess with the pact."

Right, the no-sex-among-the-heirs pact that was designed to eliminate complications. After all, we all had to rule together one day. And with only three current monarchs still alive, only one more had to die before we were all thrust onto our thrones.

Gabrelle returned to her stone ledge, pulling herself up effortlessly. "I was just exploring the potency of Leif's new mating bond."

Dion's mouth opened again. "His what now?"

"It's strong," Gabrelle said. "I've never known anyone to resist me like that, especially since I added a sprinkle of Lure."

Lure could make anyone do anything. Gabrelle's mom had

ascended to Lure, and the power ran strongly through Gabrelle, too, though she wasn't yet Ascended.

"Alara owns my dick now," I said proudly. "Come on, babe, I wanna show you my mattress." I pulled her onto my jasmine mattress in the middle of the clearing, and she lay beside me. I pulled out a tennis ball, chucked it into the air, and then caught it. I focused on a tiny berry growing twenty feet up in an overhanging vine and tried to make the ball kiss it every time I threw.

"Stop shooting them dirty looks, Double D," Neela said.

I patted the mattress beside me, where Dion usually sat. "There's room for you too, bro."

He shook his head and sat on a bush instead, which caught him neatly. Out of all the heirs, Dion hated change the most. He was pissed when Neela turned up and wheedled her way into the group, and he was pissed when Ronan fell in love with her. Now, he was pissed at me for mating with Alara. Well, he'd just have to get used to it because she wasn't going anywhere.

Ronan ran into the clearing, late as usual. Neela filled him in on my mating bond, and he beamed at Alara and me in a way only another happily coupled guy could. I recapped the ceremony and last night's celebrations, but words could never explain the depth of the bond.

"Congratulations, man," Ronan said. Then he outlined a bow for Alara. "You too, Alphaess, and welcome to the team."

Alara snorted a laugh. "Female alphas are just called alpha. And I'm still just a normal shifter."

I snatched the tennis ball out of the air and kissed her neck. "You were never just a normal shifter, babe. And now you're the alpha's mate."

Dion grumbled at the warm welcome Ronan was giving Alara,

and I tried not to hold it against him. She would win him over in time.

"Trial time," Ronan declared. He held five scrolls, each with a name on them. He handed them to each heir, shrugging. "Different instructions for each of us for this trial, I guess."

Neela's scroll was labeled 'Flora, open first,' so she broke the wax seal and read. "Mating bonds are a blessing from Gaia and must be respected." Everybody looked at the mattress where my hand was intertwined with Alara's. "In today's trial, each heir must demonstrate that they are willing to protect, comfort, and nourish Alara Everly because the realm's future may depend on it. Leif Caro will not contribute to the realm's security if his mate's safety is in question."

"Yes!" I yelled. "You all gotta protect and nourish my female. Plus, I'm going to kick your asses in this trial, so double yes."

As Neela stepped forward for her task, I reassured Alara with a supportive smile. "You got this, babe," I whispered. If anything went sideways, I would rescue her instantly so she was in no danger.

The forest melted away, and a desert grew in its place, harsh and hot, with yellow sand stretching in all directions. Fuck, Gaia was good at creating illusions. Even me and the other heirs had disappeared, leaving just Neela and Alara. I could still feel the mattress beneath my butt, but Alara obviously felt the sand that blew hard and hot against her body.

She shut her eyes and looked around, scared. She couldn't see me, and I felt her fear through the bond. I leaped up and bounded to her, but I slammed into an invisible wall. "Fucking Gaia." I was helpless and could only watch with mounting anxiety.

Neela looked around for a moment, searching for a way to

nourish or protect my mate. There wasn't much a Grower could do in the middle of a desert, and I sensed my mate's thirst and her growing heat.

"Do something!" I yelled.

"They can't hear you." It was Ronan's voice, although I couldn't see him. "But don't worry, Neela's got this. They're both safe."

That wasn't true, not one bit. Gaia was a kill-happy bitch who had a long history of destroying heirs who didn't meet her standards, and she wouldn't hesitate to murder a lowly shifter. She did it all the fucking time.

I pounded on the invisible barrier, looking for a way in. Neela's eyes were closed in concentration, though I didn't see how she could find even the hint of plant life in that sand.

A growling slobbering sound from nearby raised my hackles, and I had an awful feeling that Neela's psychotic pet grass tufts were trying to get through the invisible barrier to help her. Hopefully, they wouldn't stumble across one of us and blame us for their mistress's danger. Surely, there wasn't much a Grower could do in a desert.

But I underestimated her Growing skills. A green vine snaked up from beneath the sand and grew fast, making a green canopy above my mate. More joined it, and soon there were enough plants and trunks to make a wall against the sandstorm and shelter from the beating sun.

With Alara's relief radiating from her face and through our bond, I sank back onto the jasmine mattress, my gaze fixed on her mesmerizing beauty. Absently, I twirled the tennis ball between my fingers, savoring the moment of respite.

The desert scene vanished, returning us to the clearing in Rosenia Forest. Two large creatures, more mouth than body, shrank back into their grassy forms when they saw Neela was okay.

"Well done, tomcat," Ronan said, pulling Neela close for a kiss. The snuffle tuffs growled, and Ronan growled back, but peace was restored when the two grass tufts shuffled over to Neela, and one of them climbed onto her lap with a little helping hand under its butt. There was some weird dynamic in that twisted snuffle tuff family that I couldn't figure out, and I never saw both of them on Neela's lap at once. I supposed they took it in turns.

Ronan's scroll was marked 'Mentium, open second,' so he was up next. He left Neela with her shrubs and crossed to the clearing's center. He and Alara were transported to an empty room with a single wooden chair, and the rest of us disappeared from view, along with the forest around us.

Alara sat on the chair and started sobbing. I whimpered, looking at her distraught face, her tears dousing the fire in her orange eyes.

"Fuck you, Gaia," I muttered, knowing there was nothing I could do to help her.

Ronan went to her side and put his arms around her, which was Comforting 101 when it came to wolves, but he had to do better than that.

"Fix her damn mood, Ro," I snarled. He wasn't Ascended yet, but he was the heir of House Mentium and should have decent control over his inner power. But he was doing a shitty job of making my mate feel better. I would fucking kill him for this.

After an eternity, she finally stopped crying but never beamed with happiness. The scene dissolved, and I ran to her, licking her face and holding her tight until she felt better.

"Not good enough, Ronan," I growled over my shoulder.

"Sorry, Leif. I tried."

I would deal with him later.

Dion was up next. He and Alara materialized in a stainless steel kitchen, and his task was to prepare her a meal that reminded her of her favorite childhood memory. I settled down to watch. Thank Gaia, she wasn't in pain or distress. She just watched with interest as D whizzed around the kitchen, clanging pans and creating steam I couldn't smell.

When Alara ate, her eyes lit up.

"What does it taste of?" Dion asked. His curly hair had turned orange after whatever he tasted, making it a good match for my mate's.

"It tastes like the first time Pa took me fishing. We went out on a rickety boat that I was sure would sink, but it didn't. I still remember the feel of the fish tugging on the line, pulling so hard I thought it would be a shark from Requin Bay, but it turned out to be so small we had to throw it back." She laughed in delight, and I chuckled too.

Next was Gabrelle, who had to sneak Alara past a guard outside a museum.

"Do you think she'll use Stealth or Lure?" Dion asked. Gabrelle hadn't ascended. Her mother had Lure, and her father had Stealth, and both traits were strong in her.

"Lure, for sure," Ronan said. "She'll definitely ascend to Lure."

"I don't know," Neela said. "She's pretty Stealthy."

We all remembered how Gabrelle had used her Stealth to cast an illusion over a massive hole in the ground so Neela would fall in and break her leg.

Ronan squeezed her now-healed leg while we all considered

whether our friend would use Stealth or Lure.

Gabrelle used neither. She distracted the guard with her own beauty while Alara walked past. The scene dissolved, and Dion looked up at her with a question on his lips.

"Why didn't you use an inner power?"

"I wanted to challenge myself," Gabrelle said. "Besides, after this one turned me down, I needed an ego boost." She waved a hand in my direction.

Finally, it was my turn. "I got you, babe," I said, giving Alara a kiss that went so long that Gabrelle and Ronan both tossed grass at us to break it up.

I read my scroll. "Leif, your task is different. There is no question that you will protect and nourish your mate. Your task is to ensure you will protect and nourish the realm, even when distracted by her. You must resist her for as long as possible, and you must remain in wolf form."

A groan escaped me. "Fuck."

I shifted, and the world around me disappeared, replaced with a grassy field filled with flowers. Alara was there, too, also in wolf form. I was pulled toward her, but I stayed put, resisting her as best as I could.

A furry white rabbit jumped, and Alara's tail wagged, drawing my attention to her ass, which was cute even in wolf form. She pounced on the rabbit with a playful sound and chased it around in circles.

The rabbit smelled gamey, and it was practically impossible not to join the chase, running alongside my mate. I stayed in a sitting position, but my butt was wriggling with excitement.

The scene shifted into a moonlit scene, with furs and cushions laid on the grass. Alara was in fae form and completely naked, and without a moment's thought, I pounced on her, shifting out of my wolf form in mid-air, and taking her to the soft furs as I landed, pulling her smooth body against mine and losing myself in her taste.

"Okay, okay, cut it out." Ronan's voice filtered into the scene, which disappeared, leaving me lying on the dirt and leaves of the clearing with Alara, who was now, annoyingly, fully clothed.

My dick didn't get the message the sex part was over, and it stayed up and hard between us. It wasn't until Ronan and Gabrelle showered us in grass that Alara finally pulled away from me, then yanked me to my feet.

"You sucked at that," Neela observed.

I slumped onto the jasmine mattress, pulling my mate down beside me. "What? I resisted her for about an hour. I deserve a fucking medal."

The others all snorted in some kind of orchestrated group snort. "You lasted about three seconds, wolf boy," Gabrelle said.

They must be kidding. That felt like an eternity. I didn't believe them until the scores came out, and a big silver number one hovered over my head, showing I'd come in last place.

"Suck it, fae assholes," Neela said, beaming under her shimmering number five. "You thought I'd never win. And here I am, a mortal girl already kicking your asses."

Ronan hugged her tight. "You're fae too, tomcat."

She nodded. "A better fae than the rest of you. Except you, toy boy," she added, although Ronan only scored two points in this trial.

Dion looked proud of his four points, and Gabrelle looked satisfied with her three points. Ronan and Gabrelle used to take out the top spots, but since Dion and I ascended, we'd been slowly knocking them down. Neela had only been here a year, and she was rapidly rising in the ranks. Who knew where we'd all end up?

All I knew was that wherever it was, I'd be there with Alara.

Leif

A week later, when we'd finally crawled out of bed, I took Alara on a surprise visit to the coast.

"Surprise!" I yelled when we finally stood on the sand, the surf crashing behind us.

She grinned. "Not exactly. I mean, I told you I missed the salty air, and you promised to bring me here."

I caught her up in a kiss. "But I didn't say when I'd bring you."

Her citrus scent was intoxicating, and whenever anybody looked at her, I wondered if they noticed her divine smell too. It drove me crazy.

She laughed. "No. But coming along the moonway east and running all the way to Sylverclyff was a bit of a giveaway."

I smiled and pulled out a package from my backpack. "Maybe this will be more of a surprise."

Her eyes lit up as she ripped open the package. "Oh!" She exclaimed, withdrawing a hardcover book with an intricate silver cover. The title was written in delicate cursive calligraphy: The Ocean's Lullaby.

"This is beautiful," Alara said, running her fingers along the spine. She opened it and turned to a page in the center filled with a detailed hand-drawn illustration of a mermaid swimming under the sea.

"I thought you'd like it," I said proudly, grinning from ear to ear. "It was one of my favorite books growing up, and I wanted to share it with you."

She swatted me cheekily. "I didn't even know you could read."

"Wench!" I wrestled her to the warm sand, and we both laughed.

The afternoon passed in the blink of an eye. I taught her how to catch and throw a tennis ball in the surf, then she taught me how to make sandcastles with glassy shells, and then we sat on the beach for hours talking about anything that came to mind.

The sun set over the horizon like a burning fire, painting the sky in hues of orange and pink that made Alara's eyes shine even brighter. The waves lapped softly against the shore, lulling us into a peaceful trance. The salty air was invigorating and alive with possibility. We were simply content to be together, to huddle in each other's warmth as night fell. Together we watched stars fill the night sky like shining diamonds in a sea of glittering eternity.

"We'll come back whenever you want to," I said. "We can build a summer den here—maybe something less gross than your old one."

She whacked me playfully. "City dick."

I chuckled. "And we can bring your Pa to come and live with us. Or have some staff move in with him. Whatever you want."

I felt her joy pulsing down our mating bond, warm and glowing.

"Whatever I want," she repeated, leaning in to press her soft lips against mine. "Now, tell me more about this book."

She opened her gift on her lap and traced her finger over the foil-embossed images inside. "It's so beautiful."

I'd rarely spoken of my mother since she died, but somehow the words flowed easily. "Mom used to read it to me every night. I used to beg her to read it, even when I knew it by heart. She always said that the best stories were the ones you never got tired of hearing."

Alara smiled softly, her eyes filled with understanding. "Sounds like she was a wonderful mother."

I nodded, my throat tightening. "Yeah, she was. I mean, she could be tough but also sweet. I saw a side of her that nobody else did, especially when I was a faeling. And now, whenever I read this book, it's like she's still with me."

Alara nuzzled against me, her fiery hair tickling my face as comfort poured from her body into mine.

We sat in silence for a few moments, watching the stars twinkle in the night sky. The sound of the waves and our breathing was the only thing filling the air. It was peaceful, but my mind was already racing with thoughts of what we could do next.

"Hey, bumpkin," I said, turning to her with a mischievous grin. "Wanna go for a swim?"

She raised an eyebrow, but a smirk played at her lips. "At night? In the ocean?"

I nodded, already standing up and pulling her along with me. "Why not? It'll be fun."

She laughed, the sound like music to my ears. "You're insane."

"Only for you," I replied, brushing sand off my bare chest.

Alara pulled off her light summer dress, revealing her luscious curves to the moonlit beach. "Fine. But if any sharks eat me, I'm gonna haunt you for eternity."

I grabbed her hand and pulled her toward the water. The cold spray hit us as we waded in, and she giggled as we splashed around. The waves were stronger now, and I felt the surge of adrenaline as I swam deeper, pulling Alara with me.

The water was dark and cool, and the sound of the waves was muffled as we dove beneath the surface. I could see her clearly, even in the dim light, her hair swirling around her like dark flames. The moon above lit up the ocean, casting a silver glow everywhere. It was like swimming in a dream world.

Finally, we emerged from the water, both breathless with wonder. The stars seemed even brighter now, and a million colors were washing over us.

Alara's face was alight, and I knew in that moment that this would be a place we'd return to often.

"Are you ready?" I asked.

"Ready for what?"

"To go visit your Pa. He and I have been conspiring, and—"

"You what? Why?"

I kissed her temple. "Don't worry, babe. You'll like it. I hope."

She let me dry her with a towel, and it took every ounce of my willpower to keep it clean, but we didn't have time for a screw. We had an appointment to keep.

"An appointment?" she asked when I shared that news. "With Pa? How very formal."

"You'll see."

Her old den wasn't far from the beach, and it didn't take us long to lope up the narrow winding path that led to the clifftop, then along the grassy plain.

As we approached the den, my heart raced in anticipation

of her reaction. The old structure had been replaced by a much larger one, but still modest and rustic—just as her Pa had requested.

Over the past two weeks, my Crafters had worked hard on renovating that little cottage according to Rooni's vision. I hadn't seen it because I'd been enveloped in Alara's arms in our bed, and it was even better than I had imagined.

The walls were made from clay bricks, with an ochre-red roof gently sloping down to the sandstone floor. The shutters and doors were completely new and painted in a pop of orange.

Inside, it was beautiful. A large stone fireplace dominated one wall, with two inviting couches around it. The floors were covered in thick rugs, and there were plenty of bookshelves filled with stories, both old and new. An intricate tapestry hung above the mantlepiece, depicting a scene from Alara's childhood when she and her Pa had gone fishing out at sea in a tiny boat.

But what caught Alara's attention was seeing that her Pa had kept some of her mother's furniture and decorations intact to honor her memory. He said it was an effort to keep his wife's spirit alive.

Alara's eyes filled with tears as she took her father into her arms, and he smiled broadly, nuzzling into her embrace.

"It's beautiful," she said.

"Of course it is. You come visit often, you hear."

"Every week, Pa."

"Nonsense, Al," he said. "That's far too often. I'll be visiting you in Verda City too. Your mate said he'd built a moonway from here straight to his den."

She looked up at me, and I nodded. I would do anything for her. Seriously.

Any. Fucking. Thing.

Epilogue

Apparently, Gaia was slow at math because it took two months for the final rankings to come out. As a lowly fae from the coast, I'd always assumed the kings and queens ruled equally, but actually, there was some complicated ranking system based on their performance in the trials over the years.

It was traditional among the heirs to celebrate—or commiserate—at the Ogre's Nose when Gaia finally got her shit together and released the cumulative rankings. Leif and I were the first to arrive. The lighting was dim and the drinks were flowing, so I was happy.

"Ronan keeps trying to calculate the final ranking, but he never gets it right. It isn't just a simple average or some shit. It's weighted by difficulty or something. I don't know. As long as I'm not last, I don't care."

Leif and I sat on one side of a booth, thigh to thigh. We were still deep in the aftereffects of the honeymoon, unable to spend longer than five minutes away from each other. Honestly, I didn't see why we'd ever have to part. He was everything I needed.

"You won't be last, Leif. Although you kind of sucked in that last challenge."

"Even Gaia can't keep me away from you," he said, looking

all kinds of sexy as he smoldered at me, and I sensed blood pumping to his cock.

The rest of our group arrived, entering together with an air of camaraderie. Gabrelle silkily slipped into the booth, deliberately choosing a seat opposite me, her sly wink acknowledging the delicate dynamics between us. She knew I was still volatile and possessive, and she wouldn't resume their close friendship until the honeymoon aftereffects had passed. It was a wise decision because her ethereal beauty, the cascade of loose pink curls atop her head, and the alluring way her sheer jumpsuit accentuated her figure stirred the beast within me.

"I told you we should have brought a forklift to separate these two," Neela said, sitting on Ronan's lap on a chair at the top of the booth. She was so tiny on his huge lap that she almost disappeared into the black folds of his shirt.

Gabrelle waved a finger at Neela and her toy boy. "You can talk."

Dion slid in beside Gabrelle, his curls a subdued blond. "What's a forklift? Like, a hand or something? I just use my hand to lift my fork."

Neela looked around for support but got blank expressions from all of us. "It's a big machiney thing humans use to build skyscrapers and move stuff around." She huffed. "I don't know. Read a book, fae."

Leif licked my cheek. "She still always talks like she isn't one of us." I grinned.

Neela huffed. "Sometimes I wish I wasn't. You're all so insular."

"So what-now?" Leif asked, nuzzling me again until my skin pebbled in goosebumps.

"Forget it." The tiny blue-haired princess called out to the bartender. "Can we get a round here, please? My tattoo is playing up."

I looked at Leif. "Her tattoo?"

"That's what she calls the Floran Bracelet."

"Oh. Sure, I'm dismissive of all my priceless family heirlooms, too," I teased, earning a grin from Neela.

The bartender brought a round of Fae Fizz, and Neela ordered a second round immediately. "What?" she said, looking around at our raised eyebrows. "The tatt needs its meds."

Ronan raised a glass of Fae Fizz. "To me. The best heir, yet again."

"To the toy boy," Leif said, raising his glass.

"He can't afford a new pair of shoes, but he can lift heavy things," Dion added, downing his Fae Fizz in one.

Everybody guffawed.

Ronan had scored eleven points this year, which was worse than usual for him but wasn't bad enough to drag his average down from thirteen. Gabrelle had only scored nine points but maintained her average of eleven.

"I'm coming for you guys," Neela said. "You used to be best, but you'll be eating my dust in a couple of years." With ten points in the bag this year, she was becoming a real threat. Her average was only six points, but she'd started with zero two years ago and was definitely the biggest mover on the leaderboard. "When I get a bit more practice with my spellwork, you'll all be staring at my ass." Everyone laughed. Dion, whose hair was turning pale pink from the drink, even expelled a spray of liquid across the table. "Because I'll be so far ahead of you, idiots," she said, dipping her fingers in her drink and sprinkling everyone with Fae Fizz.

A group of tiny winged faeries buzzed past us and perched on a table up in the roof rafters. The barman had to ferry their little drinks up using a pulley system. Thank Gaia they weren't directly above our table because it didn't take long for them to get raucous and start spilling sticky liquid out of their little cups.

Leif was the only heir whose average went down, going from nine last year to eight this year because he didn't even turn up to the first trial, and his last one was torpedoed by our bond. But he was still coming third overall, so he was happy. If he was happy, I was happy. I nuzzled my cheek into his shoulder, rubbing against him for a moment and reveling in his warmth and strength.

"We might not have many more years left for you to get ahead, tomcat," Ronan said, bringing everybody's mood down. These last couple of months were my first time hanging out with such a diverse bunch of fae—previously, it had been all shifters. I was rapidly learning that fae from House Mentium were awesome to hang out with at a party, but they could also be real downers. Especially Ronan, who didn't have great control over his power. The slightest shift in his mood sent us all spiraling.

"Yeah, only one more monarch has to crisp, and then we're all fucking alphas," Leif said. I squeezed his hand. He'd finally learned how to balance his responsibility for the shifter packs with his role as heir and his natural cheekiness, and I knew he didn't look forward to shouldering even more stress and pressure. I pulled a tennis ball out of my pocket, where I always kept one these days, and handed it to him.

"Thanks, babe." He started tossing it against the wall, and I instantly felt his calmness through the bond.

"What are we going to do about the Shadow Walkers?" I asked. I wasn't an heir or a princess, but I felt comfortable among them. They treated me as an equal and took my question seriously. We'd discussed the scroll at length, my discovery that the Shadow Walkers could be defeated by something called the Stone of Veritas, a relic of truth, but we kept delaying action.

"The Stone of Veritas has to be in the Realm of Fen, right?" Dion said, twisting a light pink curl around a finger. Fen was the truth-telling realm, and nobody could tell a lie inside its borders. It was the natural place for a relic of truth to dwell. "So somebody has to go and find it."

"Fen ain't a great place to visit at the moment," Leif said. "Arrow died in the Shadow Walker attack at the temple, and their king just karked it too. They're not exactly accepting social calls."

The Realm of Fen was undergoing massive political turmoil. Word reached us yesterday that King Sanctus, who had ruled the realm for three hundred years, had died. The missive came with no extra information, so we didn't know if he died of natural causes, in a Shadow Walker attack, or some other assassination. For a truth-telling realm, the fae of Fen could be awfully mean with information.

Normally, power would pass peacefully and easily to the heir, who had been groomed for the role for a hundred years or more. But in this case, the heir to the Fen throne was Arrow, who died at the attack in the temple at our Ascension party here in Verda.

Ronan sighed. "We can't put it off any longer. We'll have to go and give our condolences to Thorne Sanctus and maybe ask for the Stone of Veritas."

Dion spluttered, spraying the table again. Honestly, that fae needed lessons on how to drink without drowning his companions. "Thorne Sanctus is not our friend. He's a sanctimonious bastard. He's the last fae who'll help us with anything."

Leif nodded thoughtfully. "Yeah, he's a cunt. He won't give us shit."

"Worse than his sister?" I asked. I met Arrow at the Ascension party. She'd barrelled up to us, insulted us, then refused an invitation to chat, all in the name of honesty. If her brother was even worse, I'd hate to meet him.

"He hates us all. Every single one of us," Ronan said.

I squeezed Leif's thigh. "No, babe," he whispered, guessing my intention.

But I had to say it. "Thorne Sanctus doesn't hate me. He doesn't even know me. I could try."

Leif growled. "Absolutely not. You're not leaving my side, mate. And I have a bunch of unruly wolves to keep in line."

I didn't fight it. I couldn't. The thought of being away from Leif was like a physical pain, and I knew our bond wouldn't allow it.

We sat in thoughtful silence, trying to figure a way out of the problem. The Stone of Veritas had to be in the truthtelling Realm of Fen, and a relic that important would be in the monarch's possession. But the king had just died, Princess Arrow, who our heirs had spent their lives getting to know, had been killed on our lands, and her younger brother hated every single one of us.

Gabrelle smoothly placed her Fae Fizz on the table, not making the barest sound of glass against the wood. "Thorne Sanctus doesn't hate me."

Dion rolled his eyes. "Oh, because you're so loveable, nobody could hate you?"

She barely glanced at the Magirus. "No, because we've never met. You've all made courtly visits to Fen, and so have I, but the time I went, he was away on business in the Realm of Caprice. And when he visited here, I was tending to my ailing mother. So he and I have never actually met." She smiled tightly. "I suppose that makes me the best candidate to coax the Stone of Veritas out of his possession."

Music floated around us, with ethereal strings and heavy notes, while we watched the ice princess. Her expression was guarded and unreadable, as always, her dusty pink irises betraying no emotion.

"We'll come with you," Ronan said, his hand resting casually on Neela's hip.

Gabrelle flicked her gaze to him. "I don't want a homeless fae ruining my chance, moody. Besides, we can't have three of our heirs out of the realm for an extended period." She looked at each of us. "It has to be me."

Good luck to her. If Thorne was worse than Arrow, she would need it.

I whined softly, and Leif put his arm around my shoulders, sending me warmth and energy from his body and our bond. Now and forever.

* * *

Hi, I hope you enjoyed A Court of Fur and Fangs!

The third book in the series, A Court of Verity and Lies, features our favorite princess of beauty and stealth, Gabrelle, clashing with the devastating Prince of Fen in a realm where she cannot lie. She needs the Stone of Veritas, but she'll get more than she can handle.

And of course, you'll get to meet up with old friends. Get A Court of Verity and Lies now.

Free novella

If you'd like a FREE NOVELLA set in the same world, sign up for my newsletter at zaradusk.com. It's a prequel novella set in the Realm of Caprice, where the weather is affected by the fae king's mood...and the king is NOT happy. A moody king, a badass heroine, and a beautiful but dangerous world—what's not to love?!

By signing up for my newsletter, you'll also get all the latest info about new releases, some character art, and other good stuff.

* * *

You can also follow me on Amazon, Facebook, TikTok, all the places. And I never say no to a good review.

xxx Zara

About the Author

Zara has a pretty sweet life – hubby, kids, and a kick-ass Dyson hairdryer. But that doesn't stop her from inventing new worlds and having steamy affairs with her book boyfriends. Angels and demons and fae, oh my!

Lucky Zara, she gets to spend hours with those sexy beasts every day. The rest of the time she's working in health, negotiating with her kids, and beating her husband to the remote.

But mostly it's angels and fae.

Come along for the ride with Zara and her feisty heroines. You can provide the mulled wine.

You can connect with me on:
- https://zaradusk.com
- https://www.facebook.com/zaraduskauthor
- https://www.tiktok.com/@zaradusk

Subscribe to my newsletter:

✉ https://dl.bookfunnel.com/jtbq9u1oeu

Also by Zara Dusk

I write badass women and bad men, with twisty plots and plenty of action.

She is the dark Angel's obsession

She has something the dark Angel wants, and he won't stop until he gets it. She might be a mere mortal, but she is every bit as powerful as he is.

Meet Zaden and Scarla in this completed trilogy.

Made in the USA
Middletown, DE
27 November 2023